ChangelingPress.com

# Beast/Thor Duet

*A Riptide MC Romance*

Anne Kane

**Beast/Thor Duet**
*A Riptide MC Romance*
**Anne Kane**



ISBN: 978-1-60521-956-1

Publisher:
Changeling Press LLC
315 N. Centre St.
Martinsburg, WV 25404
ChangelingPress.com

Printed in the U.S.A.

Editor: Crystal Esau
Cover Artist: Marteeka Karland

The individual stories in this anthology have been previously released in E-Book format.



This book contains sexually explicit scenes and adult language which some may find offensive and which is not appropriate for a young audience. Changeling Press books are for sale to adults, only, as defined by the laws of the country in which you made your purchase.

# Table of Contents

**Beast (Riptide MC 3)**

*A Riptide MC Romance*

**Anne Kane**

**Piper -- Discovering my ex was heir to the Las Vegas mafia totally freaked me out, but we parted as friends. Or so I thought. Now he wants me dead. I barely made it out of my house alive. I knew I couldn't go back, so I called my father in Georgia for help. His solution? He sent a biker to bring me home. Imagine my surprise when the biker turned out to be my one-night stand from a few months back.**

**Beast -- A one-night stand with a sassy stripper in Las Vegas left me wanting more. I couldn't get her out of my mind, so a few months later I went back to find her. That didn't go so well. She'd disappeared, with no forwarding address. Fate's way of telling me to forget her?**

**I was getting ready to head home to Georgia when Ace called and asked me to do a favor for Riptide's FBI contact. His daughter was in San Diego, and some thugs were gunning for her. She needed protection and transportation. I was close enough to offer both in a hurry. Turns out Fate has a sense of humor, though I'm not sure how happy my little stripper was when I showed up to rescue her.**

## Chapter One

**Piper**

The bullet went right over my head and lodged itself in the wall. I stared at the hole in disbelief, too shocked to be afraid. When a second hole blossomed beside the first, I bolted inside and slammed the door shut. A third bullet ripped through the door and I dropped to the carpet, whimpering in fear.

I wasn't thinking about my safety when I unlocked the front door. I was wondering what to have for supper. If I hadn't bent down to pick up the newspaper, I'd be dead.

"Give it up, you little slut. Drake wants you dead, you're dead," a male voice bellowed from outside.

Presumably the guy holding the smoking gun. Shit! Drake was heir apparent to a mafia don. We'd dated briefly, back when I was working at the blackjack tables in Vegas, waiting for my big break. That was months ago, though.

The sound of heavy footsteps approaching spurred me into action. I needed to get out of here.

The front door was out of the question, and the back door seemed like a bad idea. Stood to reason these guys were pros. They'd timed this for when my neighbors were all at work, and the guns had barely made a sound. That meant they had high end silencers. They'd have someone watching the obvious escape route.

I stayed low and crawled to the bedroom, still confused as hell. Drake and I parted ways just after I discovered his mafia ties. I thought it had been a mutually agreeable split. I didn't want anything to do with the mafia, and he was the kind of guy who liked new conquests. Once he had me, I quickly lost my appeal. Why would he suddenly want me dead? Not like I knew anything that could hurt him.

My head snapped up as I heard pounding against the front door. Sounded like someone was attempting to kick it down.

"Let me in, bitch!"

I didn't bother to answer. Thank goodness I'd automatically turned the deadbolt when I slammed it shut. That bought me a few precious extra seconds.

Cautiously raising myself up, I peered out the bedroom window on the north side of the house. There was no one in sight, and a thick hedge separated the side yard from the view of the street.

The sound of wood splintering in the front hallway made the decision for me. After opening the window, I clambered out, shutting it as quietly as possible behind me so as not to give myself away.

The last time I'd done the window escape act, it had been to avoid the landlord when my mom failed to pay the rent. I'd become a pro at it as a kid. Who knew that talent would come in handy years later?

Dropping to the ground, I scurried to the fence and climbed over it into the neighbor's yard. Luckily, they weren't home, so their pack of yappy little dogs weren't outside to give me away. I hurried to the garden shed at the bottom of the yard, putting the solid building between me and the danger.

I heard the back door to my house open. "She come out here?"

"Nah. I would have seen her. Little slut must still be inside."

"Yeah. You keep watching. I'll go find her."

"Sure thing. Remember, he said he wants pictures."

"He also said we could play with her first so long as we get the job done."

"Yeah. I got excited when it looked like an easy kill and forgot about that. Try to knock her out if you get the chance. We could take her to the warehouse. I could use some fun, and I like them scared."

I covered my mouth to muffle an involuntary whimper. I had to get out of here fast. Taking a deep breath, I carefully peeked around the corner. A dogwood tree shielded me from sight as I watched one of the thugs head toward the house, pausing when he reached the door. The other stayed put, a gun held casually in his right hand. Both were concentrating on the house.

I withdrew to safety behind the shed, looking around wildly at the unkempt ground. I needed something to distract the guy outside once the first was inside. Spying a good-sized rock, I picked it up and waited. Two against one weren't great odds.

Finally, the first guy disappeared back inside. Counting to ten to make sure he wasn't going to reappear, I hefted the rock high in the air, aiming for the yard on the far side of my house. I held my breath, watching it arc through the air before heading downward.

The rock must have hit something metal, making a satisfyingly loud clatter as it landed. The creep watching the back door automatically turned toward the sound and started in that direction.

I sent a quick prayer of thanks up to the heavens. Staying low to avoid detection, I sprinted in the opposite direction. Working my way through backyards, I put as much distance as I could between me and Drake's minions before I dared to slow down. When I felt I'd gone far enough to be safe, I plunked myself on the ground under the branches of a weeping willow in a vacant lot and took a deep breath. My heart was pounding so hard it felt like it was going to explode. I needed to calm down and figure out what to do next.

I hadn't had time to shed my cross-body purse when things went south, so I still had my wallet and phone. My car was back at the house and there was no way I was going to try going back to retrieve it. I needed to get as far away as possible though, and without wheels that meant public transport. I had no idea how far-reaching Drake's network went, but I had to assume that as the heir to a mafia syndicate, it was wide. *Would they be able to tell if I bought a ticket on a bus or a plane*?

And where the hell would I go? Sure, I had my wallet, but I wasn't exactly rich, and I didn't have a supportive family to fall back on. My mom was still in Vegas but that was the worst move I could make. Vegas was Drake's home base. Someone would be sure to spot me and report back to him.

That left my father.

Having a Vegas stripper as your mom, you grow up fast. And cynical. All the time I was growing up, my mom swore she had no idea who my father was, and I believed her. I'd seen the endlessly changing parade of bed partners while I was a child. The list of possibilities for my father was probably longer than the line up for free booze at a frat house party. When I turned legal age, I did one of those DNA ancestry things, though, and I'd found him.

An FBI agent. How ironic is that?

Turns out he was a pretty good guy though. He didn't bat an eye when I confronted him, just asked why he'd never heard of me before. I have a feeling he already knew the answer to that one.

I wasn't a "Daddy's little princess" kind of girl -- too late to go down that road. He wasn't the doting father type either, so we got along okay. It helped that I lived in the West, and he lived in Georgia. We'd only met in person once, but we kept in touch, and just knowing I had one stable parent kind of made me feel almost normal. Almost.

Now it was time to find out just how much he cared. I tapped on his number in my contact list and waited for him to answer.

"Hello, Piper. What's up?" He sounded relaxed. Given the time zone difference between coasts, he was probably settled in for the night and watching whatever sport was currently being broadcast.

"Hey, Dad. Funny thing happened when I got off work tonight. Got a minute to talk?"

"Sure."

"Remember me telling you I'd been dating a guy named Drake, and it didn't work out so well?"

"Yeah. You're not pregnant, are you?"

I rolled my eyes. "No. That would be really bad. See, what I didn't mention was the reason I bailed was because I found out Drake had mob connections."

"Mafia? Are you serious?" He didn't sound relaxed anymore. "Exactly what kind of connection are we talking about?"

I gulped. "He's being groomed to take over his father's operations. As in he'll be the next don. They run most of the illegal activity in Vegas."

Dead silence greeted my statement.

"Dad?"

"I'm here. Just trying to digest this. Ignoring the part where you were dating a mafia kingpin, you split with that guy months ago, so what happened tonight?"

"Someone tried to kill me. They said Drake ordered it."

"That doesn't make sense. He let you go and ignored you for months. Why would he suddenly want you dead? No offence, but my experience with those kinds of guys is they're pretty casual about their affairs. Once they're done, they're done, and they move on, especially if you were never involved in family activities."

"Exactly what I thought we'd done. We said goodbye and both moved on. I even took a gig in San Diego and left the area so I'm nowhere near him. Haven't seen him since the break-up. I have no idea what the hell is going on, or why he suddenly wants me dead."

"Did he ever discuss his business dealings with you, or did you ever overhear anything you shouldn't have?"

"No. I was clueless, until he suddenly decided to fess up. I had a feeling he wanted out. He knew I wouldn't hang around once I found out."

"Okay. We can figure that out later. Right now, we need to get you safe. Where are you?"

I looked around. "Hiding under a willow tree a couple of blocks from my house. Empty lot on the corner."

"Right. I'm going to send someone to pick you up and bring you here. Give me a few minutes, and I'll call you back with details."

"Thanks." I let out a sigh of relief. Glancing down at my phone, I realized it had been less than an hour since I'd left work. Amazing how quickly life could change.

Ten minutes later, my phone buzzed. Dad. I hit accept.

"Good news. One of the groups we use for security happens to have an agent in your area. He should be there to pick you up in twenty minutes or so, depending on traffic. Just a heads up, he's on a bike. You okay with that?"

"A bike, as in a motorcycle?"

"Yeah. He's a big guy, lots of leather and tattoos. He looks a little rough, but he's decent and I told him to get you a helmet. Luckily, he was out there on personal business and was just getting ready to head back here to his home base. There's a hamburger joint two blocks east of your position. He'll meet you there. I sent him a picture so he'd recognize you. He'll ask if you like the ocean. You answer yes, but the riptides are dangerous. Got that?"

I knew the place he was talking about. I stopped in there occasionally for takeout. Despite the shabby exterior they made damn good hamburgers. This was starting to sound like a B-rated movie, though, with code phrases and clandestine meetings. "Are you serious? About the ocean question?"

"You need some way to recognize each other. Code phrases work just fine for that."

"Okay. I got it. Yes, I like the ocean, but the riptides are dangerous." I paused. "Dad?"

"Yeah, Piper?"

"I appreciate this. I'll make it up to you somehow."

"Don't sweat it. I'm glad I can help." He made a sound halfway between a chuckle and cough. "Not like I have a ton of kids running around, and we're just getting to know each other."

"Thanks anyway." I stood up and brushed the dried grass and dirt off my backside.

"Call me when you're safe with Beast."

"Beast?" That didn't sound comforting.

"Just what the guys call him. He looks like someone you'd cross the street to avoid. Might look scary if you don't know him, so Beast. He's an ex-SEAL and they tend to come with muscles."

"Okay. A Beast on a bike." I tried to sound cheerful. "Talk to you soon." Disconnecting the call, I slung my purse across my shoulder. I tucked the phone into my hip pocket so I'd feel it if it vibrated. It occurred to me that Drake had this number. Once I was safely out of California, I'd have to do something about that. Right now, I needed it.

The burger joint was packed, but I managed to squeeze into a booth toward the back. I had a good view of the parking lot out the window, and anyone looking for me would have a hard time seeing me through the crowd at the front.

I ordered fries and a coke. Having someone take shots at me had killed my appetite, but I needed to order something to justify taking up a table. I was pushing the food around on the plate when the sound of a motorcycle penetrated the chatter of the dinner time crowd.

The biker pulled his machine up to the front of the building and dismounted. Dad was right. That guy was huge. Tossing his helmet onto the seat, he raked his hands through his hair and grabbed a duffel bag from under a cargo net on the back seat before heading inside. The door hadn't closed behind him before his gaze rested on me, pinning me in place.

Picking up a toothpick from the counter, he stuck it in his mouth like a cigar. A grumpy frown marred his rugged features as he strode between the tables to where I was sitting.

Shit. I knew that face. And that body as well,

although there were a lot fewer clothes on it the last time I saw it.

And the last time I'd seen him, his name was Johnny, not Beast.

He slid into the seat across from me, his gaze pinning me in place. "So, how do like the ocean, Piper?" he asked.

* * *

**Beast**

I almost laughed when Piper rolled her eyes. "This can't be happening! You said your name was Johnny."

I inclined my head. "As in John Doe. Anonymous enough for anything. I use it when I'm just out for some fun. No point in using my real name." It might be a formality, but I needed her to give me the code phrase. "You like the ocean?"

"Yes, but the riptides can be dangerous." She wrinkled her nose. "And so can guys you're never supposed to see again. Especially ones who give you a false name."

"And yet here I am, with a real name. Funny how things turn out, isn't it. The food any good here?"

You could have knocked me over with a feather when Ace had sent me the picture of the woman needing an escort back to my side of the country. She'd been a whole lot more naked the last time I'd seen her. Who would have thought an FBI agent's daughter would turn out to be the Las Vegas stripper I'd had a one-night stand with a few months back?

Piper and I had spent an explosive night together. She'd been in Vegas then, working the pole at a strip club. She told me she didn't do that as a regular thing -- she was a dealer at Merlin's Casino, but she needed some fast cash and stripping in a club was an easy way to get it. It was supposed to be a no-strings-attached night. One and done. No personal connections, never see each other again. Fuck, we lived on opposite sides of the country.

I was in town on business and looking for an easy fuck before I headed back to Georgia. With two teenage daughters to raise, I had to behave myself when I was home, so I liked to get a little action whenever I was out of town. Using a false name wasn't a big deal, and I thought John Doe was amusing. Setting a good example and all that really put a crimp in my sex life.

Piper told me she was just getting out of a relationship that went sour and wanted some fun without any consequences. Sounded perfect.

Problem was, I hadn't been able to get Piper out of my mind since I'd gone home. I tried. With two teenage daughters to consider. I can't just do whatever the hell feels good.

And it did -- it felt so damn good I wanted more.

A few days ago, I finally gave in and went back to look her up. I had this vague idea that if I fucked her a few more times, I could get her out of my system and move on with my life. Luck wasn't on my side there. Turns out the reason she needed fast cash was to leave Las Vegas, and she did just that. Disappeared without a trace. No forwarding address. No one knew where she was or how to get in touch. We hadn't talked all that much so it's not like I could call up her friends or anything. The manager at the casino she mentioned working at said they'd mailed her final pay to San Diego. It wasn't much, just a day's pay, but it had come back as undeliverable. I took it from him and promised I'd give it to her if I found her. At least it had an address on it, a place to start.

I figured looping down to San Diego wasn't going to add much time to my trip. If I didn't find her, I'd know it was Karma's way of telling me to grow up and go home to my kids. I fuelled up my Harley and hit the road.

Four hours later, the address in San Diego turned out to be a vacant lot. Even I can take a hint if you bust me over the head with it enough times. Piper didn't want to be found.

Just as I was about to leave town, Ace called and asked if I was up to bringing back the grown daughter of one the Bureau agents we worked with. Seemed she'd gotten herself in a little trouble. Someone was gunning for her, so she needed to get out of town in a hurry. I'd agreed, as long as she was okay with riding bitch on the back of my bike. No way was I leaving my bike behind, and I was feeling much too grumpy to do the airport thing.

He checked and assured me the girl was fine with the bike. He didn't have many details other than the woman needed to get out of town fast, and her father was willing to pay to see she got to him safely. Sounded like a routine mission. When Ace sent me a picture of my tagalong, though, the trip got a whole lot more interesting. Seems like Karma was on my side after all.

"Food's nothing fancy." Piper picked up one of the fries. "But if you like burgers and fries then yeah, it's good. Are you seriously planning on eating with two guys running around out there somewhere, looking to kill me?"

"Assuming they managed to figure out where you were, they're not likely to start shooting in a crowded restaurant with a couple dozen witnesses," I pointed out. "Besides…"

"Besides what?"

I grinned, my sense of humor restored. "I'm hungry and those hamburgers smell damn good." I motioned to the waitress and ordered a burger with everything on it, along with a side of fries and gravy. Turning my attention back to Piper, I narrowed my eyes. "So your dad didn't mention you were a stripper. Then again, he's FBI so probably not a detail he likes to toss around."

"I'm a singer, not a stripper. And I worked as a dealer at the card tables between gigs to make ends meet. That was just one night to raise some quick cash. I told you that in Vegas." She took a sip of her drink, wrapping those luscious lips of hers around the straw. My cock swelled to attention as I remembered how those lips felt wrapped around it.

"Yeah, you did. But when we met you were working that pole like a pro so I'm a little skeptical."

She raised one brow. "You spend enough time in strip clubs to know how a pro looks?"

Score one for Piper. I snagged a fry off her plate and crammed it in my mouth to avoid answering.

"And you're with some kind of security firm that contracts out to the FBI?" She tilted her head and studied me. "I don't remember you telling me that."

I shrugged. "I don't think my career came up. We didn't do much talking last time we were together."

"No," she agreed. "We did not."

Thinking about that night was giving me the hard-on from hell. I shifted in my seat, trying to get comfortable. "You weren't a target then, or we wouldn't have had that awesome night together. What changed?"

The stricken look on her face made me regret the question as soon as I asked it. "Forget it. None of my business. I'm just here to get you back to your father in one piece."

She toyed with the food on her plate. "I'm putting you in danger, so I guess you deserve to know the score. My ex, the one I broke up with just before we had our little fling…" Her voice trailed off and she lifted her head to gaze into my eyes. Her lower lip trembled. Not much, but enough that a guy who had to deal with teenagers every day would notice.

"He tracked you to San Diego?"

She nodded. "Worse. He put out a hit on me, and made it known he'd look favorably on whoever pulled it off."

That got my attention. I sat up straight and stopped dreaming about getting her back in the sack. "Who the hell is your ex?"

"His name is Drake. Drake Rossili."

I shook my head. "Never heard of him."

She looked sad. "Probably not. He likes to keep that part of his life under the radar. When I met him he said his last name was Smith. I suppose that should have been my first clue. Smith. Almost as bad as John Doe."

She laid it all out for me. The whirlwind affair, finding out about the mafia ties, and what she thought was an amicable break up. She shrugged. "Now he wants me dead, and I have no idea why."

The waitress placed my food on the table. "Anything else for you two?"

Piper and I both shook our heads.

"If you need me, just holler." She spun on her heel, consulting her order pad as she headed back to the kitchen.

"Even the mafia doesn't put hits out on people for no reason." I took a bite out of the burger. "Damn, this is good!"

That earned me a ghost of a smile. "Told you so."

"Did you overhear something you shouldn't have? See something you shouldn't have?" I took another bite of the burger. I hadn't been kidding about being hungry.

Piper shrugged, a helpless look on her face. "I don't think so. If I did, I have no idea what it was."

I didn't want to make her feel worse by telling her those mafia guys weren't the type to give up if their first attempt failed. And the heir to a mafia don? There would be dozens of punks looking to score points with him by offing her. She'd be looking over her shoulder for the rest of her life unless something happened to this Drake asshole. "Doesn't matter. I'll get you back to your father safely." I chomped down a few of the fries.

She gave me a quizzical look. "What exactly do you do for this security company you work for?"

"It's really more of a motorcycle club than a security agency. That's just what we do to earn our keep. Me? I'm the enforcer."

"You kill people?" Her eyes widened.

I held a finger to my lips. "Shh. Not so loud. We're trying not to be noticed, remember?"

"You didn't answer my question."

I shrugged. "Only if they deserve it."

"So, an ex trying to kill me? Would he deserve to die?"

"Not my call. I just follow orders, and so far they don't include offing your ex. I just need to get you safely back to your father."

I wasn't called Beast for nothing. I could arrange

for Drake to cease to be a problem. Hell, I'd even enjoy doing it. But first I needed to get Piper safely out of the way. I made short work of the rest of my meal, while Piper pushed the fries around on her plate. "You going to eat those?"

"I'm not really hungry." She scowled. "Getting shot at seems to have put a damper on my appetite. Plus, my career just got going. My agent got me an offer to sing lead with a group touring the southern states starting next month. I was all ready to accept too. This was supposed to be my big break, and now I don't know what to do."

"Public tour might not be such a good idea, at least until we figure this out." I needed more info.

"If I don't accept this, it could end my career before it even gets started. No telling when or if I'll get another offer."

"Being dead won't do much for your career either."

She stared at me, a reluctant smile curving her mouth. "I suppose. Maybe I can figure this out quick. It's got to be a mistake."

I doubted it. The mob wasn't into those kind of mistakes, and even if it was, chances were they'd carry through just to keep it under control. Maybe her father, or Ace could talk some sense into her once we made it back. My job was to keep her alive long enough to get there.

I turned and picked up the bag I'd brought in with me, tossing it onto the seat beside her. "I picked you up a leather jacket and some chaps. I got you a helmet too, as per your father's orders. It's out on the bike. By the time you get all that on, you won't be so easy to recognize. Plus, you'll be riding behind me, so you'll blend right in against my bulk."

She looked down at the bag and then back up at me. "It's summer. This is going to be way too hot."

"Not once we get moving. And I did promise to keep you safe. Those aren't just for show."

She looked doubtful but obediently stood and picked the chaps out of the bag, a frown creasing her forehead. "Exactly how do I put these on? I'm guessing they go over my clothes, right?"

Fuck! A picture of her in chaps with nothing underneath was just about my undoing. "Yeah, they go over your clothes." I stood up and quickly showed her how to buckle the belt and then zip the legs shut.

This close to her, I could smell the sweet fragrance that was uniquely her. This could be the best road trip of my life. Or my worst. She'd be nestled up tight to my back for days on end, her arms around me as we cruised across the nation.

Riding the Harley wasn't like being in a vehicle where you can switch drivers and make the journey non-stop. I figured it would take us three, maybe four days to get back home. I didn't know if the connection I'd felt in Vegas was all in my head or if she'd felt it too.

Didn't matter. "How old are you?"

"Twenty-four. Why?"

"Shit." I shook my head in disgust at the way my body reacted to her. A one-night stand with a willing younger chick was one thing, but now that I knew more about her, she was off limits. Not to mention the fact that mixing business with pleasure never worked out well. Someone always got hurt.

Piper frowned. "Excuse me?"

"You're way too young." Kind of made me feel like a lecher. An old lecher.

She looked confused. "Too young for what?"

"Forget it." I tossed some bills on the table to cover our check. "Time to get moving."

Grabbing the empty duffel bag, I motioned her to stay behind me as I headed to the door. Chances were the would-be assassins weren't anywhere around here anymore. They'd be staking out the airports and bus stations by now.

I picked up the helmet I'd bought for her, a nice generic black, and tossed it to her. "Put that on." I put mine on, flipping the face shield up to keep an eye on her while she snugged the buckle up tight under her chin.

Slinging one leg over the bike, I took a deep breath. "Climb on behind me and wrap your arms around me to hold on."

She squirmed around a bit, and then leaned right against me, her arms barely managing to span my waist. I reached down and placed them on my belt, giving her something to hang on to.

Despite my self-lecture on keeping my hands, and every other part of my body to myself, my cock instantly went rock hard.

I had a feeling it was going to stay that way from here to Georgia.

## Chapter Two

**Piper**

*Leather and musk, a lethal combination.*

When Beast put his arms around me to show me how to put on the chaps, I had to steel myself not to melt right into his muscular embrace. I felt heat flood my face as his unique scent went right to my groin, reminding me of how great he was in bed. Now here I was, with my arms wrapped around him and my hands tucked into the leather belt at his waist.

*If I let my hands drift a little lower, what would they find?*

He pulled out onto the highway and the bike picked up speed. Maybe it wasn't a good idea to tease him while we were flying down the interstate.

I'd never been on a motorcycle before. When my father asked if I'd be okay with it, I hadn't given it much thought beyond anything being fine as long as it got me safely away from those thugs. Now I was glad I'd said yes.

My feet rested on a set of rubber-clad pegs, and I could feel the vibration of the engine beneath me. Once I got past being a little nervous, a sensation of freedom and exhilaration crept over me. The wind whipped past, and Beast's solid bulk in front of me had me feeling safe for the first time since this nightmare started. As we left the city behind, the traffic thinned out. The bike swooped around the corners, and I clung to Beast as he leaned into the curves. I had no idea where we were, and I didn't care. Drake couldn't find me racing down the interstate on the back of a motorcycle.

I don't know how long we were on the road. It had been late when we started out, so when Beast slowed and pulled onto a side road, I wasn't sure whether it was for a quick pit stop or if we were done for the day. To be honest, now that the adrenaline had worn off, I was exhausted.

The road twisted and turned, winding its way past fields of weeds and grass until we were in front of a shabby-looking motel with a vacant sign flashing.

Beast pulled around the back of the main building, out of sight of the road. Killing the engine, he pulled his helmet off and hung it on handlebars. "Off you get, Piper. We'll bunk down here for the night."

I swung my leg over the bike and almost slid to the ground. I hadn't realized how stiff I'd be after spending a couple of hours snuggled up behind a great big Beast on a vibrating machine like the Harley. Regaining my balance, I pulled my helmet off and ran my fingers through my hair.

"Here." Beast took the helmet from me and hung it beside his. Unlatching the leather saddlebags, he strung them over one shoulder and reached for my hand.

A little confused, I slipped my hand into his and he led me over to the back door.

"Buddy of mine from back in the SEALs owns this place. I stop here from time to time, but I don't want to get him involved in anything so pretend we're a thing."

"A thing?" I wrinkled my nose.

"Yeah. Like we're together. You know. Guy and girl shit."

"Oh, that kind of thing." I suddenly had this insane urge to tease him. "Like I can't wait to get you out of those clothes and into me?"

The stunned look he turned on me had me spluttering with laughter. "You should see your face!

You look like I just suggested you sell your precious bike and buy a Volkswagen."

Beast shook his head. "You're going to be trouble, aren't you?"

I grinned, holding onto his hand with both of mine. "Yeah. I guess I am."

"Did I ever tell you I have twin girls at home? You're going to have to up your game if you want to be more trouble than them."

"No." I felt my stomach drop. I had a strict rule against playing around with someone else's man. "You're married?"

He shook his head. "Hell no. That ended a few years ago, but the girls live with me, and they've taught me a lot."

I felt the weight lift off me. "Like what?"

"Like how to turn the tables on females who think they can shock me."

I grinned. Maybe it was the fact that Drake couldn't possibly find me here, but I felt almost giddy. "Am I supposed to be scared now?"

"If you're smart, you'll wonder how I plan to do that."

I laughed, just as someone opened the door and beckoned us inside.

"Hey, Tinker. How's it going?" Beast gave my hand a little squeeze, warning me to be quiet.

"Pretty good. Enough business to pay the bills without making me work too hard. You?"

"Taking a road trip with Piper here. She wanted to see the country from the back of a bike."

Tinker held out his hand. "Nice to meet you. Enjoying the trip?"

"So far. Haven't seen much yet."

"No?" Tinker looked confused.

Beast wrapped an arm around me. "Piper's from the West Coast. Met her on the last trip out, and we hit it off. Came back to get her so we're heading back to the clubhouse now." He looked down at me. "Can't wait for you to meet the gang."

I felt out of my depth. I had no idea what the heck was going on, so I played along. "Me either. Should be fun."

"They're a good bunch." Tinker turned and headed inside. "I'll put you in the suite on the second floor, okay? Bigger room and I just redid the ensuite. Watched one of those 'how to tile a bathroom' videos on YouTube and wanted to try it. Might have overdone it a tad. The shower's big enough to hold a party in." He threw an amused look over his shoulder. "Or in your case, a party for two."

I felt my face heat up and I flashed a look up at Beast. He just shrugged slightly, but I could see he was trying not to laugh. So much for me trying to embarrass him. I needed to meet those twins of his.

Tinker slipped behind the reception desk and grabbed an old metal key off a pegboard on the wall. "Room 214. The cleaning girl put fresh sheets and towels in there this morning so you should be good to go. You going to want anything else before you turn in?"

"You have a couple beers handy?" Beast looked down at me. "Beer okay or did you want something else?"

"Beer's fine." Anything wet would be good at this point.

"Coming right up." Tinker disappeared for a moment and returned with a six pack of beer. "This do?"

"Looks great. Put it on our tab." Beast snagged

the beer and the key without letting go of me. "See you in the morning."

Tinker nodded. "You need a wake-up call?"

"Nah. We don't have a schedule to keep."

"Good night then. Nice to meet you, Piper."

"You too."

Beast and I headed up the stairs. No elevator, but not a surprise. I imagine anyone who couldn't handle stairs simply stayed on the main floor. This wasn't exactly the Ritz, but it had a quaint charm and its out-of-the way location was a plus right now.

Our room was at the end of the hallway, and when Beast opened the door, I was pleasantly surprised. The room was large, with a king-sized bed in the middle and a sitting area in front of a picture window off to the right. I took a deep breath. "It smells so clean!"

"You can smell 'clean'?" Beast looked amused.

"Yeah, of course." I took another deep breath. "See? It smells just like this room."

"Huh." He didn't look convinced. Crossing the floor, he flipped the light switch to the ensuite and let out a low whistle. "Damn, Tinker wasn't kidding. This is the king of bathrooms!"

I moved over to him and peered through the doorway. "Nice! Hope the water's hot." Striding back into the main room, I started peeling off my clothing. "Nothing like a hot shower to wash away a crappy day."

Beast raised one brow.

"What?" I paused with one hand on the waist belt of the chaps. "I'm too tired to pretend I'm shy. You've seen me naked."

"That was before you turned out to be the daughter of a client."

"Not really." I discarded the chaps and started to shimmy out of my pants. "I've always been his daughter. You just didn't know it."

"And you are now officially my assignment." He shook his head. "Not a good idea to mix business with pleasure."

I smiled sweetly. "Your choice, but I'm going to have a nice, hot shower and I'm not doing it with clothes on." My pants pooled at my ankles, and I kicked them aside. Dressed in nothing but a bra and panties I strode back to the bathroom and removed them before I stepped into the gigantic shower stall. I fiddled with the knobs for a few minutes until I had a delightful torrent of hot water streaming down on me from the rainfall showerhead.

I closed my eyes and let out a happy sigh.

When Beast didn't join me, I felt a pang of disappointment. He had to be the sexiest man I'd ever seen. Well over six feet of rock-hard muscles and tattoos. My mouth watered as I remembered how he'd made me come multiple times that night we'd spent together.

Drake had been exciting, but he'd never made me feel the way Beast did. In hindsight, I think I'd been more in love with being in a relationship with such a suave, well-heeled man than with the actual man.

Beast wasn't as sophisticated or polished as Drake, not even remotely, but he appealed to me on a more basic level. Just the thought of what he could do with those big hands of his had me reaching down to touch myself.

I opened my eyes. Through the streaming water, I could just see him standing by the bed, his eyes hooded as he watched me.

I slid the tip of my tongue out to trace the shape

of my lips as I started to play with myself.

* * *

**Beast**

I told myself I should just ignore her. The little witch knew exactly what she was doing, but I couldn't turn away. She probably wasn't much more than five feet four, maybe five feet five if you were being generous, but she had just enough curves and they were all in the right places. My cock was semi-hard just remembering what it felt like to run my hands over those curves.

Giving myself a stern talking to, I deposited the saddlebags on the dresser and pulled out my gun. I sat on the edge of the bed and checked that the safety was engaged before I placed it on the bedside table. I always made sure it was close at hand when I slept. Some people keep a glass of water by the bed. Some people keep their phones handy. I found I slept better knowing I could protect myself in a second if things went south.

I glanced over at the shower. Bad idea. But I couldn't look away.

The water sluiced over Piper, glistening on her bare mound as she slid a finger between the folds of flesh hiding her entrance. She opened her eyes and stared right at me as she added another finger and slid them in and out. Spreading her feet wide she tilted her head, letting her long dark hair ripple in wet torrents down her back.

I lowered my hand to my crotch and undid the zipper on my jeans. Yeah. She was a client, but she was the sexiest damn thing I'd ever seen, and I already knew how tight she was, and how responsive to every touch of my hands and my mouth. No one had ever accused me of being a saint.

I stood up, slipping my jeans and jockey shorts down and stepping out of them. My cock sprang free, hard as a rock. She glanced over at me, and I pinned her with my gaze as I took my cock in hand, giving it a slow stroke from base to tip.

That got her attention.

Her mouth opened slightly, letting the pink tip of her tongue slip out as her fingers moved faster, slipping in and out of her pussy.

I quickly stripped off the rest of my clothes, tossing them carelessly aside.

Piper narrowed her eyes. Withdrawing her fingers, she moved her hands up to cup her breasts, fondling them suggestively. She pinched one nipple and scored her thumbnail across it. Fuck, my mouth watered just thinking about how it would taste if I sucked one into my mouth.

As if she could read my thoughts, Piper lowered her head and snaked her tongue out to lick one tightly pebbled nipple. My cock jerked in response, and I gave it a couple of slow pumps, getting the satisfaction of watching Piper's eyes widen at the sight. She'd be a bust at poker with that expressive face of hers.

Reaching up, she grabbed a tiny bottle of body wash off the corner shelf and squirted some of the liquid out on her hands. Working the soap into a foamy lather, she kept eye contact as she layered it over her glisteningly wet body. She slid her hands everywhere, over her belly, down her thighs and then back up to outline the shape of her hips. Turning slightly so I could see her shapely behind, she soaped that up too.

Fuck this. I might be too damn old for her, but I wasn't too old to know when a woman wanted me.

I grabbed my pants and dug out my wallet. Flipping it open, I pulled out a condom and ripped it out of the foil package. Quickly sheathing myself, I strode across the room and paused in the doorway to give my cock another slow stroke. Piper's gaze followed my hands, and I saw her throat move as she gulped in a deep breath.

She wanted me, and she wanted me to know it.

Yeah. This trip was definitely going to have a lot of pleasure mixed in with the business. I stepped into the shower and cupped the back of her head, my fingers tangling in the wet mass of her hair. Blazing a kiss across those gorgeous lips, I trailed a finger down her spine.

Piper lifted her arms and wrapped them around my neck. Opening her mouth, she kissed me back. Damn, the woman had my number. I let go of her hair and ran my palms down her sides. The soap and water formed a slippery film that added an extra layer of sensual pleasure. We clung together, greedily exploring each other's mouths with our lips and tongues.

Piper lowered her arms and placed her hands on my chest. She explored with her fingers, tracing the faint scars of battles long forgotten. Then she let one hand drift down, and her fingers circled the base of my cock.

I let out a muffled grunt as she tightened her hand around me and slid her fingers from the base to the tip of my shaft and back again.

"You're huge." She murmured the words against my mouth.

"And you're trouble. You know we shouldn't be doing this."

"But I'm a good kind of trouble, yes?" She

reached lower to cup my balls.

"I'm not sure there's a good kind of trouble, but if there is, you definitely are it." I lifted my head. "Turn around." I guided her, my hands on her hips until she was facing away from me. "You might want to use those roaming hands to brace yourself."

She lifted her arms, reaching out to lean against the shower wall.

I slipped a foot between hers, urging her to spread her legs wider. The sight of her waiting obediently, her back to me, trusting me to make the next move had my cock swelling even more. I ran one finger down the crack of her ass. Damn, that was inviting but I had something else in mind right now.

Dropping to my knees, I used my hands to urge her to lean her ass toward me, pushing that adorable cleft of hers right up to my face. I stuck out my tongue and gave her pussy a nice, long lick.

She let out a little squeal, and I had to tighten my grip on her hips, holding her in place as I feasted on her pussy. Damned if she wasn't already dripping and ready for me. I slipped a finger inside her, circling until I found that one spot that made her gasp and bounce up on her toes.

I licked and sucked, feasting on her sweet juices until I could feel her getting ready to climax. I inserted a second finger, pumping them in and out until she came, letting out a squeal as her inner muscles clamped down hard on my fingers.

"Atta girl. Come for the Beast." I kept pumping my fingers as waves of aftershocks rocked her.

When she was done, I pulled my fingers out and stuck them in my mouth, licking the taste of her off me. Getting to my feet, I positioned myself at her entrance from behind.

I could feel faint aftershocks still racing through her as I slowly worked my way into her slick channel. Fuck, the woman was tight. Inch by inch I sank my cock deeper. Piper lowered her head, pushed her ass back against me, and met me thrust for thrust, letting out little moans of pleasure as I filled her. When my balls slapped up against her I held still for a moment, savoring the feeling of her tight pussy surrounding me.

She whimpered softly.

"Tell me what you want." I wrapped one arm around her and cupped her breast.

"I want you to fuck me. Hard!" She breathed the words out.

"What's the magic word?" I teased her, waited a few precious seconds, running my fingers over her tightly pebbled nipple.

"Please!"

"Such a good girl." I wrapped my other arm around her, holding her against me as I pulled out almost completely, then rammed my cock back inside her. She took it all, took everything I could give her. I drilled into her again and again. Faster and harder, holding her tight as we bucked against each other.

I felt my balls draw up, ready to shoot their load.

"You ready?"

"Yeah." It wasn't really a word, more of an exhale.

Her pussy clamped down on my cock, a second climax racing through her as I rammed into her one last time, letting out a primal yell of triumph as I came. I could feel her inner channel pulsing around me.

She went limp in my arms, and I closed my eyes and held her close against me for a long moment.

I nuzzled her neck. "You okay?"

"Mmmm." She yawned. "Just tired."

Probably exhausted. Between a day at work and the drama that followed, it was amazing she was still conscious. I scooped her up in my arms and stepped out onto the bathmat. Reaching over, I grabbed the biggest towel I could see and wrapped it around her. I carried her over to bed and laid her down on it.

Dripping my way back to the bathroom, I disposed of the condom, picked up a second towel, and dried myself off. Glancing out at the bed, I could see Piper propped up on one elbow, watching me.

"You know we shouldn't be doing that, don't you?" I toweled my hair dry and tossed the towel aside. One of the nice things about hotels was the room service. Used towels magically disappeared to be replaced by clean folded ones.

"Why not? We're both single and enjoy it." She frowned. "Are you afraid Drake will find out and come after you?"

"Hell no. He's done for as soon as we find him. He comes after me, saves us the trouble of looking for him." I strode over to the far side of the bed and pulled the sheets down. "But I never screw around with clients, and I don't think this is what your father had in mind when he hired me."

"He hired your club. Or company. Or whatever it is. He didn't hire you specifically. Besides, why would he care? It's none of his business who I sleep with."

She had to be kidding. I could just imagine how I would react if I found out some old fart was playing hide the wiener with one of my daughters. I'd probably kill him. If he was lucky. "He's not going to be pleased to know you're fucking a biker who's this much older than you." I climbed into the bed and sat up, pulling the sheets over me. "Not to mention the fact that he's paying me."

"You're not that old." She tossed her head, and all that wet hair flowed around her face. "And I'm almost twenty-five. You can't be that much older than me." She sat up and tossed the towel on the floor before she swung her legs over the edge of the bed.

"I'm thirty-four, so yeah. I'm that much older." I held up the sheets so she could climb under the covers with me.

"Age is just a number." She rolled onto her side and squirmed back toward me.

I draped an arm over her and spooned up against her. Nuzzling her neck, I whispered, "I'm only sleeping in the bed with you because it makes it easier to protect you."

A soft chuckle escaped her. "Yeah. That's why."

## Chapter Three

**Piper**

I awoke slowly, feeling pleasantly warm. I'd rolled over at some point during the night, and I was draped halfway across Beast, with one leg tangled between his. My head was cradled in the hollow of his shoulder, and he had one arm wrapped around me, his hand brushing up against my breast.

I lay still, my eyes closed as I savored the feeling of being safe, of having someone other than myself looking out for me. But would it be enough? The mob wasn't known to let things go.

Maybe I was overthinking. If I left the state, moved to the other side of the country, maybe Drake would decide I wasn't worth the effort. From what I knew from movies, the mob ran just like any other business, with an eye on the bottom line. Why pay to axe someone who'd moved that far away? I'd just have to make sure my agent never booked me into a gig in California.

Not that bookings were coming in thick and fast these days anyway. Making it as a singer was about more than having talent. You needed connections, exposure, and a whole lot of luck. I didn't have much of any of those, and if I bailed on the one gig I'd been offered I might as well give up. But what choice did I have?

"You awake?"

I realized Beast's eyes were open. "Yeah. Just being lazy."

"Get a little more rest. Tinker has a gym down on the main floor. I'm going down and do some lifts before breakfast. I'll be back in an hour or so."

"You could just stay here and do some push-ups." I could feel his stiff shaft poking against my belly. "Feels like you might be into that."

He wrapped one arm around me and rolled us both. Suddenly on top, he grinned down at me. "I was going to be a gentleman and let you sleep, but I've changed my mind."

Over an hour later, he sauntered downstairs, and I got up to get dressed for the day, still feeling the pleasant aftereffects of our morning activity.

Unfortunately, I'd run away with literally just the clothes on my back, so I had nothing clean to put on. I made a mental note to ask Beast to stop somewhere so I could pick up at least a change of under things. Luckily, I did have a hairbrush in my purse, and the hotel bathroom had enough supplies for my morning routine.

Beast hadn't returned by the time I was done, so I ventured out of the room to find him. A sign in the lobby pointed the way to an exercise room down a long hallway. I paused outside the room's glass door. A shirtless Beast had his back to the door as he worked on some kind of machine with lots of cables and pulleys. The muscles in his arms and shoulders bulged as a series of weights slid up and down in opposition to his movements.

Just watching him made my breath hitch in my throat.

From here, I could see the intricate tattoos on his back. I recognized one as the club patch that he had on the back of his leather jacket. I'd have to ask him what the rest of them meant sometime, but right now I was content to drool over his well-honed muscles and the way he worked those weights without breaking a sweat. The man was gorgeous. Sexy as hell. He had a rugged beauty that sent flickers of heat dancing down my spine even after all the times he'd made me come last night and this morning.

He was right. My father probably wouldn't be thrilled to find out we were hooking up. We were both adults, though, engaging in normal adult activities. The fact that Beast was a little older than me just made him all the more attractive, a primal gut-deep reaction on my part. He had experience, and he knew just how to please a woman. He was all sleek, well-honed muscle, with scars that hinted at an ability to fight and win. I need that right now, needed to know he was capable of protecting me from Drake and his minions.

Okay. Beast had a couple of daughters and that could be awkward, but it wasn't like we were planning a serious relationship. Once we got to Georgia and I was out of danger, we would go our separate ways. No harm, no foul. Chances were, neither my father nor Beast's kids would ever know about our relationship. In the meantime, I intended to enjoy it.

Beast rose to his feet and turned around. His gaze settled on me, and a slow smile etched its way across his face. He grabbed his shirt and shrugged into it while he crossed the room.

I opened the door and met him inside. "I found you."

He grabbed me by one hand and pulled me in close. Lowering his head, he seared a kiss across my lips. "You couldn't lose me if you tried."

I blushed, glancing around to see if there was anyone else in the room. He had a way of making everything sound so damn intimate.

"Ready for breakfast? There's a little place just around the corner, and if we ask nicely, they'll pack a picnic lunch for us as well. We can hit the road after that and not worry about stopping for a while."

"Sounds good." I let him keep my hand captive while we headed back to our room. "But I was hoping we could stop somewhere and get me a few things. I didn't have time to pack before I left, and I don't fancy wearing the same clothes from one side of the country to the other."

He looked thoughtful. "We pass through a couple smaller towns. We could probably stop at one of those big discount stores."

"I have money." The thought of Beast paying for my underthings had me blushing all over again.

"Cash money?"

"Some. But I can get more from an ATM."

He shook his head. "We pay cash so there's no chance of your ex tracing us. Don't worry. I have enough on me to pay for shit."

"You carry that much cash on you? Aren't you worried about getting robbed?" As soon as I said it, I realized what a dumb question it was. Anyone looking for a victim to rob wouldn't give Beast a second glance. He looked like exactly what he was -- a big, tough, battle-hardened biker who probably had a weapon or two hidden somewhere on him.

He laughed. "Nah. Some days I'd welcome the distraction. Work off a little steam and claim self-defense."

He opened the door to our hotel room and did a quick visual sweep before allowing me to enter. "Put the leathers on and get the rest of your stuff together." He eyed up my purse. "You want to carry that or put it in the saddlebags?"

I hesitated, then pulled out my phone and wallet before handing him the purse. I managed to get the chaps on quicker this time, buckling up the waist belt before attempting to wrap the legs around and zip them up. After pulling on the jacket, I slipped my wallet and phone into the interior pockets. "Thanks. It will be more comfortable without the purse."

He nodded. "Ready to go?"

"Yup." I squirmed a bit, rearranging my pants and the chaps to a more comfortable position.

He slung the saddlebags over his shoulder and took my hand as we headed downstairs. It had felt strange at first, but I was starting to get used to this handholding thing.

Tinker was at the front desk, checking off items on an order sheet. He glanced up at us. "You two have a good night's sleep?" The twinkle in his eye made me wonder if we'd made enough noise to be heard outside the privacy of our room.

"Great as always. Thanks for the hospitality." Beast let go of my hand for a minute and pulled out a wad of cash that had me gasping. Peeling off a few bills, he dropped them on the counter. "Thanks, buddy."

Tinker looked at the cash and nodded. "You were never here."

Beast pocketed the rest of the cash and retrieved my hand. "See you next trip."

The trip to the restaurant was hardly worth starting the bike for, but I understood that Beast valued the machine enough not to leave it behind. That, and after we ate we would be headed back out on the road.

I looked at the laminated menu card, surprised to realize how hungry I felt.

"Can I start you two out with some coffee?" The waitress looked to be in her early twenties, and I felt a twinge of something dark when she ignored me and smiled at Beast.

"Coffee for me. Black. How about you,

sweetheart?" Ignoring the waitress, Beast looked over at me.

I frowned at the endearment. "Coffee with cream, please."

"Coming right up." The waitress bustled away, and Beast reached over to take possession of my hand.

"Should have mentioned this before," Beast said. "I won't use your name in public. A small thing, but it's always the little things that trip people up. Anyone could come in looking for a girl named Piper, and the waitress or someone might just remember you."

I tilted my head. "I'd say you were paranoid but given the circumstances I appreciate it. Can I use your name or is that a no-no as well?"

He shrugged. "No one's looking for me, so it doesn't matter."

The waitress returned with the coffee and took our orders. Beast ordered a full breakfast with bacon, eggs, sausage, hash browns, pancakes, and toast. After giving him an incredulous look, I settled on bacon and eggs with sourdough toast. The waitress included both of us in her smile this time and headed back toward the kitchen.

I waited until she was out of earshot. "Can I ask you something personal?"

"You can ask. I might not answer."

"So you're not married, and you have twin girls that live with you. How does that happen? Most kids live with their mothers, or at least custody is shared."

"You want to know if I intimidated her into giving up her kids?" He narrowed his eyes.

I shook my head. "No, just curious."

"Their mother remarried, and they don't like the guy very much so they opted to live with me. It suited their mom to let them, although she still sees them and they go visit her. Neither of us wanted to put the kids through a nasty custody battle so we let them decide."

"How old are they?" I'd been picturing cute little toddlers but if they were allowed to decide which parent they wanted to live with, they had to be older than that.

"Teenagers. They'll be sixteen this fall and are all excited about getting to drive. Now that's something that scares me."

"Teenagers!"

He grinned. "Yeah. Major reason why we're not doing this once we get back to Georgia."

I wrinkled my nose. "Guess I'll just have to get my fill while we're on the road then."

"What about you? Anything juicy in your past, besides dating the heir to a mafia family?"

"Nope. Other than hunting down my father once I was old enough, my life's been pretty boring."

"Hunting him down?"

I explained that my mother had no idea who he was, and I'd had to go the DNA route to find him. "So we're actually not that close. We've visited once, and we keep in touch by email and phone calls, but when this happened he was the only one I could think of who might be able to help."

Beast let out a low whistle. "Must have sucked growing up without a father."

I shrugged. "Mom did the best she could, but yeah. I really envied the kids who had two parents."

The waitress came back with our food and placed it down in front of us. "Anything else?"

"No, we're good, thanks."

We stopped talking while we ate. I was impressed that Beast managed to polish off the enormous pile of food on his plate in the time it took me to eat my bacon and eggs. The waitress came by and refilled our coffees without being asked. It felt so normal, I almost managed to forget about Drake and the death threat.

At least, I did until my cell phone rang.

* * *

**Beast**

I watched Piper pull out her phone and glance at the number displayed on the screen. "My boss. I forgot to call and let them know I wasn't available." She hit accept and put the phone to her ear. Her eyes widened, and her face went white.

I grabbed the phone from her and held it up to my ear. A man's voice spewed out of the speaker, detailing the horrific way he planned to torture her before he killed her. I disconnected the call and looked over at Piper.

"That was your ex?"

She shivered. "I think so. He said it was, and it sounded like his voice."

"And call display said it was your work calling?"

"It did. I don't understand."

"Your scumbag of an ex had this number, did he?"

She nodded. "Yeah, but that wasn't him on the call display. I wouldn't have answered if it was."

"Tech guys can spoof a call to make it look like it came from somewhere else. Scammers do it all the time. Anything on this phone you can't afford to lose? Like your father's number? Mother? Friends?"

Piper chewed nervously on her bottom lip. "Just a few of the contacts. My father. My mom. Work. That kind of thing."

"You okay with me pulling your contact list, and

destroying the phone?"

"You can do that?"

"Not me, but Shadow can. He's the club's tech expert. I'm going to call him on your phone. He can grab your contact list, then delete everything. Once he's done, we're going to smash this all to hell. We'll get you a new phone when we stop for clothes. You can tell him which contacts you want, and he'll turf the rest. If Shadow can access phone data just by being connected, chances are this Drake asshole has someone who can too. Let's hope that call wasn't long enough for him to pinpoint our location."

I didn't like the way that call had put the fear back on her face. I made a quick call to Shadow and explained what was going on. He instructed me to pull the SIM card out and burn it before I trashed the phone. Overkill, but I liked it.

Piper sat quietly until Shadow completed his work, and I killed the call. "I'm sorry."

I frowned at her. "For what?"

"I knew Drake had that number, and I meant to tell you and get rid of the phone but then I just forgot."

I captured her hand and held it in both of mine. I detested the fact that I could now feel it shaking. "You don't have to apologize to me. I am here to keep you safe. That's my job, and even if it wasn't, I would kill any asshole who tried to harm you. Got that?"

She nodded silently.

"Good. Then let's get out of here."

I threw some bills on the table, making sure to leave a good tip but not a great one. No reason to remember us after we were gone. I shrugged into my cut and led the way outside.

Standing beside my bike, I pulled the SIM card out and casually dropped Piper's cell on the ground, crushing it with the heel of my boot. Placing the SIM on top of a metal post, I flamed it with a lighter and watched it shrink and melt under the heat. Satisfied there was no way to revive either, I picked up the shattered remains of the phone and used a shard of the plastic casing to scoop up the smoldering drop that was all that remained of the SIM card.

Seeing the glimmer of a smile on Piper's face as I tossed the useless lot in the trash can on the sidewalk made it all the more satisfying.

I slung a leg over the bike and waited for Piper to climb behind me. I had planned a straight run back to Georgia but on the off chance someone managed to tag our location with that call, I decided to detour and take a more Northern route. It would add a couple of hours to the trip, but it had the plus of being on less traveled roads. If anyone was following us, they'd be easier to spot.

After that nasty start, the day got better. The sun shone down on us, and the road was high and dry. I spotted a bargain store in a mid-sized town in New Mexico in the early afternoon and pulled into the parking lot. Piper slid off the back of my bike and stretched.

"You okay?" I knew she'd be stiff. She wasn't used to spending hours at a time riding on the back of a bike.

"Just sore. I'll be okay. It felt so good, with the wind blowing past and all." She bent down to touch her toes and winced.

"I wanted to put as much distance as possible between us and where we ditched the phone." I frowned. "From now on we'll stop from time to time to stretch our legs." I could feel the effects of the long ride, but I'd learned to ignore minor aches and pains a long time ago. Being an ex-SEAL gave me an advantage in that area.

"There must be a restroom in there, right?" Piper gazed at the bargain store.

"Let's go find out." I held out my hand and she placed hers in it.

"You have a thing about holding hands, don't you?"

I shrugged. "Probably. Started when the twins were little. If I made them hold my hands, I was less likely to lose them in a crowd. Some people put harnesses on their kids. Some of us just hang on to them. I guess it became a habit." I gave her hand a little squeeze. "Don't want to lose you."

"Not a lot of chance of that." She tilted her head. "Do you think Drake managed to trace that phone call?"

"I'm going to give Shadow a quick call and see. We can pick up a new phone for you while we're here." I held the door open for her.

"Won't he be able to trace your phone? If he knows I'm with you?"

"First thing, I don't see how he'd know you were with me. Second, my phone is on a secure, scrambled network. No one is hacking or tracing it."

"Oh, wow." She looked impressed.

"Restrooms are that way." I pointed to a sign hanging from the ceiling. We worked our way to the back of the store, and I made note of the position of the phone counter and the women's section. We reached the restrooms and I let go of Piper's hand and watched her disappear into the ladies' room.

Pulling my phone out, I glanced around to make sure no one was close before calling Shadow. "Anyone trace that last call to her phone?" I didn't waste time on niceties.

"No. But they've been trying to ping it since. Did you make sure it was out of commission?"

"Yeah." A picture of the mangled mess I'd tossed in the garbage flashed through my mind. "Melted that SIM card thing too."

"Good. I'm trying to run a backward trace on the pings, but they're encoded. It's going to take a bit of time."

"We're in New Mexico, should have a new phone for her shortly. When we do, I'll give you a shout for those contacts."

"Sounds good. I'd suggest she just put absolutely necessary ones in for now. Friends she isn't going to call right away, we can deal with later. Might be an idea to make this one a burner. Get rid of it when you get here."

"Good plan."

"And, Beast, if you can, get a second cheap phone and let me program it to her old number. Put it on a truck or whatever you can manage that is heading in the opposite direction from you. Hopefully the assholes will pick up on it and waste time chasing off in the wrong direction."

I chuckled. "You're a devious fucker, Shadow. I'll do that. You manage to find anything out about this Drake asshole?"

"Negative. Just that he's the heir to a mafia don and has managed to stay out of jail so far."

"Typical. They let the underlings take the rap if something goes sideways. No hint as to why he'd put a hit out on Piper?"

"Nothing. No mention of her on the dark web at all. Strange. Usually there would be something, if only details of the hit contract."

"Huh." I looked up as I heard the door to the restroom open. "Be in touch soon." I ended the call.

"Who was that?" Piper watched me put my phone back in my pocket.

"Shadow. Just letting him know we'd have a new phone for you soon. He suggests getting a burner, just put in numbers absolutely necessary for now. We can get you a permanent phone with your friends and family in it once we're safely back in Georgia."

"I suppose that makes sense. Since you have the super secure one maybe we use yours for everything, and just put your number and my father's in there in case we get separated for some reason?"

"That makes a lot of sense." I appreciated that she was taking this threat seriously. "Let's go get the phone, and you can pick out some clothes and stuff."

We ended up with a cheap Android phone, and some girly stuff that I didn't look at too closely. My pants were tight enough, what with the semi hard-on she inspired just by being near me without adding to the problem.

Back outside, I handed the new phone to Piper and stuffed the rest of the items into the saddlebags. If we kept this up, I'd have to buy bigger ones. I wasn't used to having a passenger on a road trip. "Hang onto that. We'll pull off up the road a bit and call Shadow to set it up."

"Why not do it now?" Piper frowned.

"Because there's a lot of networks in a town, and we don't want to chance any of them hooking into your phone before we get it secured. If we're out on the road, less chance a hacker will stumble across it." I held out my hand and she gave me the phone back. I plugged it into the battery pack I kept handy and put them both into the other saddlebag. "We also need to charge it."

"Right." Piper rolled her eyes. "I knew that."

I pulled up a map on my phone. "There's a pullout about twenty miles up the road. We can stop there, have something to eat and get your phone set up."

"How much longer will it take us to get to… where is it we're going? I know it's in Georgia but I'm not sure where."

"It's a little town south of Atlanta. It will take us a couple more days to get there. We stop for meals and sleep." I didn't mention the fact that I was enjoying our alone time, and didn't want to rush back to the club and have it end.

"How long does it usually take you? When you're on your own?"

"Normally, it takes me about 30 hours riding, coast to coast, but I don't want to push it this time. So, a day and a half. Two at the most. I just grab takeout to gobble down and cat nap when I feel tired."

"So I'm slowing you down."

I shook my head. "The point is to keep you safe, not to go as fast as we can. We're doing just fine. While we're out on the road, the club and your father's team can spend their time trying to figure out what the hell is going on without worrying about you. Now that your ex can't track you with the phone, you're going to be even harder to find. If they can't find you, they can't hurt you."

Piper looked doubtful. "True, I suppose."

"And just to make it more fun…" I pulled the second cell phone out and turned it on. "I sweet talked one of the workers into plugging it into the charger while we were shopping. It should be good for a couple of hours at least."

## Chapter Four

**Piper**

My brows furrowed as I watched him stalk over to a big rig with Massachusetts plates on it and tuck the extra phone under the back bumper before walking back to me with a huge grin on his face.

"What are you doing?"

"Sending those thugs your ex sicced on you on a wild goose chase. Shadow made sure this phone mimics the one we destroyed, and I overhead the driver say he'd emptied his rig earlier and was headed home to Boston."

"You sure that's his truck?"

"Only one out here with Massachusetts plates on it. If it isn't his, it's probably still heading that way."

"Sneaky!" I had to admire him for it though.

"Yeah." He grinned. "I have my moments."

The rest of the day went smoothly. I'd been accustomed to the vibrations of the bike beneath me and the way Beast leaned into the curves. I relaxed against him and enjoyed the scenery as we raced along the ribbon of asphalt. From time to time we stopped to stretch our legs or get a drink and a bite to eat. Those saddlebags were starting to feel like Mary Poppins's carpetbag. I was never sure what Beast would pull out next.

At dusk we pulled into the parking lot of a cozy looking little motel with a bar attached. The sign over the bar proclaimed it to be the *Best Cowboy Tavern* in town, and it looked to be pretty busy. I was more interested in getting off the bike and working the kinks out. That last chunk of road had been a long one. I loved the feeling of freedom and all, but staying in one position for the better part of the day left me feeling stiff. I wasn't sure if I'd ever get comfortable with it.

"Let's get a room and see if the manager can recommend somewhere to grab a bite to eat before we turn in for the night." Beast once again slung the saddlebags over his shoulder and reached for my hand. Yup, the guy had a real thing for handholding.

The motel office was staffed by a girl who looked young enough to be carded if she tried to get into the bar next door. "Just one night?" The girl reached for a pad of papers behind her.

Beast nodded. "Yeah. Just passing through."

"Fill this out." She ripped off the top page and handed him the form. "That your bike out there?"

He nodded, scribbling something down on the paper she'd given him. Reading over his shoulder, I could see that we were Mr. and Mrs. Beamish. I suppose Smith would have been a dead giveaway.

"Nice." She included me in her smile. "You're in Room 11. It's right next to the office here so the noise from the bar shouldn't bother you too much. It's karaoke night so it's packed and they're open till two am."

"They serve food over there, or is there anywhere close by you'd recommend?" Beast handed back the slip of paper and reached in his pocket for his wallet. I noticed he didn't just pull out a wad of cash this time.

"If you just want hamburgers and fries, the bar is great. You want a full menu, you'll have to go downtown." She giggled. "There's only one main street in this place, and there's a restaurant at the far end. Nothing fancy there either but you can get a meat and potatoes meal." She reached under the counter and pulled out a key. "That will be eighty dollars. Cash or credit card?"

"Cash, thanks." He pulled a few bills out and laid them on the counter. Picking up the key, he turned and grabbed my hand again.

I wasn't sure whether to be flattered or feel like a toddler in danger of wandering off. I waited at the door to number 11 while Beast moved the bike a few yards to park it outside our room. He dismounted and grabbed the saddlebags again before unlocking the door so I could enter. The room wasn't fancy, but it was clean, and the shower had that faint bleachy smell that told me it had been disinfected recently. I'd stayed in worse.

"Hamburgers okay with you?" Beast put the saddlebags down.

"Sounds great." I could hear the faint sound of music coming from the bar. I wondered if Beast would be okay with me joining the karaoke fun. It wasn't quite the same as singing with a band, but it would be nice to stretch my vocal cords. "Lunch was good, but it was a while ago." I stretched, wincing as a few muscles I rarely used made their presence known.

He tilted his head. "You need to freshen up first?"

I raised my brows and pretended to look hurt. "You think I look like I need to freshen up?" Teasing him was so much fun.

He crossed the room and pulled me into his arms to place a very thorough kiss on my lips. "No. I was trying to be considerate. You look like you need to get naked and let me fuck you until you can't stand up, but I figured I'd get some food into you first."

"Didn't want me fainting from hunger while you were having your way with me?"

"Yeah. Something like that." He nuzzled the side of my neck. "You smell like sunshine and fresh air."

I batted my eyelashes at him. "So I don't need to freshen up?"

He nipped my earlobe. "I'm not falling for that one again. You know I'd take you any way you'd have me, including dripping with mud, but I do think we need to get a bite to eat first."

"True." I slid out of his grip. "Just give me a minute to… *freshen up*… and I'll be ready to go."

A reluctant smile curved Beast's rugged features as he shook his head. "I knew you were going to be trouble."

I gave my face and hands a quick rinse and grimaced at my reflection in the mirror. The helmet might keep me safe, but it didn't do much for my hair. It lay flat against my head, so I tried to fluff it up with my fingers. I could have gone looking for my brush, but I doubted that would help much and I didn't want to take the time to wash and blow dry it. Maybe I could consider the new look a disguise. The girl staring back at me from the mirror didn't look much like the glamour shots my agent used.

I skipped back into the main room. "All ready."

Beast held his hand out toward me.

I wrinkled my nose. "We're still doing the handholding thing, are we?" But I put my hand in his, secretly enjoying the security it implied.

Beast shrugged. "Your ex's thugs aside, I don't want anyone thinking you're available."

"Available? Aw. Aren't you the sweet talker?" I grinned up at him.

He growled something under his breath and shoved the room key in his pocket.

The night air was just cool enough to be comfortable as we walked over to the pub. Beast held the door open for me without letting go of my hand,

and I squinted as my eyes adjusted to the dim lighting. The place was packed and true to the name there were a lot of cowboy hats and boots in the crowd. The bar covered one wall at the far side of the room, and tables and chairs were scattered around a square reserved for dancing.

The door shut behind us, and Beast led me over to a table in the far corner of the room. Taking a seat with his back to the wall, he pulled a chair around the table and set it beside his for me.

I raised my brow. "Really? You don't want me all the way over on the other side of the table?"

"I thought you'd want to be able to see the stage." He gestured toward a makeshift stage in a corner beside the bar. A karaoke machine complete with speakers was set up on the stage.

"Oh." I watched as a tall brunette picked up the microphone and said something to the guy running the machine. He gave her a thumbs up, and the soft sounds of guitar strumming filled the room. The brunette nodded her head and launched into an old country ballad.

Beast raised an arm and flagged down a barmaid. When she was close enough to hear him over the noise of the other patrons, he ordered a couple of burgers and a pitcher of beer. She nodded and disappeared into the crowd of dancers swaying to the brunette's song.

"Hope beer's okay. I should have asked." He leaned toward me.

"Beer's fine." I tapped my foot in time to the music. The brunette had a good voice, and I guessed this wasn't her first time singing to the crowd.

We sat in companionable silence enjoying the ambiance until the barmaid returned with our drinks.

She plunked a plastic jug full of beer and two glasses on the table. "Food will be up in five minutes." She gave us a quick smile before turning back to the crowd.

I picked up the jug and poured each of us a glass. Beast grabbed one and took a deep pull. He draped his other arm across the back of my chair in a casually possessive gesture. I leaned into him, resting my head in the hollow of his shoulder.

We were just another barely visible couple in a crowded bar in a small town in the middle of nowhere. It felt good. Safe. I felt safe enough to relax for the first time since this whole mess started.

The next singer got up, a cowboy complete with the boots and the hat. He picked one of those country songs with lots of whooping and foot stomping and the crowd really got into it. I looked at Beast. "You want to dance?"

He shook his head. "Nope. Not unless they slow the music down a whole lot, and I can just wrap my arms around you and sway a bit."

I laughed. "Not likely to happen. I'm getting the feeling this is a country crowd, and they're just starting to warm up."

The waitress came back with our food, and once again Beast pulled out just enough to cover the tab with a generous tip.

True to what the girl at the motel desk had said, the food was plain but good. The hamburger patties were thick and juicy, and the buns were fresh. I was hungrier than I'd realized and made short work of it. Beast looked amused. "Poor hamburger didn't stand a chance."

I shrugged, looking pointedly at his empty plate. "I don't see a lot of crumbs on your plate either."

He stretched his legs out. "Nope. That was a

damn good burger. I'll have to keep this place in mind the next time I'm out this way."

"You travel a lot for work?"

"Not a lot. I don't like to leave the twins too much."

We worked our way through the jug of beer, and watched as the next few singers went up and tried their luck. The crowd was generous and even applauded the one fellow who sang an entire song off-key.

"Most of them are probably too drunk to notice," Beast pointed out. "You told me you're a singer, right?"

"Yeah. Why?"

* * *

**Beast**

"You sing country?"

"Country. Folk. Jazz. Easy rock." She wrinkled her nose. "I'm not much on hip hop or rap, and definitely no classical."

I gestured at the stage. "You want to give it a go? I've never heard you sing."

She looked cute when she frowned. "I thought we were supposed to be keeping a low profile?"

I made a point of looking around the dimly lit bar. "I doubt there's anyone here connected to your ex. This is more of a redneck crowd, and I'm guessing if anyone did come after a woman in here, these cowboys would consider it a good excuse for a bar brawl."

I could see the longing on her face as she watched person after person get up to try out the karaoke. I'd never heard her sing, and I hadn't considered what this mess might do to her personal life or her career. I'd been too busy plotting our trip across the country and making sure she was still breathing at the end of it. "Go for it." I patted the gun hidden in its shoulder holster. "I've got you covered."

She threw her arms around my neck. "You sure?"

"Yeah, I'm sure. Just don't make it a mushy one."

"You mean like a sad one?" That grin I was starting to recognize as meaning trouble crossed her face. She dropped a quick peck on my cheek and stood up. As she headed to the stage area, I kept an eye on the crowd. No one seemed overly interested.

"This is for a special guy. He knows who he is." Piper's voice came over the speaker system with just a hint of laughter. She looked straight at me as the music started and she launched into a raunchy song about a guy in a classic car and the love of his life who liked to make love all over, under, in and out of that vehicle. The crowd roared with laughter, hooting and calling for an encore when she finished. She grinned over at me, and I nodded encouragement.

She looked happier than I'd seen her since the first time we'd met, and I didn't see any threats coming from a crowd of cowboys. The place was so packed, anyone trying to get in the door at this point would have to use a shoehorn. Sneaking in would be impossible. It was like the eye of the storm, a brief moment of calm when we could both just relax and enjoy ourselves before the real world crashed back down on us.

She finished up her second song, an old ballad I remembered from my high school days, and handed the microphone back to the guy running the show. The crowd gave her an enthusiastic round of applause as she made her way back to me.

Her face flushed, she slid back onto her seat

beside me and gave me a naughty grin. "Not mushy, right?"

I shook my head. "Definitely not mushy. You were great. The crowd would have listened to you all night if they could."

A sad look crossed her expressive face. "I was hoping to go on tour starting in a couple weeks. A few practices to get to know each other, and then I'd take over as lead singer for an up-and-coming band. Technically, I hadn't accepted it yet but only because we were still negotiating. I guess that's a no-go now."

"Your agent set this up before your ex started this shit fuckery?"

She nodded. "He was working on it. I thought it would be my big break, you know. First step on the road to an awesome career."

I wanted to tell her it was fine, that she could go ahead and accept the tour, but I wasn't into giving people false hope and chances were it would be too risky. Unless we managed to resolve the threat to her it would be like telling the hit men where to find her. Not a good idea.

"You've got a great voice, and you really played to the crowd. What do they call that? Stage presence? I bet country songs wouldn't be your first choice, but you gave the crowd exactly what they wanted. You heard them cheering you on at the end. Mark of a good performer. You might not be able to accept this tour, but there will be others."

"Yeah. Sure." She didn't look convinced. Picking up her beer, she drained the glass. "I'm getting tired. Can we go back to the room soon?"

Fuck, this sucked. I hated that look of defeat on her face. I gulped down the rest of my beer and stood up. "Sure. Let's go." I wrapped an arm around her shoulder, and we worked our way over to the door. Every few steps we had to stop as someone wanted to tell her how much they liked her singing. One woman even suggested she consider making a career out of it, which brought a smile to her face. I made a mental vow to talk to Ace and see if we could make that tour work for her.

I briefly considered going back to Las Vegas and putting an end to her ex. I'd enjoy that, but realistically I knew it wasn't an option. The mafia didn't take kindly to having one of their own executed, even if the asshole deserved it.

## Chapter Five

**Piper**

The rest of the trip was good. No calls from Drake. No ambushes. No surprises. Right now, surprises weren't something I looked forward to.

We rode hard, only stopping for food and sleep, and we made it to Georgia a couple of days later. Beast slowed the bike and pulled up to a set of wide metal gates just outside a small town. The two guys guarding the gates saw us coming and waved us through.

The driveway was long and swung in a wide arc past a row of trees that had blocked the view of the house from the road. Did I say house? It was huge, one of those old plantation type buildings from a long-ago era. Beast pulled his bike up alongside a row of motorcycles and killed the engine.

I slid off the back and undid my helmet, staring at the structure in awe. "This is your home?"

"Yes, sort of, but it's not just mine. It's the Riptide clubhouse." He pulled off his helmet and hung it on the handlebar. Reaching for mine, he placed it beside his and grabbed the saddlebags. "Come on in and meet the gang. We can let your father know you made it here safely."

He held out his hand. Apparently, we were still doing that. We climbed the front steps together and onto a wide porch that spanned the entire front of the house.

"So you live here with your kids and a bunch of other people? Like a commune or something?" I was having trouble wrapping my head around it. I hadn't given his living arrangements much thought. I guess I assumed he lived in a house, like every other normal person would.

"Yeah." He looked amused. "It's a big place, and it works out great with the twins. If I have to be away on club business, there's always someone here to keep an eye on them." He looked up at the sound of a commotion.

"Dad!" The front door flew open, and two girls came barreling out, throwing themselves at Beast.

He dropped my hand to catch them both against him. After listening to their excited chatter for a couple of minutes, he turned to me. "These are my girls, Jasmine and Jewel. Girls, this is Piper. She's from San Diego and her dad works for the Bureau. She needed a ride to this side of the country, and he asked if I'd mind bringing her with me since I was already coming back."

The shorter of the two smiled. "I'm Jewel. So, are you like, dating our dad? He never lets anyone except me and my sister ride on his bike."

I looked helplessly at Beast. How was I supposed to answer that? We weren't dating but I wasn't sure what he wanted to tell them.

"She's on my bike because I was out West when the call came in to go get her. You know I'd never leave my bike behind, so she didn't have much choice." He grinned at me. "She either rode with me or found someone else to bring her back here."

The other sister nodded. "Makes sense. Have you ever ridden on a bike before? Did you like it? Are you going to stay here or is your father coming to get you?"

Beast held up his hand. "Whoa, slow down. One question at a time and remember what we said about boundaries when we had that talk last month. You don't ask personal questions to people you've just met."

I tried not to laugh at the sight of the big bad

biker trying to instill manners in a couple of teenage girls. The man had his job cut out for him. "No, I'd never been on a bike before and yes, I did like it once I got used to it. It feels different than being in a car. I'm not sure where I'm staying. This was kind of a last-minute trip, but I think my dad made arrangements for me. I don't know him that well so I'm not sure if he has room for me at his place."

Jewel shot me a sympathetic look. "Did your parents get divorced when you were young? Some kids at school never get to see their other parent." She glanced up at Beast. "We get to see our mom lots. We just don't like the guy she's with, so we live with Dad."

"And that is a personal question." Beast made shooing motions with his hands. "Let's get inside. Piper and I need to get out of this leather. There will be lots of time for questions later."

I shot him an amused look. He made the parent thing look easy.

"Hey, about time you got back here."

I looked up to see a man with both arms covered in tattoos coming toward us.

"Ace called church for this afternoon, and he wants to see you two first." He looked over at me. "Your father should be here soon, too. Ace let him know you made it here safely."

"And this is Shadow, our tech guy." Beast slapped the other man on the back. "He can help you get that phone set up once you've had time to catch your breath."

Shadow looked young. If he was thirty, I'd be surprised. Then again, I'd never been all that good at judging ages.

"Right, good to meet you." Shadow nodded at Beast. "Sometimes my social skills aren't great. I knew who you were since you showed up with the big idiot here, but you wouldn't have any idea who I was."

I smiled. "Nice to meet you, Shadow, and thanks for the help with the phone stuff."

"It's what I do." He grinned and turned aside to say something to the twins.

"Let's get in before anyone else ambushes us." Beast led the way, and the girls trailed close behind with Shadow bringing up the rear.

I looked around as Beast led me through the main room and into the kitchen. An older couple looked up as we entered. "Beast. You're home! And this must be little Piper. Ace said you were bringing her back with you."

Beast grinned. "Not all that little, Mom, but yes, this is Piper." He turned to me. "This is Mom and that grumpy looking guy over there is her sidekick, Jake."

One of the twins spoke up. "She's not really his mom. Everyone just calls her that."

"Nice to meet you, Piper. I'm sure you two want to freshen up after spending a few days on the road. I sent clean towels and whatnot up with the twins earlier. Let me know if you need anything else."

"Thanks, Mom." Beast led me deeper into the clubhouse. The place was huge, although it would have to be if there was a whole passel of guys living there. I was surprised at how clean and tidy everything was.

"There's a cleaning crew that comes in a couple times a week," Beast explained. "And Mom is good at nagging the guys to pick their crap up, at least in the public rooms."

We went upstairs and down a long hallway. The twins skipped ahead and opened the door for us. Beast's room was more of a suite than a room. There were three bedrooms, the largest of which had an ensuite, as well as a main bathroom, a kitchen, and a living room. "This is nice!" I'd pictured something a lot less family oriented when I thought about a motorcycle clubhouse.

"Jasmine and I have our own rooms, but we can bunk together if you want to stay with us." Jewel gave her dad a sideways glance. "Unless you and Dad are sharing a room."

Beast frowned. "If she's staying here, Ace will assign her a room." He tossed the saddlebags onto a side table and looked at me. "You probably have time for a quick shower and change of clothes if you want. You can use my room for now."

One of the twins giggled, and he threw them a quelling glance.

"Thanks." I could feel my face flushing red as I crossed to the saddlebags and pulled out a change of clothes and my toiletries. "I'll be quick."

* * *

**Beast**

I sent Ace a quick text to let him know we would be down shortly. Piper's father needed to be here for the meeting as well, so that worked out. I intended to push the idea of letting her go ahead with the singing tour, and I had a few ideas about how to make it work. I remembered the look on her face at the karaoke bar. I wanted to see her face light up with joy like it had back there.

I let the twins tell me everything I'd missed while I was gone. Mom and Jake filled in for me when I had to be away on business and all the Riptide MC bikers looked out for them. They were probably better protected than someone in the witness protection program.

Piper was fast. I barely had time to rinse the road dust off my face and arms with a washcloth before she was ready. We left the twins in the room with strict instructions to behave themselves and headed down to Ace's office.

"You really think they're going to behave?" She looked up at me.

I shook my head. "Not a chance. I'm betting they're trying to come up with a way to eavesdrop on this meeting."

Ace stood up when we entered the room. He nodded his head politely. "Nice to meet you, Piper. Hope Beast has been treating you well." He gestured at a couple of chairs in front of his desk. "Have a seat. Your father should be here in a minute or two. We'll wait for him before we get started."

Piper sat down, and I opted to stay standing, one hand resting on the back of her chair.

I cleared my throat. "Something I should probably mention, Prez. Remember me telling you I was going back to look up a woman I'd met on a prior trip to Las Vegas?"

"Yeah." He narrowed his eyes, looking from me to Piper. "What about it?"

"Turns out the woman was Piper."

"I thought you said the woman you were looking for was in Las Vegas. Stripper by the name of Sparkles or some ridiculous thing."

"That was me, and it was a onetime thing to get some quick cash. I wanted to leave town ASAP." Piper let out an exasperated sigh. "Sparkles is the stage name I use when I don't want to be identified. I never told Beast my legal name, and I moved to San Diego two days later. It didn't occur to me to tell him my life story. It was supposed to be quick hook up, a one-night stand. I never asked what his name was either, so when my father said a guy named Beast was going to come get me, I didn't clue in."

Ace raised his brows and addressed me. "You must have known. I sent you her picture."

"You sent the picture after I agreed to escort her back here. All you told me originally was that she was the daughter of one of our FBI contacts."

"Still, once you realized it, you didn't mention you knew her. Don't you think that might have been important?"

"Because her father would feel better if he knew the security guy you had escorting her home could identify her without any clothes on? I can't see how that would help. And I barely knew her. Like she said, we didn't even exchange names."

Ace glanced down at his watch. "We can discuss this later."

Just then, there was a light tap at the door. "Come on in," Ace called out.

The door opened and a man I assumed to be Piper's father entered. He nodded to Ace before striding over to Piper. "You okay?"

She stood up, giving him a big hug. "Yes. Thank you. Sorry about this. I didn't know who else to call."

He dropped a fatherly kiss on her forehead. "No problem. I'm glad you thought of me."

Ace spoke up. "Beast, this is Sam, Piper's father. Sam, this is Beast. He's the one who brought your daughter back for you."

Sam looked over Piper's head at me. "Thanks, Beast, for looking out for my little girl."

Not so little, but I occasionally knew when to keep my mouth shut. "Just doing my job, sir."

Ace motioned us all to sit down, and this time I followed instructions, taking a chair on the far side of Piper where I could still see her. Being her only security all the way across the country I'd gotten used to having her in my sight at all times.

"We need to talk about next steps. The threat is still out there." Ace ignored me, talking to Piper's father.

"I can take her to the Bureau headquarters. We have a couple of apartments there for guests. She'll be safe. Lots of security."

"That works short term, but you need a solution that eliminates the threat for good." Ace leaned back in his seat, gazing at each of us in turn. "Her ex has mob connections. High level ones. The kind that don't just give up. Sooner or later, he's going to figure out where she is, and you can't protect her 24/7 for the rest of her life. She'll have to leave the headquarters eventually."

"So what do you suggest?"

"We need to investigate the ex, hopefully figure out why he wants her dead, and then find some way to neutralize the threat."

"You mean kill him?" Piper's brows shot skyward.

Ace shook his head. "Not necessarily. That might just ramp up the threat. Those guys are big on revenge. We need to find out why he put the hit out on you, and what we can do to make him decide to rescind it. The mob is a business. If there's no reason to kill you, they won't bother wasting the money or resources."

I spoke up. "I'm sure Shadow can do some more digging, but that's going to take time. I have a suggestion to keep her safe in the meantime."

All three of them looked at me.

"You told me your agent offered you a singing

gig, traveling around the southern states with a band for backup." I looked at Piper. "If it's still an option, it might just work to keep you out of sight, at least for now."

Piper looked thoughtful. "I think it is. The band's lead singer got in a car accident and is out of commission, which is why they made the offer. I'd be a stand-in for this tour, so I'm not on any of the posters or advertisements. I have until this Friday to give them an answer."

I looked at Ace. "We give her a fake identity and send her on tour. Maybe change her hair color, whatever it takes so she doesn't look like the woman they're searching for. She won't be in one place for very long, so she'll be almost impossible to track. I can go with her as a bodyguard in case they do figure it out. Lots of performers have bodyguards so it won't seem out of the ordinary. If she passes on this contract, she might not get another offer for years. Or at all. Accepting this kills two birds with one stone -- a real break for her career-wise, and a chance to hide in plain sight while we figure out what's going on."

"Would that work?" Piper looked hopeful. "I mean, the tour schedule would be public knowledge."

"It's already set, so your name won't be on the playbill." Ace steepled his fingers. "It could work."

"Does this Drake asshole know about the tour?" her father asked.

Piper shook her head. "I don't think so. The offer came months after we split up."

"How long is this tour?"

"I think they said six weeks. It's basically a loop across the southern states and back."

"Are you willing to take the time away from the twins to go on this tour with her?" Ace and Sam both looked at me.

I nodded. "Jasmine and Jewel are going to Europe with their mom. She wanted to do it as a just-us-girls thing. Mom and daughters bonding before they're all grown up and go their own way. It's been planned for over a year now, scheduled it with the summer vacation from school. They're leaving in a couple of days, so the timing is good for me."

"You okay with Beast as your bodyguard?" Ace looked at Piper.

I narrowed my eyes. What he was really asking was if she felt uncomfortable being forced into close proximity with me now that he knew we'd hooked up.

I felt a flash of anger. Ace was not going to send another one of the Riptide guys with her.

"You mean am I okay being shadowed by the big, bad Biker Beast?" She smiled sweetly, the little brat. She knew what Ace was implying, and she knew neither of us were going to voice it in front of her dad. "Yes, I'm good with that. He makes me feel safe."

"That's reassuring. When does this tour start?" her dad asked.

"A week from Friday. Starts in a pub in Atlanta and then it swings down to Florida, and across the bottom states." She grimaced. "I don't have the itinerary on me. It was on my phone, the one that got trashed. I can get another copy from my agent when I call to accept the tour. We can arrange names and things then too. Lots of people use a stage name."

"So it's a done deal? She's going on tour, and Beast is tagging along as bodyguard?" Ace straightened up and scribbled something down on the pad on his desk.

"Sounds like it." Sam stood and turned to Piper. "How about we spend a few days together before you leave on the tour? There's a spare room in my condo, and we can get you whatever you need in the way of clothes. You can use my credit card." He glanced over at me. "I take it you didn't go back to retrieve any of her things once you picked her up?"

I shook my head. "Nope. Lost no time getting as far away from the thugs taking pot shots as we could. Stuff can always be replaced. People, not so much. We picked her up a few things at one of those discount retail stores but only the necessities. It made Wal-Mart look high end. She'll need a few decent outfits for performing, and some casual clothes for travel." I glanced over at Ace. "I'm guessing her place got tossed pretty thoroughly when they realized she'd escaped. We could send someone to pick up anything with sentimental value, or we could just leave it until this is settled. As long as the rent is paid, it should be fine."

"I don't have anything I need right away." Piper sighed. "Never even considered paying the rent."

"Don't worry, I can take care of that. I'll have a cleanup crew sent in as well so it's in decent shape when you return." Her father patted her arm.

"They might as well pack it up and put it in storage." She winced. "I'm never going to feel safe there after this."

"Are you sure?"

Piper nodded. "Positive. It was just a place to stay, not somewhere I really cared about."

"Okay then. We'll have your things put in storage for now. Don't want to forward it here and risk having someone track it."

She looked up. "They can do that?"

"More than likely. You don't want to take the chance." Ace glanced over at me. "Computer shit can be hacked, and people can be bribed. Unless you really insist, I'd say leave it in storage for now. If we cancel the rent, you will just disappear with no forwarding address."

Her father spoke up. "I'm not much up on women's clothing but I'm sure one of the girls at the office can take you shopping. You can have a whole new wardrobe to start off your new life. Make up for all those Christmases and birthdays I've missed over the years."

Piper was starting to look shellshocked. "No offence, but this is all going pretty fast."

I took pity on her. "I have to take the twins shopping to get some stuff for their trip. I could pick you up and take you with them. They'd love to help you pick out a new wardrobe."

"They barely know me."

"Any female under thirty years old who's willing to discuss clothes and makeup? They'll be thrilled. How about we go find them and ask them?"

"That sounds great if you really don't mind."

Her father nodded. "That's probably a better plan. No chance anyone will see her and connect her with the Bureau if she's with a couple of teenagers."

"So we're good?" Ace broke in.

Piper looked at me, and my heart melted at the trust I could see in her eyes.

"Yeah," she said. "We're good."

"How about we check with the twins before you take off with your father? Make sure they're onboard and set up a time." I always tried to respect the twins' right to have choices. They might not want to share my attention since they were going to be gone for most of the summer. If they didn't want to include Piper, I'd just take her shopping later.

She nodded. "Okay."

I took her hand. "Let's go then. They should still be up in their room."

Ace stood. "I'm going to have a word with Shadow. I'll talk to you two later."

"I'll grab a beer and go with you." Her father left the room right behind Ace.

Piper and I headed back upstairs. We found the twins sitting on the sofa watching a rerun of an old movie. They looked up when we walked in.

"Hey, Dad, what's up?" Jasmine's gaze dropped to our clasped hands, and I could see her eyes sparkle. I knew I'd hear about that later.

"Can't a guy just visit his two favorite girls without a reason?" I tried to look hurt.

They shook their heads in unison. "Nope. You have that look on your face that says there's a reason."

I gave Piper's hand a squeeze. "Fine then. I have a big favor to ask."

"Does it involve you increasing our allowance?" Jewel grinned.

"No, but it involves shopping."

"Almost as good, but you're already taking us shopping." Jasmine raised one eyebrow. "How is that a favor? Unless you're bailing on us?"

"I would never back out on spending the day with you two. This is more of an addition to the day." I glanced over at Piper. "I've been assigned as Piper's bodyguard for the next little while. Since she just got here from California, she needs a new wardrobe. I was hoping you'd be okay with her coming shopping with us this weekend."

The girls looked intrigued, and in typical teenage style dove right into plying her with questions.

"How'd you get stuck with an old grump like our dad?" asked Jasmine.

"Right place at the wrong time?" Piper wrinkled her nose.

Jewel laughed. "Sounds about right. How come you need to go shopping? Didn't you bring clothes with you?"

"I left in kind of a hurry." Piper shrugged. "And I just accepted a gig, so I need something more glamorous than anything I brought, or anything I own actually."

"What kind of gig?"

"Lead singer for a band touring the southern states." A note of pride crept into Piper's voice.

The twins squealed in excitement, throwing questions at Piper faster than she could answer. The shopping trip was obviously going to be a go. I sure hoped my credit card was up for the challenge.

Twenty minutes later, the twins had relegated me to driver and ATM machine for the shopping trip. As a bonus, they were so excited about getting to go shopping with an honest-to-goodness singer that they forgot to tease me about the handholding thing.

## Chapter Six

**Piper**

I peeked out at the crowd from behind the curtain. They were loud. Restless. The butterflies in my stomach swirled faster. I smoothed down the top of the silk outfit Jasmine had insisted I buy.

*What if they hated me? What if I froze? What if I forgot the words to the songs?*

"You ready to go?" The drummer, a young Mexican named Jose with an incredible amount of talent peeked over my head. "Nice crowd for opening night."

I sighed. "I'm nervous, Jose. What if they don't like me?"

"That's just stage fright talking." He smiled encouragingly. "They'll love you. The minute the curtains open, you'll be fine. Trust me, I've seen this lots of times."

"Thanks." I tried to smile back at him. I wasn't so sure. I looked over at Beast, standing off to the left of the stage. He was out of the way of the bustling stage crew but could still keep me in sight.

He'd become my rock. Solid. Dependable. He winked at me, and I suddenly had to squelch the urge to burst out in nervous laughter.

What could go wrong if I had big bad Biker Beast watching over me?

"You're on in five." The stage manager held up his hand as he strode by, motioning to the lighting guys above before disappearing into the sound booth. I could see him fiddling with things on the control board, lights flashing on and off randomly as he tweaked it.

The band lined up, just like they'd done every

time we practiced, and one of the roadies adjusted my microphone so it wasn't pointing over my head. He gave me a quick thumbs up before rushing off to move one of the guitar amps to a better position.

I heard the emcee giving us an enthusiastic introduction and then we were on.

The curtains swished open, the drummer counted us in, and the band started the intro music. Soon I was too busy singing to worry about stage fright.

The energy of the audience was contagious. They jumped up from their seats, singing along and swaying in time to the music. Servers had to duck and carefully work their way around the dancers as they brought food and drink to the people still seated at the tables around the perimeter of the room.

I began to relax. I could do this. The people in the crowd were enjoying the show, they loved us!

I plucked the microphone off the stand so I could move around the stage as I sang. This was what I'd always dreamed of doing. The connection with the audience was exhilarating.

I focused on one teenager in the audience as I sang about first love, and she blushed a deep red. Out of the corner of my eye I could see Beast keeping a watchful eye on the crowd. Every so often his gaze would drift back to me, and I'd feel his quiet strength bolster my confidence.

Time flew by in a mixture of songs, banter, and an occasional drum or guitar solo that let me catch my breath.

Before I knew it, the emcee came back on stage and announced the intermission. As soon as the curtains closed, I ran to Beast, throwing myself in his arms. "They loved me!"

He caught me against him and laughed. "Of course they did. You're amazing, and you connect with them. You make them feel like they're part of the show."

"They are! Did you see that kid blush? And that one couple dance a solo to that jazz number?"

"Yeah. Just don't expect me to ever try that." He handed me a bottle of water. "Here. You need to hydrate. You probably should have a bottle on stage with you."

I twisted the lid off and downed half the contents in one big, long drink. He wasn't wrong. I felt parched.

The guys in the band watched in amusement. They were all old hands at this, and I felt like a kid at her first rodeo, but I couldn't help it.

The drummer set his sticks down and sauntered over. "Congrats, Piper. I told you it was just stage fright. Everyone gets it at some point. I know performers who have been on the stage for decades and they still tense up when it's a new gig or a new venue."

"Thanks, Jose." I gave him a grateful smile. "You guys were amazing. You made me sound great."

Jose wandered back to the band area. The stage manager hurried on, checking wires and plugs to make sure everything was still secure. Glancing up at me, he nodded. "Good first set. You've got twenty minutes if you need to go do anything."

"Thanks." Beast grabbed my hand and led me off the stage area.

"Where are we going?" I frowned. "We only have twenty minutes."

"Then we'd better make this fast." His eyes danced with mischief and something else that sent a sizzling heat dancing through my veins. He led me down the back corridor and into a room marked SUPPLIES. Flipping the light on, he locked the door and turned to drag me up against him. His mouth closed over mine as I let out a squeak of alarm. "Watching you out there, singing your heart out to that crowd gave me a monster hard-on." He took my hand and guided it down to the huge bulge at his crotch.

I should have said no. I should have pushed him away. I should have been outraged.

Did he really think he could just drag me offstage for a quickie in between sets?

Yes, apparently, he did.

And my traitorous body seemed to be onboard with it. My thong was already damp as he pushed up the skirt of my outfit to my waist.

"We don't have time for this! Twenty minutes, remember?" I hissed.

"Down to fifteen, so quit talking and help me out here. I'm not stopping, and the show isn't going on without you."

The thought of all those people out in the audience, cheerfully unaware of what we were doing, turned me on. Who knew I'd get a kick out of making out in a supply closet halfway through my debut musical show?

I reached down and undid Beast's pants.

"That's my girl." He took his cock in his hand and gave it a couple of quick strokes.

My eyes fixated on a single drop of moisture glistening on the tip. I flicked my tongue out to wet my lips. "I want to taste that."

He shook his head. "Later. Right now, I need to be inside you." He produced a condom from his back pocket and quickly sheathed himself. Grasping me by the hips, he pushed my thong aside and positioned himself at my entrance.

I sucked in a deep breath as the tip of his cock slipped through my moist folds. Reaching up, I wrapped my arms around his neck to steady myself.

Beast surged forward, burying himself balls deep in my pussy with one massive thrust of his hips. His hands on my waist, he pinned me against the wall.

"Oh God, please." I let out my breath in one explosive gasp as pleasure skated across the surface of my skin.

"Please, what?"

"Fuck me. Hard. Make me come."

He slowly withdrew, then plunged back in, circling his hips to make sure he hit every raw nerve inside me. "You know what gets me all fucking hot and bothered?" he growled.

"What?" I gasped as flames of erotic heat flickered up my spine.

"Standing there, watching you up on that stage, singing your heart out to all those people? It just fucking made me crazy horny knowing that at the end of the night, I'm the one who gets to take you home and do this." He reached down between us and used one finger to toy with my clit. "I'm the one who gets to strip you naked and fuck you till you can't stand up."

"You're doing that now." I whimpered as I felt my orgasm starting to build.

"Nah." He shifted position and managed to ram his cock in even deeper. "This is a just a teaser. When we get back to the motel, I'm going to take my time and make you beg me for it."

"Not gonna happen. I don't beg." I shuddered as my climax gained momentum.

"We'll see." He rammed into me again, and my climax roared over me like a wildfire in the bone-dry

California foothills. One more thrust and he joined me, letting out a deep groan as his seed spilled into the condom. I sagged against him, and he held me tight as we both gasped for air.

"Five minutes to curtain. Take your seats, people." The muffled sound of the announcer's voice reached us as it blared over the loudspeaker. Meant as a warning to the audience, it spurred me into action.

"We need to get back!"

Beast grinned at me, every inch the conquering hero. "Yeah, we do." He removed the condom and tied it off, dropping it into the wastebasket in the corner of the room. Pulling his pants back up, he fastened them and looked over at me.

I straightened up my clothing and ran my fingers through my hair. "Do I look okay?"

"You look gorgeous."

I rolled my eyes. "Do I look like I just stepped out for a quickie?"

"No." He opened the door and checked the hallway before holding out his hand for me to follow him. "You look like you're enjoying the night, which is what you're supposed to look like. No one's going to guess what we were up to."

I had my doubts about that, but I kept them to myself.

* * *

**Beast**

Piper was on an adrenaline high after the show. Her eyes sparkled as she accepted the congratulations from the stage manager, Mark. It made me feel good to see her so happy, especially since I knew that little quickie in the supply closet had helped.

"You must remember to include us in your next

tour!" Mark beamed with joy. "The audience loved you, and I can guarantee a sold-out house if we can convince you to return."

"I'd love to come back." Piper grinned. "You need to talk to my agent, though. That's who sets these things up. I just sing, and the band does a terrific job backing me up. Without them, I wouldn't stand a chance."

"You're being modest."

Piper shook her head. "No, the band has been together a long time. They play so well they just make me look good. I was lucky they asked me to replace the lead singer when she bowed out."

"I'll call your agent." He rubbed his hands together and threw me a nervous glance. "I'd give you a hug but your watchdog over there is glaring at me."

Piper, the little wench, threw me a look that said she dared me to do anything. "Don't mind him. He always looks like that, but he's harmless."

The manager looked doubtful.

Piper giggled and threw her arms around the guy, giving him a great big hug. "See? All nasty looks, but no action. Thanks for everything, Mark. The concert went off perfectly, and I'm sure I have you to thank for all the behind-the-scenes work."

The manager was probably old enough to be her father, but his face turned an interesting shade of red. "Thanks. A lot of people don't realize how much we do back here."

A blur of motion on the far side caught my attention and I tensed, my hand going for the gun hidden under my cut. When I realized it was just one of the roadies wrapping up cords, I relaxed and let my hand fall back down to my side.

"I do, and I appreciate it." Piper looked over at

me, her brow drawn down in a frown. "We should probably get back to the motel and get a few hours' sleep before we hit the road."

I straightened up, more than ready to call it for the night.

Mark gave me another nervous look and headed over to talk to the roadie.

* * *

The band had already packed their equipment into the tour bus and headed back to the motel by the time we got outside. We climbed onto my bike and zipped back there in record time. Piper was used to riding by now, and I didn't have to worry about scaring her if I felt like going full throttle. I think she secretly enjoyed the thrill, although she always scolded me afterward for acting like a teenage idiot. Her term, not mine.

She didn't say much when we got there, heading straight for the shower and shedding her clothes carelessly on the floor. The vibe she gave off told me she was pissed, but I had no idea why.

*Women. You might as well try to figure out why the chicken crossed the road.*

I took off my cut and set it and my gun down on the side table. I'd silenced my phone earlier, leaving it on vibrate so it didn't ring while Piper was on stage. I left the ring tone off and set it beside the gun. My boots came off next, followed by my shirt. Clad in just my pants, I picked up the remote and turned on the television.

"That's too loud." Piper reappeared wrapped in a towel, her wet feet leaving damp footprints on the tiled floor.

I raised one eyebrow. "You want to tell me what's wrong, or are we going to play twenty questions?"

"I'm fine," she snapped.

"Fuck," I groaned. "I know what that means."

"What the hell are you talking about?"

"A woman says she's fine, it means I screwed up real bad."

She looked at me, her face set in a mutinous frown. "No. Yes. I don't know." The towel slipped just a bit, hinting at the fullness of those delectable breasts it covered. She stalked across the bed, pivoting to glare at me. "I don't get you. You say you don't want any kind of relationship. Just sex. Then you grab me mid show for a quickie and you know the entire band knew it. Like you were a caveman staking a claim and making sure everyone understood. Then, just for good measure, you glare at some poor guy who is probably older than my father just because he talked to me. Talked! What the hell do you plan to do if a guy actually touches me?"

"Beat the shit out of him."

"What?" She blinked. "Why? That's ridiculous. You are the most irritating, difficult man I have ever had the misfortune to meet."

She didn't get it. "Yeah, I said all those things. Said I didn't want a relationship. I've got kids, and that can get way too complicated. But you and me? We're easy. We get each other. So I'm not letting you dump me for a guy with more money, or fewer tattoos, or no kids to complicate things. You and me? We belong together. And yeah, if some asshole thinks he can take what's mine? Ain't happening, so it's best if everyone understands that from the fucking start."

"I belong to you?"

Trust her to fixate on that. "We belong to each other. Together. You have to admit you enjoyed our little quickie in the closet, and you liked that everyone knew I was so far gone I couldn't keep my hands to myself."

A reluctant smile curved the corner of her mouth. "Yeah. It was kind of awesome."

I scowled. "Then why are you so fucking mad?"

"I'm not mad at you, I'm mad at myself."

"I don't get it."

"I don't do relationships. Drake was my first, and look how badly that turned out. I fuck, and I smile, and I say goodbye. Simple. No strings attached."

"But now there's strings." I was starting to understand. "And you don't know how to deal with that."

She sighed. "Yeah. I never wanted to belong to someone. Your words, not mine. But now I do, and I see you protecting me and doing shit to make me feel good like that quickie in the closet. I don't know how to deal with it. I don't know if I want to deal with it."

"You're scared you're going to get hurt," I said quietly. Reaching out a hand, I pulled her down into my lap. The towel slipped down, and she tugged it back into place like it was some kind of armour keeping her safe from feeling anything for me.

She nodded. "I grew up watching men come and go through my mom's bedroom like a parade. And every time, every new guy, she'd get her hopes up. She'd be as giddy as a schoolgirl, and then he'd be gone and she'd be devastated. I swore I'd never do that, never care enough about a guy that him leaving would tear me apart. I used them, I let them use me. Worked just fine. But now you? Shit. You could really hurt me."

I wrapped my arms around her and rocked gently back and forth. "It's okay. I'm not going anywhere. You and me, we'll work this out."

She started to cry. Fuck. I could handle a lot, but listening to her sob quietly against my chest near broke my heart. It had been a long day, what with the opening performance nerves, stage fright, and that fear in the back of her mind, that fucking Drake would somehow track her down. I let her cry herself out, then I tucked her into bed. Shedding the rest of my clothes I climbed in beside her, pulling her up against me and cradling her in my arms as she fell into an exhausted slumber.

At some point, I dozed off only to be awakened by the faint buzz of my cell phone vibrating on the side table. I freed one hand from around Piper and checked the call display.

Ace.

*Fuck. Now what?*

## Chapter Seven

**Piper**

I woke alone in bed. The heavenly smell of fresh coffee teased my nostrils. I stretched, rolling over to see where Beast had gone. This was a motel room, not a house. He couldn't be far.

He was sitting at the rickety table by the window, a mug of coffee in his hand and his gun already holstered. The guy did not let that weapon get more than an arm's length from him at any time.

I propped myself up on one elbow, pulling the bedding up to my chin. "You going to share that?"

He turned his head toward me, a slow smile making it all the way to his eyes. "Morning, sleepyhead. You mean the coffee?"

"Of course I mean the coffee."

He stood and stalked over to the tiny kitchen area. Picking up one of the paper cups the hotel supplied, he fixed the coffee just the way I liked it -- lots of cream and sugar. Handing it to me, he sat down on the edge of the bed. "How do you feel about you and I taking the scenic route on my bike to the next gig?"

I took a sip of the coffee. "Sounds lovely, but why?" The plan was for me to ride in the tour bus and Beast to follow on his bike so he could keep an eye out for anything suspicious.

"Because I feel like taking a ride and I love it when your arms are wrapped around me?"

"Not buying it. Try again."

He sighed. "Ace called. Said Shadow found some chatter on the web. Hard to decipher, but he thinks Drake might know where you are."

"So he knows where I am, or he knows I'll be on

the tour bus?"

"Shadow couldn't get details, just the bare bones. Ace figures we need to play it safe. Keep you off the bus, and off the planned route. If the bus changes route, it can be followed. It doesn't exactly blend into the landscape. But a lone bike? Not even on the planned route? It won't attract much attention."

I took another sip of the coffee and considered. I kind of missed the days we'd spent on the bike doing the cross-country thing. "How sure is he that Drake found me?"

"About fifty percent. The intel was kind of vague. Might have been someone else. Drake's name was never mentioned but the details were suspicious."

"So this is just a precaution?"

He nodded. "A better safe than sorry kind of thing."

"What about the band? Is this going to put them in danger?"

"Nah. These guys are pros. They won't even show themselves unless they plan to strike. No female to shoot at, they'll just disappear back into whatever shithole they came from."

I gulped down more coffee. "In that case, I'd love to go for a ride on your bike."

"Good." He stood up and headed back to the coffee machine. "You hungry? I can go find some donuts or something for breakfast if you want."

I wrinkled my nose and let the bed sheets slide down to my waist. "I don't think I'm in the mood for donuts."

"Muffins, then?"

God, the man was dense. I stuck one finger in my mouth and sucked on it suggestively. "Guess again."

Half an hour later I was feeling deliciously

satisfied and ready for whatever the day brought. Or at least I thought I was. I had a quick shower and got dressed while he went to find me that donut he'd mentioned and explain the change of plans to the band.

"You going to tell them about Drake and his band of hit men?" We had agreed not to mention my insane ex, the mafia connection, or the contract out on me to my agent or the band when I'd agreed to the tour, but that was when it was a vague threat.

Beast shook his head. "No point. It would just freak them out, and there's nothing they can do. Best they look as innocent as they are if anyone comes sniffing around. As far as they are aware, I'm your bodyguard because you needed an excuse to bring along your boy-toy. They all think you just can't keep your hands off me."

I raised one brow. "They seriously think I can't keep my hands off you?"

He grinned. "It's true."

I reached for my chaps that he'd laid out on the bed. "Yeah, it is. Help me get these chaps on."

"I thought you had this figured out."

"I did. But I like the feel of your hands on me, right?" I stuck my tongue out at him.

"Wench!"

I laughed.

He stalked over and took the chaps, wrapping them around my waist and buckling the belt. Damn, the man was freaking gorgeous. And he was right. I couldn't keep my hands to myself.

* * *

It had only been a day since the last time I'd rode on the back of Beast's bike, but that had been much too short of a ride. The wind whipping past me while I rested my head against his broad back brought me a special kind of peace. I felt safe. Cared for. Happy, even.

All my worries melted away, and the only things that mattered were the vibrations of the bike beneath me and the warmth of Beast's body in front of me as I watched the landscape race by in a blur of color. The next gig was in a little town three hours down the road from last night's performance, but Beast had warned me that the detour he had in mind would take us at least twice that long. We weren't scheduled to be on stage until the next day so there was no rush. I could relax and just enjoy the ride.

I'd never understood people who spent their whole lives moving from place to place. My childhood had been one of constant moves when my mom hadn't been able to pay the rent, found a new boyfriend, or jumped at a new job. She'd always been searching for that perfect life that was just out of reach.

Me? I'd longed to have a real home, a permanent one where I could settle, make friends, and feel like I belonged. I watched the little cliques of kids at schools who'd grown up together, friends since they were old enough to walk, and I'd envied them. Now I wasn't so sure home was a place. Beast made me feel safe, and his club, Riptide, had made me feel welcome with no judgment, no questions. My dad had helped me escape San Diego without hesitation. Despite the terror of knowing Drake wanted me dead, I felt happy. I'd found a family, a home. I just hoped they felt the same way about me.

A few hours later, Beast slowed down and turned into the parking lot of a shabby-looking diner. Parked in a row in front were several motorcycles, and he pulled up beside them.

I slid off the back and removed my helmet,

shaking my head to fluff up my hair.

"Doesn't look like much, but the food here is good." Beast took my helmet and hung it off the handlebars beside his.

I eyed a faded sign that proclaimed it to be the *Best Burger Joint in the State*. "You've been here before?"

He nodded. "It's run by an old Navy buddy of mine."

"You seem to have old Navy buddies all over the place."

"We went through a lot together in the SEALs, and we keep in touch. Like family, but with less fucking drama."

"That sounds nice. Family." I could hear the wistful note in my own voice.

Beast held out his hand, and I hid my grin.

The lady behind the counter looked up and beamed at us when we walked in. "Beast! Been too long since you visited. How are you doing?"

"Good, Ruth. How about you and Henry?"

She rolled her eyes. "He's as stubborn as ever, but I love him. I must, to put up with his shit. He wants to paint the place."

Beast glanced around. "Doesn't sound that bad. A bit of paint wouldn't hurt."

She grimaced. "He wants to paint it pink and purple."

Beast snorted. "Sounds like Henry. Probably just said that to get you riled up. You know what he's like."

Ruth sighed. "Yeah. I suggested a nice green, or blue even. He said he'd take it under consideration." She looked pointedly at our joined hands. "Are you going to introduce me to your friend?"

Beast nodded at me. "This is Piper. She's the daughter of a friend. Piper, meet Ruth. She and her hubby Henry were snipers back in the day. Saved my ass a time or two."

* * *

**Beast**

I liked that Piper didn't bat an eye at finding out the motherly-looking Ruth was a retired sniper.

"Nice to meet you." Piper smiled warmly.

"And you."

A sound behind us had me automatically turning to face the door, pushing Piper behind me and reaching for my gun.

"Speak of the devil. Here's the color blind idiot now." Ruth gave me an understanding look. "You shouldn't have your back to the door if you're that jumpy. Someone could get hurt."

I inclined my head in acknowledgment. "Yeah. Sorry about that. A little touchy today." I didn't offer an explanation. They'd just assume it was PTSD kicking in, like it did for a lot of the vets who'd seen action. "Hey, Henry. I hear you're thinking of painting the place."

"Nice of you to drop by, Beast. I see you found someone willing to overlook your many faults. At least for a day or two."

I gave Piper's hand a squeeze. "Her name's Piper, and she adores me."

Henry gave her a sympathetic look. "You obviously don't know him very well. If he's holding you hostage, just give me a sign and I'll take him out for you."

Piper laughed. "Thanks for the offer, but so far I'm enjoying myself."

Ruth shook her head, looking from Henry to me. "A person would think you two weren't friends."

Henry grinned. "We don't care what a person thinks, do we, Beast?"

I shook my head. "Nope."

"Find yourself a seat, and I'll rustle you up some grub." Ruth turned and headed to the kitchen.

I led Piper past a few of the occupied tables, nodding to the bikers I recognized. I chose a booth at the back of the diner, right beside the emergency exit. Always a good idea to have an escape route handy, even if you didn't think you needed it.

Henry followed us with a couple of glasses of water. "Hot out there today. You could probably use a drink," he said by way of explanation. "Ruth has your burgers on the grill."

Piper looked confused. "We didn't order yet."

"Not that kind of place. Ruth decides what she thinks you need, and she's never wrong."

"She doesn't know me," Piper pointed out.

"You're with this big lug here, so that tells her all she needs to know."

I patted Piper's knee under the table. "Never said my friends were normal."

Henry hooted with laughter. "Biggest frickin' understatement of the decade!" He turned and headed back to the front of the diner.

"You still okay?" I moved a ketchup bottle to the side of the table. "I know they can be a bit strange, but Henry and Ruth are some of the best people on the fucking planet."

"Don't worry about me finding things strange." Piper smiled wryly. "My mom was a Vegas stripper, remember? I'm not sure I'd recognize normal if I saw it."

Fuck, this woman was perfect.

"You planning on going much further today,

Beast?" one of the bikers hollered back at me. "Weather service says there's a storm heading this way, and it's moving fast. You might want to hunker down for the rest of the day."

"Those guys are wrong more than they're right." I glanced outside. "Sun's shining and there's not a fucking cloud in the sky."

The biker shrugged. "Your call. Just thought you should know."

I caught Piper looking out the window. "You want to stay put? I'm sure Ruth and Henry would be happy to put us up."

Piper shook her head. "No. You're right. Those guys are not very reliable. We could stay put, and the storm will blow in tomorrow when we go to leave. Or it will circle around us completely. We can always pull off somewhere up the road if it gets bad, right?"

I nodded. "Absolutely."

Ruth came bustling down the aisle balancing a couple of plates on her arm. "You always have to sit with your back in a corner, don't you, Beast."

It was a statement, not a question. Old habits died hard, especially ones intended to keep me from meeting my Maker. If I backed myself into a corner with an escape route handy, I was much more likely to make it out of a shithole alive.

"That smells heavenly!" Piper stared down at the plate Ruth set in front of her.

"Thanks, sweetie. It's a hamburger steak with fries and gravy and the salad fixings are from my garden out back. Enjoy." Ruth looked over at me and winked, letting me know she approved of Piper. Not that I needed her approval, but it was nice to have it.

We ate in companionable silence. Breakfast hadn't been all that filling, and we were both hungry.

Finishing up her salad, Piper let out a contented sigh. "That was amazing. Do you have friends all over the country just waiting to feed you or put a roof over your head on short notice?"

"Hell, yeah." I grinned and downed the last mouthful of my hamburger steak. "Seriously though, I tend to plan my routes to touch base with the guys I served with as much as possible. This is a route I take a lot. There's a motel a couple hours up the road, although we don't need a place to stop today. Might drop in and say hi, depending on how our time goes."

I pulled out my phone and checked for messages. Nothing. I took that as a good sign. I glanced at Piper. "I should touch base with the twins. They'll be expecting me to call before they take off for Europe."

"Go ahead. You want some privacy?"

"Nah. After that shopping trip, they're big fans of yours."

She grinned at me. "I think they're fans of your credit card."

"True. But you're the one who talked me into letting them spend that much."

"Well, you don't want Europe thinking you're stingy."

"Why would I care what Europe thinks of me?" I thumbed the FaceTime app and waited for Jasmine to answer before adding Jewel to the call.

"Hey, Dad!" Jewel grinned at me on the screen. "We're just trying to fit everything in the suitcases. Thanks so much for all the new stuff. And thank Piper for us."

"Thank her yourself." I angled the phone so Piper was included in the call.

"Thanks, Piper," they chimed in unison.

"You're in leather." Jasmine tilted her head. "You

and Dad biking it? I thought there was a bus."

"The weather's good so we're taking advantage." I nudged Piper's leg under the table to warn her not to mention the threat.

"Lucky! I bet it feels great."

"Better than being cooped up on a bus." Piper glanced at me.

"You two look cute together." Jewel wrinkled her nose. "Any chance there's more shopping trips in our future?"

Jasmine rolled her eyes. "That's her subtle way of asking if you two are into each other."

"Into each other?" I raised one brow. "We're fond of each other, if that's what you mean."

Jewel shook her head and looked at Piper. "You can be fond of a cat. We want to know if you and Dad are more than just friends."

"Are you okay with it if we're more than friends?" Piper asked.

Both girls nodded enthusiastically. "Definitely. It would be so great if Dad had someone to concentrate on other than us."

"You mean you think you could get away with more?" I tried to look stern.

Piper frowned at me before turning her attention back to the girls. "Good to hear. We're exploring things right now."

"Dad's a good guy." Jewel's expression sobered. "He gave up a lot for us. He deserves someone to make him happy."

Her sister nodded. "He does."

My heart melted. "You two are worth everything to me. You give me so much more than you think I gave up. I can't imagine life without you to keep me on my toes."

Jasmine turned her head at a sound in the background. "That's Mom calling us. We have to go."

"Just finishing up, Mom. Be right there," Jewel yelled at her mother, before turning back to wave at the screen. "Have fun, you two!"

"Have a great trip and send lots of pictures." Piper waved back.

"We will. Look after Dad for us, Piper." They blew kisses at the screen before the picture winked out.

I turned the screen off and slid the phone back in my pocket. "I think we can safely say they're okay with you and I being together."

Piper nodded. "They're great kids. You've done an amazing job raising them."

"Thanks. They are my world." I glanced outside. "We should probably get moving." I stood up and tossed a few bills on the table to cover our meal. I knew if I tried to pay for it, Ruth would get on her high horse and talk about friends and all that shit. Friendship didn't pay the bills, and I wasn't short on cash. This way, it saved her pride and my dignity. Henry? He was smart enough to stay out of it if Ruth got to arguing.

It was early afternoon. We still had lots of daylight left, and I was in no hurry for the ride to end. I took it easy, puttering along so slowly you could actually read the road signs. For a short time, we could forget about Drake and hit men and the rest of the world. It was just Piper and me and the open road.

Biker heaven.

Ruth had packed a snack for us to take, and we stopped at one of those roadside picnic areas to stretch our legs and sample it. Damn woman sure liked to feed people. No wonder Henry now sported a sizable beer belly, despite the fact he didn't drink.

Piper glanced up at the sky. It wasn't as bright as it had been earlier. Dark clouds had started to gather to the east. "You think it's going to storm?"

I considered it. "Maybe, but we should be safely at our destination by then. The clouds aren't moving very fast."

She nodded, her attention turning back to the food. "These scones are amazing. You don't suppose she'd be willing to share the recipe, do you?"

"You want a recipe? I've never seen you go near a kitchen, much less show any interest in cooking."

"I can cook. Just haven't had the chance lately. Cross-country bike rides, and then a concert tour? Doesn't leave much time for domestic stuff. I'll have you know people rave about my fried chicken."

What were the chances she'd know that was my favorite food? "You'll have to prove that to me the next time we're near a kitchen for more than half an hour."

She laughed. "You just want a free meal."

I tried to look hurt. "Not me. I can resist liver and onions until the end of time, free or not. Can't resist a meal that has grease dripping from it, though."

Piper shook her head. "And here I thought the way to your heart was through your pants. Turns out it's your stomach."

"Oh, the pants thing works too," I assured her. "Combine them and I will be your fucking slave for life."

Piper rolled her eyes. "You are incorrigible!"

"If that means horny, then yeah. That's me."

Piper laughed again. I loved that sound, the way her entire face lit up. Out here on the open road, she didn't worry so much about her asshole of an ex. The chances of him finding us when we were on the move were slim.

"Can I ask you a personal question?"

I narrowed my eyes. "Sure. Can't promise I'll answer."

"All the guys at Riptide, and all these friends you have on the road seem to be good guys, like not murderers or drug dealers. Heck, my father trusted you to bring me back here. You work with the FBI, and you were all in the service. How did you end up being a biker gang?"

"Fair question, but it's kind of a long story."

"Short version?" She didn't plan on letting this go.

Everything Riptide meant to me flashed through my mind. I took a deep breath and looked her in the eyes, hoping she could understand. "War is hell, and trying to fit in when you land back stateside is tough. We found each other and figured out a way to make it work for us. We make a difference, get to do something that makes the world a better place, and we have a family. Not one made from blood ties, but one we made for ourselves."

"Wow." Her expression softened. "That sounds amazing. I'd love to hear the long version some day when we have more time."

I glanced up at the sky. The clouds were moving faster now, and getting stuck out in the rain on a bike was no fun. "You will, I promise. Right now, though, we'd better get back on the road."

"I'll hold you to that." Piper helped gather up the remains of our snack and dumped the garbage in the cans provided for it. I had a strict no littering policy.

We were back on the bike, cruising down the road at top speed within minutes. Those fucking clouds were moving faster though, and we'd barely made five miles before the first fat droplets hit us.

I felt Piper try to squirm in closer behind me to avoid them, and I doubled down on the throttle. There was a deserted cabin up ahead that I sometimes camped out in overnight when I was out this way. Door didn't really close, and most of the windows were boarded over. It was surrounded by mounds of wild peppermint, and the pungent odor of the plants kept most of the native rodents and insects away. It wasn't much, but at least we'd be dry while we waited for the rain to pass.

The storm ramped up, gusts of wind pushing the bike sideways at irregular intervals. I struggled to keep the machine under control. Between the slick pavement, the unpredictable wind gusts, and the water streaming off my helmet, it was a fight. If I'd been on my own, I would have just pulled over and waited it out. Piper hung on like a trooper, though, and I was determined to get her to shelter.

The cabin finally came into sight and I let off on the throttle just as the bike hit one big-assed puddle and started to skid.

*Shit*!

## Chapter Eight

**Piper**

The bike started to skid sideways just as a rickety old shack came into sight on the right side of the highway and I felt Beast tense.

This couldn't be good. Beast was my rock, and rocks didn't scare easily.

I tightened my grip around his waist and sent up a silent prayer to whatever gods were listening. Up to now, we'd always headed for shelter if the weather looked threatening. This was my first time on a bike in a storm.

*Focus on the little things you can control.*

The one thing I'd learned on that cross-country trip on the back of Beast's motorcycle was that my body needed to follow his at all times. If he leaned right, I leaned right. Whatever he did, I imitated it exactly. Balance is key, he'd told me, when you only have two wheels under you. Made sense. I took a deep breath, trying to ignore my gut feeling, and focused on his body language.

Beast turned the handlebars and leaned right, steering in the direction of the skid. At the same time, he shifted his weight back. The bike moved sluggishly, and I tried to squelch down a growing twinge of alarm. Moments later, the bike wobbled slightly as the rear wheel regained traction and the bike stopped its sideways slide.

The butterflies in my belly settled back into place. Of course Beast managed to regain control. Why had I doubted him? He'd probably done this a hundred times.

The bike slowed, and we turned onto the weed-covered path leading to the cabin. Beast circled the structure completely before bringing the bike to a stop at the back of the building. I wasn't sure if he was checking to make sure it was safe or just trying to find the dryest spot to park. If he was looking for a dry spot, he was wasting his time. The torrential downpour showed no signs of easing up.

He pulled up as close to the building as he could get, and I slithered off the back of the bike. Not bothering to take my helmet off, I bolted for the door. Beast grabbed the saddlebags and followed hot on my heels.

I squelched down an insane urge to giggle. I knew it was caused by nerves but that didn't make it any easier. We made it. We were safe. And bonus, as derelict as the cabin appeared from the outside, the roof didn't leak, and I didn't see any signs of rodents or insects scurrying around. The powers that be were feeling generous for a change.

I dropped the helmet on the shelf beside the door and shrugged out of my jacket and chaps, grateful for the water shedding ability of leather. My backside was a little damp but considering the monsoon rains we'd come through that was hardly worth noting. Tossing his helmet beside mine, Beast strode to the table on the far side of the room and lit the candle sitting on it with the matches someone had left handily beside it.

He cast me a sideways look. "That got a little rough at the end. You okay?"

I nodded, running my fingers through my hair. "Yeah. It wasn't so bad."

"At least there's one good thing." He grinned.

"And that is?"

"We can be fairly sure Drake had nothing to do with this."

"True." I gave him a rueful smile. "But I can

blame him anyway, right? I've kind of got into the habit of blaming him for anything that goes wrong in my life."

Beast took off his chaps and cut, hanging them over the back of a wooden chair to dry out. "You're a fierce little wench, aren't you? Who would have thought a pint-sized singer could hold such a mean grudge?"

I bowed mockingly. "That's me. Small but fierce. He did try to have me killed so I think I'm justified. You might want to keep that in mind if you ever cross me."

"Wouldn't dream of it." He moved to the kitchen counter and looked at an old-fashioned metal coffee maker, the kind you set on a stove. Ground coffee, sugar, and powdered creamer were neatly stowed in glass jars beside it. "Looks like whoever was here last left us some supplies."

"A stovetop coffee maker? Do you know how to use that thing?" I remembered the type well from all the times Mom hadn't paid the power bill.

"Yeah. Not my first time here. It's kind of a community shelter for whoever is passing by and needs to stop. Unwritten rule is you leave it stocked for the next guy. It doesn't always work out, but it's nice when it does. Should be one of those green camp stove things in the cupboard, and hopefully some fuel for it."

He reached over and turned the tap. A trickle of orangish colored water splashed down into the sink.

I wrinkled my nose. "I think I'll pass on the coffee. That looks nasty."

"Good thing we still have a couple bottles of water left from our picnic. You want coffee, I can make it happen."

"No, but thanks." He really could be sweet

despite his name.

"Hard to say how long we're going to be stuck here." He glanced over at one of the windows. "I'd better check in with Ace." He pulled out his phone, holding it up and walking around the room.

"No signal?"

"Nope. Don't read anything scary into it. These storms tend to interfere with cell phone signals."

"If this were a spy movie, there would be a guy outside with a hi-tech device blocking the signal so no one would know we were being butchered," I pointed out.

"And if this were a tropical storm in the southern states, there would be a lot of weather blocking the satellite signals. Possibly a tree or two down over the lines to kill the power, although that really isn't an issue here. No power to kill." He put the cell phone back in his pocket. "Come hold the door for me while I bring the bike inside out of the weather."

"You're bringing the bike inside the cabin?"

He nodded. "Damn straight. It's our transportation and it'll be a whole lot safer inside than being blown around in that wind, not to mention wet electronics and very wet seats."

"Good point." My hand went to the damp material on my ass as I followed him to the door. I tried to hide behind it from the pelting rain as I held it wide open for him to wheel the bike inside. Even having the door open for that brief period of time caused a big puddle to gather inside the doorway. I hunted through the kitchen cupboards and came up with a pile of rags to help dry things up. When we were done, the bike was safely parked against the wall where we wouldn't be tripping over it.

He walked over to the fireplace. Crouching

down, he peered up the chimney.

I frowned. "What are you looking for?"

"Just checking nothing's taken up residence in the chimney before I light a fire. Birds. Squirrels. Badgers. That sort of thing." Apparently satisfied, he proceeded to build a fire with the paper and wood stacked neatly against the wall. When the flames were crackling cheerfully, he turned with a big grin on his face. "Pretty good for someone who's not a boy scout, huh?"

I laughed. "Yeah. I'm impressed." The damp chill was already disappearing. I guess it didn't take long to warm up a small open space like this.

"So now what?" I placed one of the chairs in front of the fireplace and hung the rags over the back to dry off.

"We find some way to kill time until the storm passes." He shrugged. "These things usually blow themselves out in an hour or so."

"We could play spy." I batted my lashes at him. He'd taken off his wet shirt after bringing the bike in, and all that bare skin and muscle caused naughty thoughts to flood my brain.

He cocked his head. "Never been much of one for games. I can think of better ways to kill time."

"You'll like this game, I promise." I smirked. "You're the enemy general, and I'm the sexy spy. It's my job to get you to tell me your super-secret plans."

"And how do you plan to do that?"

I dropped to my knees in front of him. "Guess."

Reaching up, I held his gaze as I undid his pants. His cock was already hardening as I slid my hand down its length. Beast pushed his pants down further, and I cupped his balls, squeezing gently.

"Going to have to try harder if you want those

plans." He leaned back against the table.

"By the time I'm done, you're going to be begging me to take them." I swirled my tongue across the head of his cock.

Beast let out a low groan. "We'll see."

I took that as a challenge, opening my mouth and taking him in. Gods, he was magnificent. His shaft, fully engorged, was long and thick. I sucked enthusiastically, my cheeks hollowing. Running my tongue down his hard length, I could feel the thick vein on the side throbbing.

"That feels so fucking good." He reached down to fist his hands in my hair.

I angled my head to take the last few inches. His cock bumped the back of my throat, and I fought down a gag reflex. Beast threw his head back, eyes closed tight as he fucked my mouth.

I loved the feeling of control, of being able to give him what he wanted on my own terms. With Beast, there weren't any power games. We were both here because we wanted to be, and as much as that scared me, I realized I was okay with it.

"Piper…"

"Mmm?" It's hard to talk with a massive cock in your mouth.

"If you don't stop, I'm going to come in your mouth."

"Mmmm?" I failed to see the problem.

He tugged gently on my hair. "I want to be inside you when I come."

Technically, he was inside me now, but I knew what he meant. I let his cock slide out of my mouth and lifted my head to see him staring down at me, his eyes sparkling with lust. "Oh." I was almost back on my feet when he scooped me up and tossed me on the bed in the corner of the room.

"Hey!" I sat up and glared at him. "I'm still dressed."

"So you are. You might want to take care of that so I don't rip anything that can't be replaced." He stood right beside the bed as he casually stripped the remainder of his clothes off. Within seconds he was naked. That's one thing I loved about him -- the way he was so casual about his body. Not that he had any reason to hide it. The man was absolutely gorgeous -- all muscle and sinew and beautifully artistic tattoos. Well-endowed was an understatement. His cock was so thick and long it was almost scary.

I quickly wriggled out of my clothing and laid back on the bed, spreading my legs wide.

Beast's eyes lit up and his gaze slid across me, coming to rest on my pussy. "I bet you're already wet down there." Reaching over to his cut, he pulled a condom out of one of the pockets and ripped it open with his teeth.

I raised one brow. "You have one or two of those hiding all over the place?"

He rolled it on. "I like to be prepared." Climbing onto the bed, he knelt between my thighs, his gaze fixed on my sex.

I held my breath as he reached down and gently teased one finger through the soft folds of flesh. "Fuck yeah. Dripping wet. You want me."

I peeked up at him through my lashes. Absolutely, I wanted him. Parting my lips, I slid my tongue out to moisten them. Excitement swirled in my belly as I waited for him to make the next move.

He grinned, sliding up until his body completely covered me, his rock-hard shaft positioned at the entrance to my sex. Resting his weight on his massive forearms, he paused. "About those super-secret plans you wanted me to reveal? I could go get them for you right now."

I growled in annoyance. "Fuck the plans. I want you. Now!"

"Fuck the plans, or fuck that tight little pussy of yours?"

"I swear, Beast, if you don't fuck me right now -- "

He cut off the rest of my sentence with one powerful thrust of his hips, burying himself balls deep inside me. Damn, that felt good!

He pulled out slowly, making sure I felt every delicious inch of his retreat, then slammed back into me. Flames of lust swirled across my skin as he shafted me again and again with that gorgeous cock.

I wrapped my legs around his hips, locking my heels together as I met him thrust for thrust. I'd never had such an attentive lover, one who made sure I enjoyed myself as much or more than they did. He lowered his head to capture my lips, plundering them like a conquering hero as he drilled into me.

Everything faded away except the feel of Beast inside me, on top of me, surrounding me. Nothing mattered but this moment and the flickers of erotic fire racing through my body. He lifted his head, and I opened my eyes. He was staring straight down at me. I couldn't look away, pinned in place by the naked want on his face.

I scored my nails down his back as my climax started to build, stoking the fire in my belly until it exploded across every nerve, wringing a cry of pleasure from somewhere deep inside me.

Beast reared up and slammed into me one last time, his body tensing as he came. I could see it in his eyes, his gaze still fixed on me. Something passed between us, unspoken but binding. Both thrilling and terrifying at the same time.

This was not a casual fling I would be able to walk away from.

I quickly buried that thought deep, where I didn't have to think about it.

Beast rolled onto his side, taking me with him, his cock still inside me. I buried my face in his shoulder, not wanting to talk about anything right now, especially that look we'd shared.

"Piper?"

Damn, the man did not know when to let things go. "What?"

His voice held a hint of amusement. "I think I won the game."

* * *

**Beast**

Piper was still deep asleep, snuggled up at my side with one of my arms wrapped around her. Her warm body against mine felt fucking awesome. She might still think she could walk away after we dealt with her ex, but I knew better. She was mine for keeps.

It was late afternoon, and the rain had let up an hour ago, but I didn't have the heart to wake her. She'd been through so much lately she deserved some rest. Besides, that had been one hell of a rainstorm, and it made sense to let the roads dry up, or at least let the excess water run off before we ventured out again. Next show wasn't scheduled until tomorrow, so we had lots of time. I didn't want a repeat of that traction issue. Never been so damned scared in my life. Not for me, but for Piper. Just the thought of her being hurt because of me made me want to puke.

I reached over and snagged my phone off the bedside table. Unlocking the screen, I was surprised to see there was still no signal.

I rested my chin on Piper's head and closed my eyes.

"We have to go yet?" Sleep tinged her voice.

"No, still got time. Go back to sleep."

"K." Her warm breath teased across my chest. I hadn't bothered to put my clothes back on. Not like someone was going to come knocking at the door.

As if to prove me wrong, I heard the loud thrumming of Harley engines pulling up outside.

Quickly disentangling myself from Piper, I pulled on my pants and grabbed my gun. Barefoot, I padded over to the side of the window and peered out.

Parked in front of the cabin in full sight were two mud splashed Harleys. The bikers were just taking off their helmets, and I knew they were aware of my scrutiny.

*Hawke and Thor.*

I turned to Piper. "Better get some clothes on. We got company, but it's friendly. Hawke and Thor."

She let out a little squeak and gathered her clothes from around the room. We hadn't been real careful with where they were thrown. I stalked over to the door, keeping it closed until she was fully dressed. I'm not a sharing kind of guy.

Satisfied she was decently covered, I opened the door wide enough to stick my head out. "What's up?"

"Sociable as always, Beast. You going to let us in?" Hawke raised one brow.

I grudgingly opened the door wider. "I suppose. You going to tell me what the hell you're doing out here in the middle of nowhere?"

"Checking up on you and your old lady." He

nodded at Piper. "Ace was worried."

"She's not my old lady. Yet." I planned to fix that real soon. "Piper, meet Hawke and Thor. You weren't at the clubhouse long enough to be introduced to all the riffraff."

Piper crossed to my side and I draped an arm around her shoulder. "Nice to meet you."

"Delighted to meet anyone who's able to put up with this guy for more than ten minutes." Thor crossed to the kitchen, eyeing up the counter. "Coffee and everything." He turned a chair sideways and straddled it. "You're not answering your phone. Given the circumstances, Ace wanted to make sure you were just too busy to bother with the phone."

"Network's down here. You know I'd never go offline without a good reason."

"Which is why Ace got his shit in a knot," Hawke grunted.

"A good host would offer to make us a coffee after we came all this way to save his ass." Thor looked pointedly at the kitchen counter.

"You want to make these idiots coffee?" I looked down at Piper.

"Tap water or bottle?" she asked with a trace of laughter in her voice.

"Better make it bottled. They did come to check on us after all. Almost like they care." I pulled a chair out and sat down, and Hawke did the same.

Piper pulled the camp stove out of the cupboard and lit it, setting the coffee pot on one of the two burners. Satisfied it was working properly, she came and sat on my lap. I liked that. I noticed Hawke narrowing his eyes as he took it in.

The room was silent except for the sound of the coffee dripping into the pot. Hawke held up his phone, staring at the screen. "You're right. No signal."

I snorted. "I already said that. I may not be a tech genius, but I can read a phone."

"So here's the deal." Thor sat up straight. "The concert bus slid off the road during the storm. No way to prove it wasn't an accident given the fucking storm, but Rattler and Deuce were following because of that threat Shadow intercepted. They say a big-assed pickup sideswiped it just as it hit a big puddle and lost traction."

"Everyone okay?" Piper tensed.

"Yeah. Two guys got out of the truck, heading to the bus. Rattler says they were armed but when they saw our guys pull up, they aborted. Got back in the truck and took off. Rattler and Deuce made sure everyone on the bus was okay before they followed, and so far we haven't heard back from them. Ace told them to bring the guys back to the pen if they manage to catch them."

Piper frowned at me. "What's the pen?"

I hesitated. Some things you don't share except with patched members of the club, and their old ladies if it's important. Piper belonged to me though, even if it wasn't official yet. "It's where we take people to interrogate them. Like the holding pens at a livestock auction."

She nodded and looked back at Thor. "You sure the band is okay? And what about the bus?"

He shook his head. "Bus landed on its side in the ditch. Gonna need a crane truck to set it upright and back on the road. Until then, hard to say how much damage it took."

"And the guys?"

"Mostly bumps and bruises. The driver broke his arm. They took him into the hospital to have it set and cast. Not so sure about the equipment though. It probably got tossed around a bit. At least it was contained in the back of the bus, so it didn't get thrown out when the bus went down. Can't think all that water would have done it much good."

Piper looked at me. "You think this is Drake's doing?"

I nodded. "Yeah. Smacks of mafia tactics."

The grim look on her face didn't bode well for Drake if she ever ran into him again. Not that that was likely. I planned to introduce him to his Maker as soon as possible. He'd put a hit out on my woman. Nothing forgivable about that.

"I suggest we saddle up pronto and get to the rally point. Ace is not going to be happy with all three of us going phone silent." Hawke made a motion to stand up, but Thor put out a hand to stop him.

"Beast's woman put coffee on for us. It wouldn't be polite to leave without drinking it. And they're coming with us, so it would be wasted. Not cool."

"My name is Piper. Not Beast's woman." But she didn't sound upset. "Coffee looks like it's done. You two take cream and sugar?"

"None for me. I like mine black as a moonless night," Hawke spoke up.

"Both for me." Thor shrugged. "I need all the sweetening I can get."

"Yeah. Janet mentioned something like that." Hawke smirked.

"Who's Janet?" Piper hopped off my lap and I got up and reached for her hand as we crossed to the counter together. Hawke snickered softly, and I glared at him. He stopped, but I could still see the amusement dancing in his eyes.

"Janet is the woman who likes to sleep with Thor

but won't take him seriously." Hawke grinned. "I'd say she's playing hard to get, but I don't think she has any intention of getting got at all."

Thor grimaced. "Ouch. Maybe I'm just using her for sex."

"Sure. Keep telling yourself that. Better for your ego." I reached around Piper and turned off the camp stove burner.

"So where are we going?" Piper poured coffee into four cups and carried two of them back to the table. I grabbed the other two along with the jars of creamer and sugar and followed her.

"Ace set up a rally point in that hotel you were heading to. We're taking the top floor so we have lots of room and some privacy for meetings. He sent one of the prospects with a van to pick up the band and ferry them there. Joker, our medic, will meet them at the hotel. He can take care of any minor injuries they have."

"Wow." Piper looked impressed. "You guys are really organized."

Hawke shrugged. "Sometimes you don't want to wait in a crowded emergency room, and sometimes you don't want anyone to know where you are or how bad you're hurt. Joker may not be a licensed doctor, but I'd trust him with my life. He just doesn't have quite as much fancy equipment as you see in a hospital."

"Ace is working on that too, though," Thor pointed out. "Plans on adding a clinic to the clubhouse next summer."

My cell phone vibrated in my pocket and moments later both Hawke and Thor pulled theirs out as well. The network must have been restored. I used my thumbprint to unlock the screen and pulled up the list of missed text messages, reading each one at a glance. The last one elicited a low whistle from me.

Piper tilted her head, and I turned to the phone so she could see it. Her eyes grew wide as she realized the implications.

## Chapter Nine

**Piper**

I read the message again. Rattler and Deuce had managed to intercept the guys who ran the bus off the road. One was dead -- he'd pulled a gun on the bikers and paid the price. Self-defense was a reasonable argument in court, but I doubted it would ever come to that. They'd taken the second guy prisoner and were headed to the pen with him.

I suppose I should have been horrified at the casual mention of murder, self-defense notwithstanding, but it could easily have been Jose or one of the other guys in the band lying dead on the road, so it felt justified. That guy wouldn't run any other innocent people off a rain-soaked highway.

As for the guy who was still alive, I knew in my gut that interrogation was just a fancy word for torture until he spat out whatever information he had. If he was smart, he'd give everything up right away. I had the feeling Ace wasn't a guy to be toyed with, and like his dead partner in crime, this guy had deliberately run a bus full of people under the protection of Riptide MC off the road, endangering their lives. He didn't deserve mercy.

I wondered if Drake had any idea what kind of hornet's nest he'd stirred up when he put that hit out on me.

Hawke and Thor both muttered as they stared at their phones, and Beast moved his back to reply to the message. The three of them lifted their heads at the same time, exchanging a look I didn't quite understand.

"Time to get on the road." Beast tucked his phone back into his pocket and motioned me to stand.

Hawke and Thor nodded, getting to their feet. "We'll get to the rally point with you and see how Ace wants to play this. We don't think Drake knows where you are, but no point in taking chances."

"They targeted the bus because they thought I was on it, didn't they?" I looked from one biker to the other.

"Yeah, they did." Beast took my hand. "But it's not your fault so don't go there."

He was right. This one was squarely on Drake's shoulders. I looked around the cabin, trying to focus on something else. "Shouldn't we clean up a bit first? Someone left it in great shape for us."

"That's why we have prospects." Thor grinned. "They get to do the grunt work. We need to move fast, before Drake realizes we have one of his minions."

Beast packed what little we had back in the saddlebags and Hawke held the door open so he could wheel the bike back outside. They didn't waste any time getting organized. Within minutes, we were back on the road with Hawke in the lead and Thor bringing up the rear. I clung to Beast's back, feeling right at home. I'd probably spent more time like this in the past weeks than anywhere else. Except in his bed maybe. We definitely spent a lot of time there.

* * *

Before long we pulled up in front of a hotel with my father pacing across the entranceway. Beast stopped and let me slide off before he followed Thor and Hawke over to the side where a number of bikes were parked in a row.

"I thought I'd lost you!" My father grabbed me in a bear hug before I managed to get my helmet off. "Ace said Beast wasn't responding to calls or texts, and what with the bus getting run off the road…" His voice trailed off.

"I'm fine. The storm. It cut off cell service." I wriggled in his tight grasp, and he immediately loosened his arms slightly, but he didn't let go. I could get used to this. It was kind of nice having my father worry about me.

"I thought you'd be safer over on this side of the country. I was wrong. Damn, was I wrong."

"Made sense, Dad. Really. What doesn't make sense is why Drake is so intent on having me killed. I just can't figure it out."

"Well, he picked a fight with the wrong guy." His words hardened to a steely edge. "He wasn't on our radar before, but he is now. Every club he owns. Every casino. Every bar. Every betting syndicate. I will take them apart one by one, and I'll make sure he knows why." He looked over my head. "That would be if your man there doesn't take him apart piece by piece. He's not known for his pacifist nature when it comes to things he cares about."

I turned my head and saw Beast stalking toward us. "He's not my man." It was an automatic denial, but even as the words left my mouth, I realized it was a lie.

My father looked skeptical, but didn't say anything, releasing his grip on me as Beast came up to us.

"Ace inside?"

My father nodded. "Just waiting for you three to get back."

"There's four of us," I pointed out.

My father looked at Beast.

"You're not part of Riptide. When it comes to strategy and attack plans, we're a team. Have been for years. You're welcome to come along and listen. This is about you, after all," Beast explained. "But you're the target which means we need to keep you safe while we take care of the threat. Plus, I need to focus, and I won't be able to do that if I'm worried about you."

That made sense. I didn't want Beast to get hurt because he was worried about me instead of focusing on what he needed to do.

Between the bikers, the guys from the band, and the operatives from the Bureau, the top floor of the hotel had been taken over. One room was reserved for the war council. A whiteboard and a huge monitor took up one side, and a scary looking bunch of men lounged around the room on chairs and sofas.

Beast fit right in, and I made sure I kept as close to his side as possible. The atmosphere in the room was tense, and these guys did not look friendly.

My father introduced me and explained the situation so far. Maps were drawn on the whiteboard, wiped out and redrawn. Pros and cons were discussed, and a plan was formulated. The men were divided into teams. A group they labeled the cleaners was going to take care of the truck and the dead thug. Another group would help with the retrieval of the bus and comb the area for clues. It seemed like an awfully convenient set up with the hoodlums in the truck knowing exactly where to be when the bus came by.

The largest group was waiting in reserve, ready to spring into action once the prisoner spilled his guts. They discussed sending a delegation to Las Vegas to deal with Drake directly, but since no one was sure of his whereabouts, it was decided to put that part of the plan on hold until they had more information. By now, he'd know his plan had failed and he'd be expecting retaliation.

Beast, Hawke, and Ace were heading back to interrogate the guy they'd captured. I offered to go with them, but Beast quickly squashed that idea. I was to stay put, with Thor and my father along with a couple of the Bureau guys to protect me. Until this was over, I wasn't allowed to leave the hotel.

I wanted to object, especially when they used the word "allowed." I didn't like being told what to do, but it made sense. I was the one with a price on her head. If I ventured out, I'd endanger myself and everyone who came with me.

* * *

**Beast**

I was not happy leaving Piper behind. She hadn't been out of my sight since I'd picked her up in San Diego. I didn't want her anywhere near when we interrogated the prisoner, though. It was one thing to know it was going to be ugly. It would be something else to see or hear what we might have to do. The prisoner was dead no matter what. He'd targeted my woman. His only choice was how hard that death would be.

Ace understood my reluctance to part from Piper, but he'd already given me the pep talk about her being safer where she was. Thor and a gang of Bureau agents, including her father, would provide more than enough protection to keep her safe.

Hell, even Piper understood, although she didn't look any happier than me. Kind of made me feel better, knowing she didn't want us to be apart.

The trip back to the clubhouse was somber. We rode straight through at speeds the local cops would not have approved. Lucky for us the Bureau had smoothed the way, and the cars with the radar traps looked the other way as we sped by.

The prospects guarding the gate back at the

clubhouse were expecting us and opened up when we approached. We parked in front of the clubhouse, and Jake met us at the door. He handed us each a bottle of beer, and I downed the first half of mine in one long gulp. Ace and Hawke did the same.

"You've got him in the pen?" Ace asked.

"Affirmative."

"Anyone talk to him yet?"

Jake shook his head. "Thought it best to wait for you."

"Good." Ace looked over at me. "You want some time, or you ready?"

"Let's get this over with."

Ace nodded. "You take the lead. Hawke and I will back you up if you need us."

I stalked through the kitchen and down the hall, exiting by the back door. The pen was back behind the shooting range, and I saw a couple of prospects lounging there, waiting for us to get started. They'd shoot at targets while we questioned the prisoner. No chance of anyone hearing him scream over the sound of the guns.

I opened the door, and we entered. The prospect standing guard straightened up and nodded to Ace before heading out, shutting the door firmly behind him.

I circled the prisoner. He was tied to the one chair in the room, bolted down to the concrete floor. A gag stopped him from making a sound, and I nodded to Hawke who stepped forward and removed it. Ace stood back by the door, his eyes narrowed as he studied the man.

He didn't look like much. Straggly hair and a skinny frame that showed no effort at keeping in shape. This was the kind of guy the mafia relied on?

Hard to believe. He looked defiant, though. He must have known he was dead meat, after seeing his buddy bite the dust. Maybe he figured he had nothing to lose. I was about to disabuse him of that fucking notion. There are easy ways to die, and really hard ways.

I was hoping he'd choose the hard way.

I stopped in front of him. "You want to tell us who sent you?"

He glared at me.

I backhanded him across the face, leaving him with blood dripping from his nose and a split lip.

"We know it was Drake, so why not give him up?" I caught a quick glimpse of confusion in the asshole's eyes when I named Drake. Maybe this guy knew less than we thought.

"Don't know no Drake. It was a contract. Blind paywall." He spat out a mouthful of blood.

I narrowed my eyes and turned to Ace. A blind paywall didn't make sense. Drake's name had been bandied about enough. Why would he suddenly be hiding behind a paywall?

Ace shrugged, and I turned back to the asshole. "Tell me about the contract."

He sneered. "You're going to kill me anyway. Why should I tell you anything?"

"Because there's two ways to die. Easy or hard. Your choice."

He didn't believe me at first, but it took less than an hour before he spilled everything he knew. Working him over gave me an outlet for the rage that had lodged itself in my gut when I realized how determined this Drake fucker was to kill my Piper. I felt calmer now. The rage was still there, but focused.

Drake needed to die.

I went outside to use the hand pump and trough

to wash the blood off me and motioned the two prospects from the shooting range to clean up the mess inside. Hawke and Ace followed me out.

"Something doesn't add up here," Ace mused.

"I agree." I splashed cold water on my face. "First Drake wanted everyone to know he was behind this, and now he's trying to backpedal? Hide behind a blind paywall? Mafia doesn't fucking backpedal. They own their shit."

"Exactly. I'm going to see if Shadow can find anything else out." Ace headed for the clubhouse.

"You feeling better now?" Hawke stayed behind and I knew it was in case I needed to talk.

"Yeah. Kind of. I need to end this bullshit so I can concentrate on Piper."

"You going to officially make her your old lady?"

"If she'll have me. And if her father doesn't kill me for trying."

Hawke laughed, slapping me on the back. "Her father seemed okay with you, and by the look on her face when you left, I'd say your chances are pretty good."

He slung an arm around my shoulders as we walked back to the clubhouse together. Jake handed us another beer when we entered the kitchen. He looked from me to Hawke. "Well?"

I shrugged. "Not much to tell, really. They were given the bus route and told where the best section of road was to run it off. The storm was an added bonus, making it easier to approach without being seen, and to push the bus off the road when it had less traction due to the water. They weren't expecting the biker escort though, and they panicked."

"It was a contract on the dark web. Blind paywall and all that." Hawke shook his head. "That's not how the mafia works. Usually, they send their own guys if it's a kill contract. They want to make sure the job gets done. The contract didn't even require proof that she was dead, although they'd be able to check that through normal channels. Something smells fishy."

"You're right." Ace and Shadow joined us in the kitchen. "The contract disappeared off the dark web as soon as this went down, and no mention was ever made of Drake or any of his top lieutenants."

"You think someone else is behind this?" Jake frowned.

"I'm not sure what to think, but someone is definitely trying to get to Piper. We need to figure it out before that happens."

"Any ideas on how to do that?"

Just then, my phone lit up.

*Piper. What the fuck*?

She should be safe with her father and Thor. I glanced wildly at Ace as I hit accept. She didn't mince words.

"Drake texted me. I have no idea how he got this number, but he wants to talk. What should I do?"

## Chapter Ten

**Piper**

The silence was so long I thought I'd dropped the connection. "Beast?"

"Yeah. I'm here."

"So what do you want me to do?" My gaze collided with my father's steely stare. "About Drake?"

"Are you sure it's Drake?"

"I suppose. It's not like I can recognize a voice on a text. Why would anyone lie about that?"

He ignored the question. "Text him back. Ask him something only the two of you would know."

He sounded cold. Distant. Something was up. Those damn butterflies in my stomach flew a little harder and faster. "Why? What's going on?"

"Not sure yet. Just need to cover the bases."

My father motioned me to give him the phone.

"Here. Dad wants to talk to you." I handed the phone over and watched my father's face. He would have made a great poker player. His expression never changed. He nodded a few times, but his side of the conversation mostly consisted of grunts and one-word answers.

He finally handed the phone back to me, and motioned Thor over to the side of the room. They conferred in muted whispers.

I held the phone back up to my ear. "You figure things out with my father?"

"Yeah. I want you to text Drake back. Make sure it's him and then give me his number. I'll take it from there."

"What do you mean you'll take it from there? Not that I care about Drake, but I'm not sitting here waiting while you do time for murder."

Beast chuckled. Actually chuckled, which made me want to smack him. Pity he was so far away. "You won't have to. I promise whatever goes down, I'm not doing time for it."

I wasn't exactly comforted by that. "Then what's your plan?"

"If that really is Drake, I arrange a meeting and the boys and I discuss the situation with him. Neutral ground. Truce in place. No one gets hurt."

It sounded simple but I could see a few issues. Mafia and bikers. Neither one was known for their peaceful natures. "Can I be there?"

"Why?"

Trust him to question my motives. "Because I'm kind of fond of you and I want you in one piece. Starting a war with a mafia don-to-be is not a good way to stay safe."

"I could point out I didn't start this."

"I get it, Beast, and that's what scares me. I'm serious." I could see my father and Thor both watching me, and at this point I didn't care. "Either I'm there, or I don't put you in touch with Drake."

"You know I can find him on my own if you do that."

"Yes, but it would take you longer. Like long enough for you to cool off and behave."

"This is me behaving. I want you safe, Piper. No way in hell am I okay with you being within ten miles of a guy who wants you dead."

We were both silent, and I mulled over my options. I didn't want to be left in the dark, but I had to give Beast credit for honesty. He was just trying to protect me, the same way I was trying to protect him.

I looked up as my father crossed the room and put a hand on my shoulder. He took the phone from my hand and put it on speaker. "What if I bring a couple of snipers with me and stay with Piper, back from the action? They're damn good. They could take a person out before they get anywhere near her."

"I suppose that could work." Beast did not sound happy. "If things go south, you promise to get her the fuck out of there ASAP? I don't care if you have to hog-tie her to do it. Promise?"

"Promise." My father handed me back the phone with a wry smile. "You really picked a charmer. Hog-tied?"

Ignoring Thor's snicker, I took the phone. "Now what?"

"Verify it's Drake. What's something only he would know?"

I thought about it. "The first night we were together, it didn't go so well. I'm pretty sure he wouldn't have bragged about that to anyone."

"How do you mean didn't go so well?"

I grinned, knowing this would make Beast's day. "He was drunk. He couldn't get it up."

That earned me a chuckle. "Go for it."

I pulled up the message app and sent Drake a text, explaining I needed to make sure it was really him by asking something only he would know.

*Sorry, but this is the only thing I could think of. How many times did we have sex that first night you slept over at my place?*

The answer came back immediately. *None, and you know why. Good enough?*

*Yeah. I'm going to let my new guy set up the meet, okay?*

*The biker guy?*

*That's the one.*

I cut the conversation off and called Beast back.

"Yeah, it's him. He's expecting your call. I just texted you the number. Got it?"

"Got it. I'll be back in touch when I have the meet set up." He paused. "Piper?"

"Yeah?"

"I will do whatever it takes to keep you safe." He broke the connection before I could reply.

Thor stalked over to me, his expression serious. He looked straight into my eyes. "He's serious, you know. I haven't seen Beast this worked up about anyone except the twins since his POS wife walked out on him. Please don't do anything to get him hurt. Or worse."

I glanced at my father standing beside me, and he nodded solemnly.

I was touched. These guys cared about each other a whole lot more than some families I'd met. They might not be blood, but they were family in way that made me feel special to be included in their tight-knit circle.

"I promise." I took a deep breath and tried to calm the butterflies that were still swirling around in my belly. "Now what?'

"Now we wait." My father walked over to the kitchen area and picked an apple out of the basket of fruit one of the prospects had dropped off. "The hardest part of any operation."

"You think it will be today?" I asked.

Thor shook his head. "Not likely. It's already getting late. There's set-up needs to be done."

"Set-up? Like what?"

"Where they'll meet is a big one. Your ex is on the other side of the country, isn't he? And he'll want to hand pick the guys that are coming with him. So will Beast. That takes time. Both of them are going to have someone go in and discreetly scope out the meeting site, although whoever picks it will already have the logistics in mind. I'd say two days from now is likely."

"Two days!" Shock lanced through me. "The suspense is already killing me. I can't wait two days!"

Thor shrugged, picking up a cookie and examining it like it was prepared to bite him. "Not like you have a choice."

I hated it, but he was right. "Can I at least go see Beast, then? I don't want to sit here for two days without him."

Thor and my father exchanged looks.

"I'll call Beast and see how he feels about it." Thor pulled out his phone and walked out of the room.

I turned to my father. "Why can't I call him? I'm the one asking."

"Because the big bad biker has a much harder time saying no to you directly. If Thor asks, he'll reason it out and give an answer based on risks and facts."

"Oh." I gave him a wry smile. "I'm the weak link, aren't I?"

He suddenly looked sad. "Problem with caring about someone is they can be used against you." Something about the way he said that made me wonder who'd been used against him. I made a mental note to ask him about it. Later, after this whole mess got cleaned up. There was a lot we didn't know about each other.

Thor walked back into the room. "Beast said yes. He's going to have the prospects bring over a couple of trucks. One for you and one for a decoy, just in case anyone is watching."

"This is starting to sound like a James Bond knockoff," I muttered, but I was willing to do whatever it took to get back to Beast.

"Gets better." The grin on Thor's face should have warned me. "Once those two set off on a wild goose chase, we load you in a big box and put it in one of the Bureau's off-road Jeeps to make the trip home. Four of us will be in the Jeep to cover any angle we might get attacked from, and there will be half a dozen bikers on the pavement to make sure no one gets close."

"You just said two trucks -- one for me and one for a decoy." I frowned. "I'm confused. Why the Jeep?"

"The two-vehicle stunt is standard protocol, and anyone watching is going to think you're in one or the other. They won't know which, so they have to follow both. We just split the enemy force in two. Not much chance they're going to wait around for a third option, but if they do most of the firepower is in the Jeep."

"Which is bullet proof," my father pointed out.

* * *

**Beast**

I could barely contain myself when the Jeep rolled into the compound. Thor had kept me up to date during the entire transfer, but I didn't relax until Piper stepped out of the vehicle and into my arms. I didn't care who was watching, I held her to me and kissed her like we hadn't seen each other in months. Fuck, this woman had me wrapped around her pinkie.

Thor cleared his throat. "You might want to take that inside."

I gave him the finger, and he laughed. "Just saying. I'm not against free entertainment."

"I am." Her father tried to sound fierce, but I knew better. He was glad to see his little girl had someone to look after her.

I loosened my grip, and we climbed the stairs to

the front porch.

"Someday, I'd like to come here just for fun. Maybe a party, or a dinner. A barbecue. There always seems to be something hanging over my head." Piper leaned into me as we crossed the porch and entered the house. "I bet the twins love parties."

"Yeah. Sometimes a little too much. Not sure how I'm going to handle it when they start dating."

Piper laughed, and the sound lit up my heart. "You'll handle it just fine as long as the guy respects them. I'd hate to be the guy who hurt one of them."

I thought of what I'd like to do to Drake and kept the opinion to myself. "You tired from the long trip?"

"He's hoping you say yes so he can take you up to bed." Thor smirked. "Trust me. Napping is not what he has in mind."

I glared at him. He wasn't wrong. "Don't you have somewhere you have to be?"

Thor grinned. "Nope."

Ace appeared in the doorway. "Need to talk to you. My office." He nodded at Piper. "Welcome back."

"Thanks." Piper tilted her head. "Can I come, or is this a Riptide only kind of meeting?"

Ace looked from me to her. "This is about you, so you're welcome." He pivoted and headed down the hallway.

"Should I worry?" Piper asked.

"No." I shook my head. "Likely just finalizing plans for tomorrow's meeting."

She looked doubtful, but I took her hand and we followed Ace to his office. Ace took a seat behind his desk, and I sat on one of the chairs facing it, pulling Piper down onto my lap.

Ace steepled his fingers. "Walk me through the plan."

"First, Drake is now the don. His father officially passed the torch a couple of weeks ago, which is probably when this whole mess started. We haven't figured out why, but the theory is Piper knows something even if she's not aware of it, and that makes her a liability. They've agreed to a meeting at the old gazebo on the cypress trail. It's out in the open, so no cover for any kind of surprise attack by either side. Not that I expect one. Drake's group has a reputation for sticking to their word. Rattler and Hawke scouted the area yesterday just to make sure it was viable. They didn't see any issue. Piper and some of the Bureau guys will be holding back at the edge of the clearing. If things go south, they have clearance to protect Piper, her father, and whoever else they can cover on our side with lethal force. Meet time is noon, so neither side will be blinded by the sun in their face. Each side brings a maximum of four people, including the primary. We're going in from the east. Drake's group will come in from the parking lot side on the west."

Ace narrowed his eyes. "Who's on your team?"

"Rattler, Deuce, Thor, and me."

"Does this Drake fucker know Piper will be there?"

"Yeah. He agreed to it. As long she and whoever's guarding her are back by the tree line, they're not counted as part of the team."

"Sounds like you have it all under control, then." Ace looked at Piper. "You okay with this?"

She frowned. "I need for this to be over. I feel guilty that people are in danger because of me."

"Not your fault." A faint smile curved the corner of his mouth. "Great chance for us to put your father in our debt. Who knows when a favor from the Bureau might come in handy."

I felt Piper stiffen. "We done here?" I asked.

Ace nodded, his expression softening. "Yeah. Good luck with the meet. Hopefully you can get this thing settled without any more bloodshed."

"Any more?" Piper's brows furrowed.

"Figure of speech." I threw Ace a quelling look from behind Piper. I never told her how the interrogation had ended.

Ace stood up, signaling the meeting was over. "Anything changes, let me know."

"I will. Thanks, Prez." I nudged Piper off my lap and got to my feet. Reaching for her hand, I headed for the door. She looked up at me and caught her bottom lip between her teeth. Her gaze dropped to my crotch.

My cock jumped in response. Looked like she was on board for a quickie before the promised nap. Good way to settle the nerves.

## Chapter Eleven

**Piper**

I looked down on the meeting place from my assigned spot on the perimeter of the clearing. From a strategic point, it was likely a good choice. I could see everything from where I stood to the far side of the clearing, including the entrance to the trail where the mafia contingent was supposed to enter. The trees were limbed up high enough that you could be certain no one was hiding beneath them. A rocky cliff bordered one side of the open space, and a fast-moving creek with boulders sending the water in all directions framed the other side. No chance of anyone sneaking in either way.

Beast and his Riptide brothers looked incredibly relaxed on their bikes as they waited for Drake's group.

*How could they be so calm, waiting for the mafia to show up?*

Five minutes to noon. I felt a hysterical urge to laugh as thoughts of the showdown at OK Corral passed through my mind. I prayed this wouldn't end the same way. For the umpteenth time, I wished I'd never set eyes on Drake, never agreed to go out with him.

As if sensing my inner dread, my father reached for my hand. I pulled back, pretending not to notice. Holding hands was something I did with Beast. It felt wrong with someone else, even my father. He wrapped an arm around my shoulder instead, and I leaned against him.

"What if this is a trap?" I whispered the thought.

My father shook his head. "It's not. Drake has a reputation to uphold, especially since he just took over as don. If he breaks his word on this meet, no one will ever trust him. He'll be finished before he gets started."

I tilted my head to look up at him. "Honor amongst thieves?"

"Something like that. These guys have rules, and anyone who breaks them doesn't survive long."

I felt a chill go down my spine at his words. These guys played for keeps.

A movement at the far side of the clearing caught my attention. Drake and three men I didn't recognize strode into sight.

The Riptide team hopped off their bikes and strode to the center of the pavilion, Beast in the lead. I noticed the other three fanned out behind him as if preparing for an assault.

Drake stopped a few feet from Beast, and his minions stayed back from him, matching the Riptide guys. From this distance I couldn't hear what was being said, but the body language of both groups was telling.

Drake, dressed in business casual in all black, looked as flamboyant as I remembered. After the initial handshake that I took to be standard meeting protocol, he started to talk. I might not be able to hear him, but I could see him as he gestured wildly, looking more and more agitated.

In contrast, Beast was wearing his jeans and well-worn chaps, with his leather cut showing his Riptide affiliation. He stood at ease, his hands on his hips as he occasionally nodded or shook his head in reply to something Drake said. I felt a wave of warm affection calm the butterflies in my gut. That was my Beast. He didn't feel the need to impress anyone with expensive clothes. He was confident in his own abilities, and woe betide anyone who underestimated him.

Drake reached for his pocket and immediately Rattler, Deuce, and Thor tensed, their hands going to the guns holstered at their hips. Drake stopped, holding his hands up in surrender and saying something.

"Wish I could read lips," I muttered.

"Probably better that you can't." My father gave my shoulder a reassuring squeeze. "I doubt he was going for a weapon. Highly unlikely a kill shot would come from the main negotiator. If it was intended to be a trap, one of the other guys would be doing the shooting. They'd wait for their shadow to glance away, and bam. Target down."

I frowned up at him, and he shrugged. "Not my first time at one of these things. They rarely go bad, but when they do, it's pretty much scripted."

I glared at him. "Not helping me feel better."

I looked back at the pavilion and saw Drake hand a piece of paper to Beast. Probably what he'd been reaching for in his pocket. Beast unfolded it and studied it for a few moments. Lowering it, he nodded his head and the two talked for a few more minutes before he handed the paper back then reached out and the two men shook hands.

A few more words were exchanged before Drake turned and headed back the way he'd come, followed by his henchmen. I noted that two of the three men in the mafia group walked backwards, keeping the Riptide gang in sight until their leader disappeared into the tree-lined trail. Turning they hurried after him.

Beast and his group didn't move until the mafia contingent was out of sight. Then Beast looked up to where I was standing and gave me an open-handed salute before mounting his bike and heading straight toward me.

My father withdrew his arm, and I ran toward my lover.

* * *

**Beast**

The information Drake shared at the meeting cleared up so many of the inconsistencies I'd noticed ever since I'd picked Piper up that day. Not that I was okay with the asshole, but at least I now understood what was going on. And of course he'd brought proof of what he'd said, not expecting me to take his word for it. Smart. Frankly, the whole thing was twisted. I should have demanded to keep that paper to hand around at church. It was going to be fun explaining it.

I throttled back, hitting the brakes when I reached Piper. She threw her arms around my neck, and I swear she hugged me tight enough to strangle me. I used one hand to hit the kill switch and kicked the stand down so the bike wouldn't fall over when I dismounted.

"Easy, babe. It's over. You're safe." I held her gently against me.

Her head came up and she glared at me. "Safe? Watching you and Drake do a Mexican standoff was the worst time of my life. I kept imagining one of his goons pulling a gun or a knife on you. Why I ever agreed to this is beyond me. You are not going to put yourself in harm's way again. Not ever!" She burst into tears.

I looked helplessly over her head at her father, who had come up behind her. He just shrugged and shook his head. No help there.

"Shh. I'm fine. You're fine. It's going to be okay. I'll explain it all once we get back to the clubhouse, okay? Ace will want to know the whole story and I don't want to have to tell it half a dozen times." I gently untangled her arms from my neck. "You want to ride with me?"

Piper sniffled, wiping her face with the sleeve of her shirt. "Well, I'm not letting you out of my sight, so yeah. I'm riding with you." She glared at me as she grabbed her helmet off its perch on the back seat and jammed it on her head.

I swear her father was laughing as he turned away and headed back to his snipers.

I took it easy on the way back to the clubhouse, giving Piper time to pull herself together. The fact that having her snuggled up against my back helped soothe the rage I felt when I contemplated what I'd just learned was a bonus.

The prospects guarding the gates opened them wide when they saw us coming, and I swooped in, gliding my bike up the driveway to park in front of the clubhouse. I pulled off my helmet and helped Piper with hers. She'd managed to calm down somewhere between the meeting place and here, and no trace of tears showed on her face.

"So?" Ace lounged against the porch railing.

"A little complicated. Can we call church, so I only have to explain it once?"

Ace nodded, pushing himself upright. "In ten. Give the other guys time to get situated."

"Okay if I bring Piper in? She needs to hear this too."

Usually, church was only for patched members, but as President, Ace had the authority to bend the rules. He hesitated long enough to make me nervous before finally nodding his head. "Sure. One time only. Her father will want to hear it too, unless you already briefed him."

"Fuck no." There was a strict chain of command, and I followed it at all times. No way I'd debrief an outsider, even an FBI contact and the father of the intended target, without first clearing it with Ace.

Just then, the van carrying the FBI contingent rounded the corner of the sweeping driveway and pulled up alongside the bikes.

"Speak of the devil. I'll let him know he's in for church. Mom can keep the rest of them contained in the kitchen." Ace strode over to the van.

I turned to Piper. "You need a drink before this goes down?"

She wrinkled her nose. "Whiskey?"

I almost laughed. "I had water or coffee in mind. You can do the hard liquor thing once church is over."

She let out an exaggerated sigh. "Fine. Water it is."

We grabbed a couple bottles of water and walked out back to the building Riptide used to hold church. It wasn't much, but it worked. I held Piper's hand and led her to the front of the room. I sat her beside me, taking a seat facing the rest of the club members who were straggling in one by one. The atmosphere was relaxed. The boys knew we'd had a meeting and things went well. How well, they were waiting to find out.

When Ace walked in with Piper's father, the room went silent. He nodded at a seat near the back, and her dad immediately sat down.

Walking up to the front, Ace held up a hand. "Beast is going to brief us on how the meet went down. I gave Piper and her father permission to be here. Hold your questions till the end. Anyone got a problem with any of that?"

He waited a few minutes, scanning the room. When no one spoke up, he gestured to me. "Floor's all yours, Beast."

I gave Piper's hand a final squeeze and stood up. Looking around the crowded room, I saw guys I'd served with, guys I'd fought with, and guys I'd sworn to protect with my life. They'd do the same for me.

I cleared my throat.

"Seems like there's a turf war going on back in Las Vegas. Piper's ex, Drake, just inherited the position of head of the mafia there. A cartel out of Mexico isn't happy with that. They run drugs and hookers, but they're greedy. They want a hundred percent share of the action, so they came up with a plan. They knew Piper was seeing Drake and they found out Piper's dad was FBI. The plan was pretty simple. Kill Piper and make it look like some kind of revenge hit by Drake. Her father would be understandably upset and use every resource at his disposal to get back at Drake. Shut down his operations, arrest all his top lieutenants, and possibly take out Drake or put him in the slammer for an extended stay. That would leave the action wide open for the cartel to stage a takeover without putting a target on their own back. Hence, the use of the dark web and contracts without any traces. If you think back, Drake's name was only tossed about by the guys trying to cash in on the contracts. Shadow could find no trace of it on the contracts on the dark web, could you?"

I looked over at Shadow, who shook his head slowly. "It never made sense why he suddenly turned on Piper, and no, his name wasn't on the contracts or discussions on the dark web. Just a blind paywall. Which did raise a red flag, because that's not how the mafia works. They like people to fear crossing them."

"Exactly. Plan was Drake would never find out he was being set up until it was too late."

"But we got involved," Ace said. "And that got his attention, especially when Shadow started looking into him."

"Exactly." I smiled grimly. "The cartel's plan started to unravel at that point. They expected Piper to die in that first attempt at her house, but she evaded them. Things started to go badly for them from there."

"So now what?" Rattler spoke up. "We going to Las Vegas to take them down?"

I shook my head. "Fuck, no." I glanced over at Ace, who nodded his approval. "The FBI has assets on that coast, and they have an interest in this. They were being set up as much as Drake and his mafia contacts. The cartel will be dealt with by their black ops division over there. They'll let us know when it's done."

"Another thing," Shadow spoke up. "I couldn't understand how Drake got Piper's new phone number, or how the cartel found out about the tour, so I dug around a bit more. Not even on the dark web, just searching. Looks like one of the dealers she worked with in Vegas was willing to sell her out."

"They wouldn't know anything about the tour."

"No, but they knew what agency her agent worked for, and it doesn't take much to hack into that system. Their passwords are embarrassingly simple."

"Ouch." Ace shook his head. "Should we worry going forward? I don't like one of our own being at risk."

Shadow shook his head. "Nah. I'll contact them and offer to up their security for free. Given they almost got one of their clients killed, not to mention the damage to the bus and the equipment, I'm sure they'll take me up on it. Especially if I point out, nicely of course, that Piper isn't going to sue their asses off."

"So we're in the clear? Your old lady is safe?"

Thor always did like things to be spelled out in black and white.

"Yeah. The club is in the clear. We've talked to Piper's agent about postponing the rest of her singing tour until this is cleared up, but we're using the bus accident and finding replacement equipment as the public reason. That should satisfy them. Once the cartel is out of the picture, she can go back on the road again. With luck, the tour will finish up before the twins get home."

And I needed to give the twins a call and let them know what I had planned.

## Chapter Twelve

**Piper**

My head was spinning with everything Beast had explained at the meeting. Church, they called it. Before leaving, my father gave me a big hug and promised to be in touch real soon. After this mess, we both agreed we wanted a closer relationship. First though, he was off to coordinate the takedown of the cartel. From the steely look in his eyes when he mentioned them, I almost felt sorry for them.

We exited the church building to find a roaring fire going in the pit behind the clubhouse. Mom had coaxed the FBI contingent to carry the wood over and start one. She also enlisted their help to bring out coolers full of beer and ice. She had steaks sizzling on the king-sized barbecue, and the old ladies and some of the club groupies had set up a table laden with a variety of salads and desserts.

I was impressed and told her so.

"Not a biggie. Organizing food is my thing." She grinned. "I knew the guys would come back hungry, and we haven't had a barbecue in weeks. Jake loves barbecue and he's been hinting loudly that it's about time. So, I made a bunch of salads up ahead of time and pulled some steak out of the freezer. I figured if the news was good, they'd want to celebrate, and if the news was bad, they'd need fuel up for whatever they had to do next. Either way, I was prepared." She looked around at the bikers laughing as they grabbed beers out of the coolers. "I take it the news was good?"

I nodded as Beast strode over and draped his arm around my shoulders. "Yup. Short version -- her ex isn't quite as much of an asshole as we thought. He was set up. We know the source. The Bureau is taking care of it, and we just have to sit back and wait for things to shake out."

"Celebration it is, then." She tilted her head. "And what about you two? I heard Ace referring to you as Beast's old lady."

"Yeah, he did mention it that way during church." Beast looked down at me, the corner of his mouth twitching with a suppressed smile. "And she didn't object."

"I was being polite." I feigned disinterest. "He might have made a mistake. I don't recall anyone asking me to be their old lady."

"Well then." Beast held up his hand and hollered for everyone to pay attention.

I felt my face go red as everyone turned to stare at us. "Beast," I hissed, "what are you doing?"

He grinned and got down on one knee, keeping a firm grip on my hand so I couldn't escape. "Making an honest woman out of you. I was hoping your father would be here, but I got his blessing before he left."

"His blessing?" Could my face possibly get any redder as I tried to ignore the snickers from the crowd. "What century are you living in?"

Beast ignored my outburst. "Piper, love of my life, keeper of my heart, will you do me the honor of being my old lady and wearing my cut?"

"Your cut?" I knew he called his jacket with the Riptide patch on it a cut, but me wearing it made no sense.

"Yes or no? Please say yes." He actually looked nervous. Like he thought I might reject him.

"Yes. Of course, yes, but --"

Jake interrupted, stepping forward to hand him something.

Beast let go of my hand and stood, holding the

item Jake had given him at arm's length so I could see it. A leather vest, my size. He turned it around. The Riptide Logo was emblazoned on the back, and in bold letters around the logo it proclaimed --"Property of Beast."

I held my arms out, and he put it on me to the cheers and hoots of the club. Ace walked over, a half empty beer bottle in his hand. "Welcome to the club."

Before I could answer, Beast swept me up in his arms and kissed me so thoroughly I could barely breathe. The crowd whistled and hooted, and I could see Mom and Jake smiling at us from beside the fire pit.

Just like that, I had a family. A group of people who cared for each other and kept each other safe. I wrapped my arms around Beast's neck and kissed him right back.

**Thor (Riptide MC 4)**
*A Riptide MC Romance*
**Anne Kane**

Janet -- Thor is an addiction I can't seem to overcome. He's everything I've ever wanted in a man, and everything I can never have. They call him Thor for a reason -- he looks like a modern-day Viking with that shaggy blond hair, piercing blue eyes, and ropes of muscles covered in intricate tattoos. And in bed the man is definitely a god who grants my every secret desire.

I walked away from the marriage my parents tried to force me into, but I'm not naïve enough to think they're going to let me go. They have money. Power. Influence. They know how to bend people to their will. They will make sure I marry someone they approve of, and it doesn't take a genius to figure out they will never approve of Thor.

Thor -- Janet is mine. I know she knows it too. I can see it in her eyes, hear it in her voice, feel it every time we make love. But she refuses to wear my cut and freaks out if I mention anything permanent. I have no idea what the fuck her issue is, but it doesn't matter. I want her, and I'm going to have her if it takes me the rest of my fucking life to convince her. I want her to come to me willingly. I love her enough not to force her.

Now I just have to stay alive long enough for that to happen, because someone wants me dead.

## Chapter One

### Janet

Some men are thick-headed, and Thor takes it to the extreme. Why couldn't he just accept the fact that I was not into commitment?

For one thing, I'm old-fashioned in that regard. Commitment meant I had to be honest with him. And being honest could ruin a perfectly good relationship. Honesty meant telling him about my family.

"Are you ashamed of me?" Thor looked magnificent when he frowned. Of course, he looked magnificent most of the time. Kind of like a modern-day Viking with his shaggy blond hair reaching down to brush his shoulders, and those striking blue eyes. All those muscles didn't hurt either. And the full sleeves of tattoos? They made my mouth water.

I shook my head. "No. I'm not ashamed of you. But commitment changes everything. People look at us differently. We look at each other differently. There are expectations."

"Such as you not fucking other men? Those kinds of expectations?" His voice had a dangerous edge to it.

"That's not the issue and you know it." My mind flashed back to the extremely satisfying sex we'd had less than an hour ago. "I'm not looking to be the club sex toy."

He relaxed. Not a lot, but it was something. "Then what? Is it Riptide? You don't want to be one of the old ladies?"

"Well, I'm not thrilled with being called an old lady, but you know Sophia's my BFF." I toyed with the tiny umbrella in my drink. "I already feel like I'm part of the club, in a way. Why can't we just go on like we are?"

Thor scowled. "Because I want everyone to know you belong to me. Off limits. Do you have any idea how tough it is not to react when Tiny flirts with you? That needs to stop."

"So, tell him to stop." I failed to see the issue.

He shook his head. "Can't do it. Unless I claim you as my old lady, you're fair game."

"You know Tiny doesn't really want me. He's all talk. I think he does it just to bug you. He's never even tried to kiss me."

His scowl deepened. He looked cute when he scowled. If I didn't know him better, I'd think he was dangerous. "He'd better not. Brother or not, I'll take a round out of him."

I tried not to let my exasperation show. "We haven't exactly been secretive. Tiny must know we have a thing for each other. Surely that's enough."

"Nope." Thor sat back and crossed his arms on his massive chest. "I want my cut on you. I want the world to know you belong to me."

I raised one brow. "Belong to you?"

"Don't try to change the subject. You know what I meant. I want the world to know we belong to each other."

I sighed. I really did care about him. A lot. But my family had money. Power. Influence. And not necessarily in a good way. I'd walked away, but I wasn't stupid. I knew they'd let me go. For now. And I also knew they could make life extremely difficult for anyone they didn't approve of.

It didn't take a genius to figure out they wouldn't approve of Thor.

"Can we just let it go for now? I promise I'm not going to bed down with anyone else. I just don't want to do the whole till death do us part thing."

His lip twitched, and I knew he was trying to suppress a laugh at my phrasing. "Till death do us part? I'm not asking you to marry me."

"No. You're asking me to be your old lady, and that's a whole lot more serious."

He nodded. "True. But it is just as binding on me."

I shook my head. We'd argued this around in circles before, and it always ended the same. Neither of us were willing to give in. Time to change the subject. I looked over at the bar. "They serve food here? I haven't had anything to eat since lunch, and that was a long time ago."

That brought a grin to his lips. "Something help work up your appetite?" His hand caressed my thigh under the table.

I rolled my eyes. "You should know. You were there."

"Yeah, I was."

The door opened and I glanced over to see a familiar face. Joker. With a girl on his arm. I didn't recognize her, but that didn't matter. It was enough to get me out of this line of conversation for now. I raised my arm and waved.

Joker waved back, pausing to say something to the girl with him before heading over to our table.

Thor stood up and the two bikers clasped arms, slapping each other on the back. "We were just going to order something to eat. Want to join us?"

"Sure." Joker glanced down at his companion. "You okay with that?"

She nodded, giving him a shy smile. "I'm Cassie," she said by way of introduction. "Joker and I were just out at the races."

"Sorry." Joker looked sheepish. "Forgot the

introduction part. This is Cassie. We met at the tattoo parlor a couple weeks back and kind of hit it off."

"Nice to meet you, Cassie." I scooted over, and Thor slid in beside me, leaving the other side of the booth for Joker and Cassie. "What kind of races?"

"Motocross. They run them every Saturday over at the old Forman farm." Cassie glanced up at Joker. "I've never been before, but it was fun to watch."

A waitress bustled over, order pad in hand. "What can I get you two to start with?" she asked the newcomers.

Joker looked over at Cassie. "Want to split a plate of nachos?"

Cassie nodded. "Sounds good."

Joker looked up at the waitress. "A large nachos and a jug of beer with two mugs."

The waitress scribbled on her pad and glanced at me and Thor. "Are you two still okay?"

Thor looked at me, one brow raised.

"Can I get a burger with the works, and a side order of fries with gravy, please?" I smiled at her. Waitressing at a pub wasn't the easiest way to make a living.

"Sure, honey." She smiled back at me.

"Make that two. I seem to have worked up an appetite." Thor's hand wandered up my thigh, heading north. I slapped it down, ignoring his soft chuckle.

I watched as the waitress wrote down our order and hurried off, using the distraction to ignore the questioning look Joker threw at us.

"You two are spending a lot of time together?" He made it sound like a question as his gaze shuffled from Thor to me and back again.

Thor narrowed his eyes, looking ready to pick a fight. "Yeah, so? You have a problem with that?"

Joker held up his hands in mock surrender. "Just noticing. That's all."

Thor grimaced. "Sorry, man. Touchy subject."

*Shit. I did not want to do this in front of another couple.*

Feeling cornered, I turned to Cassie. "I've never been a motocross race. Is it like a car race, with a big round track?"

She shook her head. "No, it's more like a cross-country thing, with motorcycles instead of cars. There's a dirt track with bumps and hills that the bikers jump over at high speeds. They can really get some air under them on those! It's a ton of fun to watch the bikes get airborne."

"Sounds like fun." I grinned at Thor. "We should go watch some time." I could tell by the laconic smile he gave me that I wasn't fooling him. He knew I'd changed the subject on purpose. Luckily for me, he seemed willing to let it go. For now.

"So, what have you two been up to?" Joker glanced around the crowded room, then back at Thor. "I don't see Tiny anywhere, and you two are usually together."

"He had a family thing, so I called Janet up to see if she wanted to hang out." Thor lied like an expensive rug, smooth and effortless in the roll out.

Thankfully, the conversation changed directions into the types of bikes used in motocross and a debate on air-cooled vs liquid-cooled engines. I looked over at Cassie, who looked a little lost. "Don't worry. There won't be a test at the end of this."

"Do you understand any of it?" she asked.

I shrugged. "Enough to know I really don't care. Much as I like riding behind Thor or any of the guys, I can't see me ever wanting my own bike. Too much responsibility, and besides, I'd need to up my license and I'm not good at tests." I'd almost slipped up there and admitted the only one I ever rode with was Thor. I slipped a quick look at him from under my lashes and was relieved to see he hadn't noticed.

"You need a different license to ride a motorcycle?" Cassie looked surprised.

"Afraid so. A car and a bike don't have a lot in common, so you have to do the whole thing over again. Written test. Road test." I shuddered. "I'm one of those people who suddenly forgets how to spell their own name when it comes to tests. The only one I ever managed to pass on first go round is the vision test."

"Vision test?"

"Yeah. My eyes don't have a problem with tests." I gave her a wry smile. "Lucky me."

The waitress appeared with the jug of beer and glasses. "Your food will be out shortly."

She eyed up my empty glass. "Another round for you two?"

I shook my head. "I better not. I have to work later."

Thor spread a meaty palm over the top of his beer stein. "Not for me. I'm driving."

She nodded and headed back to the bar. Joker lifted a brow. "You had that many already or are you becoming one of those respected adult kind of people?"

Thor shrugged. "Adult enough to know when to quit."

"I'm going to hit the ladies' room before the food gets here." I motioned Thor to scoot over and let me out. "You want to come freshen up?" I asked Cassie.

"Sure." She chuckled. "You can give me the

scoop on Joker."

"No secrets here." Joker didn't look worried. "I'm a law-abiding ex-SEAL who's dynamite in the sack. What else do you need to know?"

I leaned over toward her and stage-whispered, "And he's modest. Incredibly modest."

Cassie laughed and blew a kiss in Joker's direction before turning to follow.

* * *

**Thor**

Fuck, that woman frustrated the hell out of me! I knew there had to be a reason she balked at making our relationship public, but she just kept evading the issue. I was a hair's breadth away from having Shadow snoop into her and see what was up. I knew that would cross a line, but I wasn't sure it was one I cared about. Did she have an ex she didn't want me to know about? Or one that still had a legal claim on her? Because I could fix that without breaking a sweat.

She didn't act like someone running from an ex though. It had a different feel to it, and that's what scared me. More like she didn't want people to know about me because they thought she could do better. Admittedly, she probably could but that was just too bad. I had her now, and I had no intention of letting her go.

"Cassie, huh?" I looked at Joker.

He shrugged. "Like I said, we met at the tattoo parlor. She was getting a dragonfly on the back of her shoulder. Said it was in honor of her grandmother who'd had a thing for them."

"And?"

"And we got to talking. You know. Families. Life. Shit like that. Ended up at the steakhouse for dinner, and I invited her to come watch the races with me today."

I nodded. "So not a long-standing secret affair you've kept from the club all this time?"

He smirked. "You mean like you and Janet? Nah. At least not yet. I haven't told her about Riptide."

I sighed. Everyone except Janet seemed to be aware of our status.

A ruckus over at the far side of the room caught my attention. Two burly guys were half leading, half dragging a woman toward the back exit, and she was not going willingly. Squirming and letting out muffled screams through the hand one of them had over her mouth.

"Fuck. Looks like she needs a hand. I'll be back in a minute."

"Need me for backup?"

The two were nearly at the door, one swearing loudly as the woman stomped on his foot. "Two against one? I think I can handle it. Keep Janet amused for me."

Joker laughed. "No problem. I'll tell her about the time you thought the monkey crying in the jungle was a kid and just about got yourself killed going to rescue it."

"Asshole." I stood and shouldered my way across the floor to the trio. By the time I reached them, they'd manhandled the girl outside and the door was closing behind them.

"Not so fast, guys." I pushed the door open and stepped outside, ready for a little exercise. I hadn't been in a decent fight in weeks.

As the door snapped shut behind me, I saw the girl standing alone on the far side of the alley. In the second that it took for my brain to register that, a fist slammed into the side of my head.

*Ambush!*

*Fuck!*

Not my first one though, and I ducked low, twisting to the left as a second blow glanced off my shoulder. I brought my fists up to protect my head, and aimed a roundhouse kick at my assailant, connecting with a satisfyingly meaty thud that drove him backward.

The second guy was quick, and he had a knife. Holding it low, he slashed upward.

I jumped back, and the blade traced a shallow path across my abs.

He bared his teeth and came at me again.

I kicked low, hitting his knee and causing him to stumble. Out of the corner of my eye, I saw the girl turn and run, waving to my attackers as she headed out of the alley. Fucking slut wasn't waiting around to see the outcome.

The first guy came in from the side, pummeling me with his fists. I ducked to the side, getting my back against the wall so they couldn't come at me from behind.

Still, two against one, with one of the two brandishing a knife.

Didn't look good, but I wasn't going out without a fight. Fuck that. Vikings had coined the term *berserker*, and they didn't call me Thor for nothing.

Letting out a furious battle cry, I threw myself at the knife-wielding thug. I got in a few good shots with my fists before a searing pain lanced through me. A quick glance down showed a crimson gash on my side.

Ignoring the pain, I grasped his wrist, the one holding the deadly blade, and twisted. The knife arched back, and wussy let out a scream of agony as it bit into his flesh. He dropped to his knees, and I turned to protect myself from his buddy.

The next few minutes stretched out like a slow-motion movie. At this point in my life, hand to hand combat was second nature.

Attack.

Defend.

Kick.

Twist out of reach.

Punch.

Duck under the next blow.

I could do this on autopilot, like a choreographed dance. If not for the wound on my side, I would have made mincemeat out of this clown in minutes.

I was holding my own, but I could feel my strength waning as a crimson trail of blood dripped from the knife wound. Not as shallow as I'd first thought.

My breathing was labored. My hits had less strength behind them. The pain was getting harder to ignore. I wasn't going to last much longer but damned if I wasn't going to take this asshole down with me.

Just as the thug came at me yet again, baring his teeth behind a split and swollen lip, the door slammed open, and Joker entered the fray. He might be a medic, dedicated to healing, but that didn't mean he couldn't fight. Faced with a fresh opponent, and his sidekick lying motionless on the concrete, the coward turned tail and ran.

"What the hell, man?" Joker took a few steps after the asshole to make sure he was gone, then turned back to me. He grabbed my arm, gently lowering me to the ground. "Where's the girl?"

"Ambush." I grasped my injured side, wincing. "She bailed somewhere between the first punch and the knife."

Joker eyed up the assailant lying motionless on the ground. "You had a knife on you?"

I shook my head. "Nah. He brought it. I just turned it back on him."

Joker nodded. "Self-defense."

I nodded. "Fuck yeah. He got in the first strike." I grimaced, trying to take shallower breaths. As the adrenaline rush of the fight receded, the pain set in. Good chance I had a broken rib under that slash.

I spared a look at the remaining attacker. "How bad is he?"

Joker shook his head. "Dead."

I looked over at the crumpled form. "Seriously?"

"Yup. Knife went straight in, sliced the main artery and took out one lung. He bled out. Probably before he hit the ground."

"Crap."

Joker pulled out his phone. "I'll get Daryl on it before the cops show up."

Daryl was the club attorney. Yeah, we had a lawyer on speed dial. Yet another ex-SEAL, but one who'd made the transition back to civilian life better than the rest of us. Used the GI bill to get an education and pass the bar. If anyone could spin things in my favor, it was Daryl. When one of us got into legal type trouble, Daryl was there to fix it.

We got into trouble more than we liked to admit.

The door swung open again, and Janet stepped outside. She looked gorgeous as always. I tried to smile past the pain that was quickly ramping up.

"I might want to take a raincheck on that burger, Cupcake."

## Chapter Two

**Janet**

When we got back from the ladies' room and found both Thor and Joker missing, my first reaction was annoyance. I did not take well to being ignored, and I somehow assumed they were outside looking at a shiny new bike or something equally asinine.

I didn't expect to see Thor on the ground covered in blood, and Joker with a worried frown on his face. The other guy wasn't moving, but I didn't care about him.

Rushing to Thor, I dropped to my knees beside him and smoothed the hair back from his face. "How bad is it?" I looked to Joker for the answer. I knew Thor wouldn't admit to being hurt unless he'd been dead for at least twenty-four hours.

"Bad." Joker had taken off his shirt and was applying pressure to Thor's side, but I could see a steady stream of blood leaking out from under the makeshift bandage. "He needs stitches, and possibly a transfusion."

I nodded. I'd interned at the local hospital while I was in college, then when I graduated, I'd accepted a position as a medical receptionist in their emergency room. That had given me lots of experience at dealing with these kinds of situations. I pulled out my phone and hit speed dial to the ER.

"What's up?" Sarah, my co-worker answered with her usual cheerful voice. "You miss me already?"

"Emergency. Thor's hurt. Bad. Knife wound. Get me an ambulance to the alley behind the Settlers Pub. FAST!"

"On it." She dropped into professional mode. "He need a transfusion?"

"Probably. He's type O positive." He'd come to the blood donor clinic with me a few weeks back, and we'd laughed that we had the same blood type.

"Hang on while I notify dispatch." The wait music came on, but not for long. "Okay, I'm back. They have a crew a few blocks from you. Should be there any minute."

"Thanks." I dropped the phone back into my pocket and took Thor's hand. Staring into his ice-blue eyes, I realized just how much he meant to me.

"Help's on the way. You're going to be all right."

A faint smile curved his lips, and his voice sounded strained. "Of course I am, now that you're here." His eyes fluttered closed.

I knew that look. He was in shock. Loss of blood could do that. He needed help. Right now.

The sound of an ambulance siren broke the silence, and I ran to the entrance of the alley to flag them down. They pulled in and a paramedic jumped out. I recognized him from multiple visits to the ER. His head swiveled between the two forms laying prone on the ground.

"Him!" I pointed to Thor. "The other guy's beyond help."

Not taking my word for it, the medic strode over to the stranger. After a quick inspection, he shook his head. "Dead. "As he talked, he dropped to one knee beside Thor, pulling a pair of scissors out of his kit. "Hey, Joker. We need to stop meeting like this. Did you notify the police?"

"Taken care of." Joker moved back to give him room to work.

The ambulance driver joined him just as the medic sliced Thor's shirt off him and lifted the shredded material away from the wound. "We need to wait for them?"

Joker shook his head. "Clear case of self-defense, and he's in no condition to answer questions. They can talk to him at the hospital once he's stable."

The medic looked at me and I nodded my approval. "Do what you need to and get him to the ER."

"Roger." The driver maneuvered the ambulance around and pulled out a stretcher. I watched as they worked on Thor. I felt so damned helpless. Despite my unwillingness to commit, I couldn't imagine my life without him.

"What the hell is going on out here?" The bartender pushed open the back door, his voice trailing off and his face going pale as he took in the scene. He looked young, early twenties at most.

"Cops are on the way," Joker assured him. "Did you see these guys come out here?"

Visibly shaken, the bartender stared at the still body of the dead man. "Yeah."

"Good. You can tell them what you saw when they get here."

The bartender shook his head. "I don't want to get involved. They could be the mob. They could come after me."

Joker stalked over to the unfortunate guy. "Did I make it sound like you had a choice? You tell them what you saw. Two guys and a girl. My buddy following. Just tell them the truth and you'll be fine. What's your name?"

The bartender stared at Joker, his eyes as wide as saucers. "Johnny. Are those guys dead?"

"One is. One better not be. Go back inside and wait for the police."

The unfortunate guy gulped and jerked his head

in a nod before retreating into the bar.

I watched the door close behind him before meeting Joker's gaze. "You scared the hell out of that kid."

He shrugged. "As long as it worked."

Joker skirted around Thor and the medics and came to put an arm around me. Watching the paramedic hook an IV into Thor's arm, I took a deep breath. He would be okay. He had to be okay. I glanced up at Joker. "Where's Cassie?"

"I called an Uber to take her home before I came out. Had a bad feeling and didn't want to spook her. I'll talk to her later."

"Good. She seems nice. Sorry to ruin your day."

"Not your fault. He was ambushed."

I frowned. In the shock of seeing him like this, I hadn't stopped to ask what happened.

"Ambushed?"

"Looked like a girl was in trouble. He followed her and her attackers out the door. When he didn't come back, I came and found him holding his side in with one hand and fighting off some guy with the other." He gestured at the man on the ground. "That guy was already down. The second guy was trying to finish Thor off. I'll have Shadow check to see if there's any cameras in the area that we can tap. We need to know who these guys are, and why the ambush."

I frowned. "Where's the second guy?"

"Ran like a scared pussy when I joined in. I would have followed him, but Thor looked like he needed my help more."

I felt that sinking sensation in my gut again. I prayed it had nothing to do with my family. I might not like them, but I didn't want the wrath of Riptide to fall on their heads.

"Thanks. For looking out for Thor, I mean." I rested my head against him.

He shrugged. "We're brothers. He'd do the same for me."

He meant it. I'd watched the Riptide bikers for some time now, ever since my BFF, Sophia, had fallen for Deuce, the treasurer of Riptide MC. These guys, these scary looking biker dudes, meant everything to each other. They supported and protected one another more than most blood families I'd known. They'd accepted Sophia into their midst, and by association, me. I felt safe with them. Safe and cared for. Unlike my biological family, I was sure they'd never use me to further their own agendas.

A wayward thought sent a chill down my spine. Had my family had something to do with this? Had they found out about me and Thor and decided to handle the situation? I locked that scary question away in a sealed compartment of my brain to be taken out and examined later. Once Thor was safe. Once I was calm enough to reason it out.

It felt like forever before the paramedics transferred Thor to the stretcher and loaded him in the ambulance. In reality, it was mere minutes. These guys were good, they knew exactly what needed to be done and how to do it. I wanted to pull rank and ride with Thor in the ambulance, but I knew better. There wasn't a lot of room in there, and it was best for Thor if I found my own way to the hospital.

I stepped forward and touched the paramedic on the arm to get his attention. "Which hospital are you taking him to?"

"Yours. It's closest and there's a trauma doc on site right now." He paused, sympathy written all over his face. "He's young and healthy. He's got a good chance."

Coming from a seasoned paramedic who had been on the site of countless medical emergencies, that was comforting. "Thanks. We'll meet you there."

He nodded curtly and turned back to his job. As the door to the ambulance closed, blocking Thor from my sight. I took an involuntary step forward.

The ambulance took off, lights and sirens shattering the quiet night and I bit back a sob.

*Would I ever see Thor alive again*?

As if by magic, a car appeared at the entrance to the alley and one of the Riptide prospects stepped out.

"Come on." Joker took my hand and pulled me toward the waiting vehicle.

When had he had the time to summon a car? I slid into the passenger seat and fastened the seatbelt. Joker drove like the car was an extension of him. He didn't slow down, even for corners, maneuvering the vehicle with incredible skill. Despite the lack of traffic-clearing sirens and lights, he pulled up to the emergency entrance of the hospital just as the medics rushed Thor inside.

"Go. I'll park and be there right behind you." Joker gave me an encouraging grin. "Thor's as tough as his Viking namesake. He'll pull through and you can keep on pretending you don't care."

I was too worried about Thor to respond to that jibe. I jumped out of the car and raced into the emergency room, skidding to a halt in the lobby. I must have caught Sarah right before shift change. She was nowhere in sight.

My attention zeroed in on the receptionist now on duty, a kid who'd just started last week. Her eyes were as wide as saucers. She stared at me like I'd grown a second head. In hindsight, I probably looked like an escapee from the lockdown ward on the third floor, and I was lucky she didn't immediately summon security.

I looked around wildly. "Where is he?"

"They, uh, you mean, um, the blond guy from the ambulance?" she stuttered.

I glared at her. "Yes, I mean the blond guy from the ambulance. Where is he?"

She flinched and gestured behind her. "Last cubicle on the right."

I shouldered my way behind her and headed past the cubicles filled with emergency patients. Some were alone, and others had a loved one hovering over them. Monitors and machines beeped quietly, keeping the nursing station informed of their conditions. Weekends were always busy, and the nurses were the front line of defense.

Thor's lips twitched upward in a weak smile when I slid behind the curtain sectioning his cubicle off from the rest of the chaos. His face was pale, and an IV line trailed from a bag of plasma into his arm. The blood had stopped dripping, which I took to be a good sign. A nurse was busy hooking up a monitor up to track his vital signs.

"Bet you didn't think the night was going to end up with you back at work quite this soon." He reached out a hand toward me, and I winced at the raw flesh on his knuckles.

I plastered a smile on my face and gently placed my hand in his. "Nope. If you wanted a tour of the place, you could have asked."

He grasped my hand. "More fun this way, don't you think?"

Joker poked his head behind the curtain. "I'm going to wait up front and direct Daryl when he gets here. I notified Ace and the guys, so once you're finished grandstanding for Janet, they might want to see you."

Thor narrowed his eyes. "Asshole."

Joker laughed. "Feeling better already, I see." The look he threw my way, though, showed how concerned he was. He'd been a medic in the SEALs and the fact that he was worried ramped up my fear.

I shied away from wondering just how bad this was.

* * *

**Thor**

The knife wound burned like fire. I fucking hoped the asshole had cleaned the damn knife recently. Dying of an infected knife wound was not how I wanted to end my life. Hell, I hadn't been patched into Riptide all that long. I wanted to enjoy bossing some of the prospects around for a while before I bit the dust.

Janet dragged the plastic chair closer to the bed without letting go of my hand. "What happened? I went to the bathroom and when I came out you and Joker were both outside."

I took a deep breath. "I saw a couple guys drag a girl out the back door. Thought she needed help, so I followed. Turned out to be an ambush." I gave her the lighter version of the story. She was already skittish about settling down with a biker. I didn't want to give her any more reasons to hesitate. I was already picturing cute little girl babies with her smile and my stubborn streak.

She frowned. "Do you know who those guys were?"

"Fuck, no. Never seen them before today. I haven't led the life of a saint, but I don't think anyone personally wants me dead. Maybe someone has a grudge against Riptide or ex-SEALs and I was just a handy target. I'll get Shadow to look into it once I get out of here."

A strange look crossed her face, but she gave my hand a squeeze just as two uniformed cops shouldered their way in. She changed from concerned girlfriend to woman in charge in less than two seconds. Jumping to her feet, she faced them with her hands on hips, barring them from approaching any closer.

"This patient is not up to being questioned yet. Who let you in here?"

The young receptionist rushed in behind the intruders. "No one. I told them they had to wait, but they pushed right past me."

"Well, you can push your way back to the waiting room." Janet raised her arm and pointed the way back to the lobby. "The doctor will let you know when this man is available to talk."

The first cop started to speak. "But there's been a --"

"Go! Now!" Janet stomped her foot, gesturing toward the exit.

I had to swallow a shit-faced grin. My woman was magnificent when she was mad.

The cops backed up slowly. They were not happy. "You know we can get a subpoena?" growled the taller of the two.

Janet took a step forward, forcing the man to back up further. "Have at it. I'm sure the judge will be thrilled to be pulled away from his family on a Saturday evening to issue a subpoena to talk to a victim in need of urgent medical care."

"Biker bitch." The cop mumbled the insult under his breath.

Janet's eyes opened wide. "Excuse me?"

The receptionist chuckled and whipped out her phone to snap a picture.

"What's that for?" the second cop demanded.

"Just something to remember you by. In case you come back some day. Plus, I need some content for the staff newsletter. I thought I'd title it *The Dragon And Her Victims.*"

He opened his mouth to reply, but his partner grabbed his sleeve and pulled him toward the exit. "Let's go."

With a final glare that took in all three of us, the cops stomped off in the direction of the waiting room. Janet turned and came back to stand beside me. "You, okay?"

I nodded. "Other than the knife wound and a few bruises? Yeah." I reached up to twine my fingers in her hair, tugging suggestively. "Wanna have some fun?"

The receptionist cleared her throat. "I'll just get back to my station. You two behave yourselves now. I'm pretty sure there's a rule against fraternizing with a patient."

"He's not my patient." Janet didn't take her eyes off me. "He's my boyfriend."

The receptionist raised one brow and eyed me up. "I'm not sure 'boy' is a fitting description, but okay." She sauntered out the door.

I started to laugh and winced as a shaft of white-hot pain lanced through my side.

Janet's face turned to a mask of concern just as a doctor bustled into the room, clipboard in hand. He hesitated a moment when he saw Janet, then turned his attention to me. "Mr. Stennson?"

"Call me Thor."

Janet straightened up, backing away from the bed to give the doctor some room to work. I missed her warm touch.

"Tell me what happened." The doctor put the clipboard down and started to examine me. I gave him the short version, leaving out the part where I thought it was an ambush.

"So, how's the other guy?" he joked.

"One dead, one ran away."

A startled look replaced the easy smile. "Two against one? You're lucky to be here." Unwinding a stethoscope from around his neck, he continued his exam. A few minutes later, he straightened up. "You are lucky. The knife missed your aorta by about half an inch, and any other major organs as well. It left a nasty gash though and we can't know how dirty the weapon was, so I'm going to clean it out and then stitch it up. I'll numb the area first." He addressed Janet, jerking his chin toward the waiting room. "You can wait out there. The nurse will let you know when we're done."

Before she could react, I reached out and grabbed her hand, pulling her back to my side. "She stays."

The doctor shook his head. "This will be messy, and we may need to restrain you. It's best if your friend isn't present."

I narrowed my eyes. "No. She stays. I'm sure she's seen worse."

The idiot actually softened his voice like he thought he was talking to someone missing a few brain cells. "I'm sure she has, but she knows you, and people don't react well to seeing someone they care about in pain, even if it's necessary."

I started to sit up. "She goes and I go with her."

"You're wounded."

"Yeah, I noticed." I pressed down on the

bandage on the wound and swung my legs over the side of the bed.

"Fine." The doctor scowled at Janet. "But if you get in the way, I'm getting security to haul your ass out of here."

That pissed me off. No one talked to my woman like that. "Touch one hair on her head, and I'll personally make sure you know why one of those guys is in the morgue."

The doctor turned on his heel and walked out without a word.

I looked at Janet, who shrugged like it was no big deal, but I could see that worried little crease on her forehead. Maybe I should have kept my mouth shut, but that wasn't something I was good at.

The doctor returned moments later, followed by a nurse pushing a cart neatly covered with what appeared to be a dish towel. You know, those big white ones they use if you have to wash the damn plates by hand. She gave me what I assumed was supposed to be a comforting smile. She greeted Janet before turning to me. "Hi there. My name is Samantha. Janet can tell you I'm the best nurse in the hospital. Just relax, and we'll try to make this as painless as possible."

Ignoring Janet completely, the doctor glared at me. His bedside manner wasn't nearly as good as the nurse. "Lie down and behave."

I looked over at Janet, and she gave me a slight nod of her head, so I did as I was told. This was her turf, and I didn't want to cause her any grief.

The doctor and the nurse conversed in hushed tones over the towel covered cart. The nurse removed the towel and picked up something. She turned, and I could see the big fucking needle in her hands. I wasn't sure if that smile was reassuring or evil. I took a deep breath and gritted my teeth.

The whole thing went as well as could be expected. I wasn't good at lying still and letting people manhandle me. Went against everything I fucking believed. Yeah, the needle was to numb the area, but it only worked after they finished playing with the fucking thing. Once that took hold, the doctor kept up a running conversation while he worked. I didn't think he was expecting me to answer so I let him ramble on. He used a needle and a synthetic thread instead of staples which were more common these days, explaining what he did and why as he worked. He was old school and thought stitches healed better with less chance of infection than staples. I didn't care what he used as long as we got this over with. Once he was done, he warned me to take it easy and left the nurse to bandage me up and clean up the mess.

She'd just finished when there was a commotion in the lobby and Ace came in, followed by Daryl, the club lawyer. The nurse packed up her little trolley and left the room. Janet was back at my side, and after a piercing appraisal of my condition, Ace turned to her. "Do you mind letting us have a few minutes alone with this idiot?"

Janet gave my hand a squeeze. "Sure. I'll just go check to see what the doctor put on his chart." She'd been around the club long enough to know we didn't discuss business in front of anyone not a patched-in member, and that included our old ladies or girlfriends.

After Janet left, I told Ace and Daryl how things had gone down. Daryl made notes in a little pad he kept on him. Most guys would use their phone and record stuff these days, but Daryl didn't trust technology for that kind of thing. "They can hack just about anything, "he'd told me once, "but they can't hack a pad of paper jammed in your pocket."

"Self-defense." Ace's mouth formed a grim line. "It sounds like someone has it in for you."

"Any witnesses? Camera footage from the pub, maybe?" That was Daryl, into proof mode.

I shrugged, wincing as the movement pulled at the stitches. Freezing sure didn't last long. "The girl was in on it, so not likely any help there even if we knew how to find her. Not sure about cameras. It would be nice, but you'll have to go ask them. I was too fucking busy trying to stay alive to check for entertainment systems."

Daryl scribbled some more notes. "The cops are going to want to talk to you. Dead bodies make more work for them, and they don't like that."

"They were here already, but Janet threw them out before they got anywhere near me."

"Good for her." Ace narrowed his eyes and turned to Daryl. "Can you set up a time for them to interview him? At the clubhouse would be great, but I doubt they'll agree to that."

"No problem. These things always go better when we control them." He eyed the bulky bandage on my torso. "If they keep Rambo here in hospital, we can do it once he's in a room. Nice neutral ground. If not, I'll make a point of you and I both being there. Play up the wounded victim thing. They've already talked to Joker, but he wasn't there until after the fact."

"It's Thor, not Rambo," I muttered.

Daryl grinned for the first time since entering the room. "Yeah. I know." He tucked his notepad back into this pocket and looked at Ace. "You can let me know if they're keeping him or not. In the meantime, no one talks to the cops unless I'm present. Understood?"

Ace nodded. "Understood. We'll be in touch."

Daryl gripped my hand. "Take it easy, bro. I'll take care of the legal shit. You just focus on getting well and maybe tying down that little chick. Not that you deserve her, but I think she's good for you."

Ace barked out a laugh. "He's been trying. She's playing hard to get."

Daryl shook his head. "Can't say as I blame her. Who wants to be tied down to a guy who doesn't even see an ambush coming?"

"Asshole." I looked around for something to throw, but he ducked out past the curtain before I had a chance.

Ace settled down beside the bed. Stretcher, actually. Calling this thing a bed was a bit optimistic. "I've got a couple of prospects out in the waiting room. I imagine your woman has spotted them. They'll be ready if you get cut loose, or they'll guard your room if you have to stay for a day or two."

I scowled. "I don't need armed guards at my room."

"Not negotiable. Until we know you weren't a target, or until you're healed up enough to defend yourself, you get a shadow."

"Who decides when I'm well enough?"

Ace smirked. "I think I'll leave that up to the woman who chased the cops out of the room. I have a feeling she cares about you a lot more than she's willing to admit."

## Chapter Three

### Janet

I read the doctor's report. He might be a bit abrupt in his bedside manner and the doctor I least liked working with, but Dr. Murphy was the best trauma doctor in the state. Although a deep cut, and definitely messy, the knife wound wasn't serious. Thor was being admitted overnight, but I suspected that was more to make sure he didn't move around and tear out any stitches than because of any concerns.

I'd taken advantage of the time Ace and the lawyer had spent with him to contact my mole in the family mansion. Montgomery's role in the family could best be described as butler/bodyguard. I don't remember a time he hadn't been around, rescuing me from the consequences of my own actions. I trusted him implicitly, even to the point of keeping my calls to him a secret from my parents. I hadn't talked to them in years.

Montgomery swore no one had been paying any attention to my dating habits or anything else about me in the past year. They knew I was dating a biker and didn't seem to care. Thought that it couldn't possibly be serious. My mother thought I just picked a biker to annoy them. He pointed out that even Maxwell, the guy my parents had decided I was to marry, hadn't shown much interest other than making sure he was never seen with another woman in public. Montgomery had his theories on that one as well, but Maxwell's sex life was of little interest to me as long as I wasn't included in it. I felt a bit better after the call but that still left the questions -- who set Thor up, and why?

Or was it really just a big coincidence?

I hesitated to call Maxwell directly. If anyone, like my family or his, caught wind of the fact I'd been in touch they might ramp up the marriage pressure all over again. That wouldn't be good for either of us. Montgomery didn't seem to think Maxwell was behind this, so maybe I should let it go for now. No point in stirring the pot.

The lawyer, Daryl, strode into the waiting area and nodded to me as he headed out the door. Moments later, Ace appeared, stopping by the admissions desk where I was sitting. "Sorry about that. Club business."

I rolled my eyes. "Yeah. I get it. So, what can I know?"

He countered with a question of his own. "Are they keeping Thor in overnight, or sending him home?"

I glanced down at the chart still in my hands. "Keeping him overnight at a minimum, but he's stable. I think the main reason is to make sure he stays in bed and lets things start to heal."

Ace snorted. "You mean they don't trust him not to jump on his bike and go after someone?"

"Pretty much."

"Good call. In that case Daryl thinks we should let the cops interview him here. Neutral ground and all. They can't try to bully him into admitting something he didn't do if there're witnesses, and it's easier to handle the narrative."

That almost made me laugh. Thor wasn't the kind of guy you could bully into doing something he didn't want to do. "Sounds good. Give them an hour or so to get him upstairs and settled, though."

"Okay. I'll call Daryl and have him set it up. Let

me know when he's ready." He pulled out his phone and paused. "Thank you for looking after him."

I looked over at the two prospects lounging against the wall in the waiting room. "Looks like you're doing some looking-after too. Joker left when those two showed up, but he made a point of telling me who they were. I let the triage nurse know to ignore them."

Ace glanced over at the prospects. "Yeah. We take care of our own."

And Thor was one of them. A good man, and an ex-SEAL who didn't quite fit back into civilian life. That was one of the things that drew me into their world. There was no jockeying for favors, no backroom politics. Just a bunch of guys looking out for each other and trying to make the world a better place.

Ace hit quick-dial and put the phone to his ear. I could hear him talking to Daryl as he headed out the door.

I hung the chart up and headed back to Thor's bedside. He reached out for me when I entered the cubicle, and I took his hand. He looked tired. Exhausted, actually. "Did you think I deserted you?" I teased.

He squeezed my hand, his mouth curving up in that sensual smile I could never resist. "Nah. I'm so incredibly sexy you'd never be able to stay away."

I laughed, even though the sight of him so weak terrified me. I could have lost him. "Don't count on it."

He let out an exaggerated sigh. "Are you saying I have to keep you locked up and chained to my bed?"

Someone behind me cleared their throat loudly. I turned, feeling my face go red with embarrassment.

Thor just grinned.

"We need to get your boy toy up to his room."

Madison, one of the on-duty aides, came into the room. "He'll be in 211, so maybe you could get anything he might need and meet us there?"

Translation -- get out of the way and let me do my job. And get the guy a toothbrush.

I turned to drop a quick kiss on Thor's forehead and gently extracted my hand from his grip. "I'll call Ace and have him send someone over with your stuff. Anything you want?"

"My cut." He looked around the room as if he'd just realized it was missing. "I had it at the pub."

"Joker took it when they started cutting stuff off you in the alley. I'm sure he kept it safe."

Thor relaxed. "Can you check to make sure? And see if you can find my phone? Not sure where I left the damn thing."

"Oh, right! It's in my purse." I'd picked it up off the table when I'd gone out to find him. In the chaos that followed I'd totally forgotten about it. "I'll bring it right up."

Madison made little shooing motions with her hands, and I blew Thor a kiss as I left the room.

* * *

The police had come and gone, and both Daryl and Ace seemed to be happy with the outcome. They were leaning toward labelling the killing self-defense, especially since Thor's story was backed up by the bartender and a couple of the other bar patrons along with a rather grainy image from the security cameras. No one knew the identity of the second man, and the officers promised to look into that. The woman they'd used as bait was wily enough that all you could see of her was the back of her head as she left the area. The dead man was a lowlife who was well-known to the police. He'd been up on murder charges a couple of times, but there was never enough evidence to convict him. They didn't seem overly concerned at his demise.

I'd been allowed to stay in the room during the interview, mostly because Thor refused to cooperate unless I was present. He sat up in bed and held onto my hand for the entire interview. I was starting to feel like his emotional support girlfriend. Or maybe he was just scared I'd disappear while he was too weak to chase me.

Fat chance of that. After this fiasco he'd be lucky if I let him out of my sight.

The interview was short, almost as if it were a forgone conclusion. Thor followed the lawyer's instructions, only answering what was asked and adding as little description or detail as possible. Daryl had pointed out that the less he said, the less chance there was of the police tripping him up on some obscure point at a later date.

Joker was waiting downstairs and as soon as the officers left, he came up. He had Thor's cut with him, along with a plate of brownies baked by Beast's twin daughters.

"You didn't bring him a toothbrush or comb?" I asked.

Joker shrugged. "You didn't ask for those, just his cut. The twins added the brownies."

I rolled my eyes. I'd just said his cut and stuff. I didn't realize I needed to be specific. "It's okay. I'll just slip over to the pharmacy and get him a few basics if you're going to be here for a bit?"

"Sure. I'll stay until you get back."

I grabbed my purse and headed out. The same two prospects were lounging just outside his room, and they nodded to me as I left. Just the fact that Riptide felt the need to place a guard on Thor's room made me nervous all over again. Montgomery had assured me my family had nothing to do with the attack, but that still left anyone who'd ever felt they had a beef with Riptide in general, or Thor in particular.

Or maybe my wannabe fiancé felt Thor was a threat to the continued falsehood that we would someday be a couple. I made a mental note to give him a call as soon as I could.

There was a pharmacy attached to the hospital, and I picked up a toothbrush and some other basic items for Thor. I added a bag of potato chips and a couple of chocolate bars for good measure. Hospital food had a reputation for a reason.

I was on my way back into the hospital when Dr. Murphy intercepted me, indicating he wanted to talk to me in his office.

Great. He might be an amazing trauma doctor, but he was a terror to the rest of the staff. He seemed to regard us as some type of lower life form that needed his constant negative remarks to keep us in line.

He followed me into the office and closed the door behind us. I put my purchases down and took a seat in front of his desk. He strode behind the desk and sat, steepling his fingers in front of him as he stared at me without saying anything.

The silence stretched out, but I refused to be intimidated. This wasn't the first time he'd called me in here, and after the day I'd had I wasn't in the mood to be browbeaten by him.

He finally spoke. "This is not going to look good on your performance evaluation."

"What's not going to look good?"

"Hanging out with criminals and murder suspects."

I lifted one brow. "I have no idea what you are talking about."

He snorted. "That man you came in with. He's a member of a biker group. The police came to talk to him about a murder."

I crossed my legs and took a deep breath, reminded myself to stay calm. "He was the victim, and the police just came to talk to him. They are tentatively labelling the death as self-defense, and they are looking for the dead man's accomplice. Feel free to check that out with whomever you please. Yes, he owns a motorcycle, but that's not a crime as far as I know."

"You should not be hanging out with people who get involved in this type of thing." He glared at me. "Everyone knows motorcycle gangs are drug dealers and criminals."

I smiled sweetly. "That's an interesting perspective. Does that include the Blue Knights?"

He frowned. "Who?"

"The Blue Knights. It's a motorcycle club. They have chapters all over the place including right here in Georgia."

He shrugged. "Then most likely, yes."

"Huh. For your information, the members of the Blue Knights are all law enforcement officers, so there goes your theory. And just FYI, what I do on my time off is none of your business. You want to bring it up at my next performance evaluation? Be my guest. Right now, I have better things to do than sit here and let you waste my time." With that, I picked up my things and walked out, closing the door quietly behind me.

Well, that felt good, even if I'd just flushed my career in healthcare down the drain.

I was not in the mood to placate Dr. Murphy's ego. Maybe he'd have me fired and I could stop worrying about whether or not I could afford to quit yet. I could always go back to teaching, although there didn't seem to be much call for that with all the budget cuts these days. My dream was to open my own flower shop. I'd taken the floral design courses at the community college, and one on running your own business. I'd planned on waiting until the fall so I could take advantage of the Christmas season when I opened. The winter might be a little slow after that, but I figured I'd be able to jump right into Valentine's Day, Mother's Day, and the summer wedding season. I'd been saving for a couple of years now, so I had a bit of a financial cushion. I just might have to speed up my timeline.

* * *

**Thor**

This lying still in bed doing nothing was driving me crazy. And I'd only been here for a few hours. If some fucking guy with glasses and a white jacket thought I'd stay put, he was the one with a problem. They'd stitched me up and given me enough blood to replace what I'd lost. I was good to go.

Janet had gone to get me some toothpaste, warning me in that bossy voice she liked to think worked that I'd better behave myself until she got back. She'd left Joker to ride herd on me. He'd gotten a call from his new arm candy, though, and left after I assured him I could survive without him watching over me. There were a couple of prospects guarding the door in case I decided to make a break for it. Yeah, Ace said they were there to protect me, but I'd bet my last helmet that Janet had warned them to make sure I stayed in bed.

Now I was stuck here with nothing to do except

flip channels on a television practically mounted on the fucking ceiling. Likely put there by some chickenshit pencil pusher who'd ordered it put up there to make sure the patient had to lie down to watch the damn thing. Not like there was anything worth watching. Not a single sports channel. Not even movies. Just news, kiddie shows, and a bunch of dumb-assed soap operas. If I had to stay here very long, I might limber up my throwing arm and see if I could knock the fucking thing off the wall.

Sex. There was another thing the dumbass doctor had weighed in on. He forbade me from having sex for at least two weeks. Forbid. The asshole seriously said forbid.

And that line of thought got me to imagining Janet in a nurse's outfit. Not those scrubby things the nurses around here wore. A skintight white outfit like you saw on Halloween. Low cut in the front, so her breasts threatened to pop out any moment, and a skirt that just barely covered her nicely curved ass.

My cock stirred to life just as the object of my wicked fantasy walked back into the room and set a package from the pharmacy down on the bedside table. "You're supposed to be behaving." She eyed the sheet, tented suggestively at my groin.

"I am behaving." I grinned like a wolf about to devour its prey. "I'm still in bed, aren't I?"

She gave me a stern look. "You're supposed to be resting." She gestured at the growing tent. "That doesn't look like you're resting."

I shrugged. "Can't help it. I was just imagining you in one of those little nurse's uniforms. Like the sexy ones in that store full of grown-up toys."

A faint smile tugged the corner of her mouth, and I knew she was having a hard time pretending to be mad. "You need to stop that. Try thinking about something boring."

I sighed theatrically. "Not working. I can't get the image of Nurse Janet out of my head. Maybe if you did something about my condition, I'd be able to sleep."

"Your condition?"

"Yeah." I reached down and gave my cock a nice long stroke from base to tip. Even with the sheet blocking the view, the effect was obvious.

She raised her brows. "That's not a condition. That's a hard-on."

"I knew you'd be able to figure it out. Now if you just had some way to fix it."

She snorted. "It's not broken, so it doesn't need fixing."

"You sure? Maybe if you took a look…" I started to push the sheet out of the way.

"Stop that!" She squealed and turned to look at the open doorway. "What if someone walked in?"

"Not really my thing, but I suppose if she was cute and you really wanted to, we could have a threeway."

The outraged look on her face was adorable. "I do not do threeways!"

"Good to know. You want me all to yourself, huh?" I waggled my eyebrows suggestively.

"I want you to stop that before someone comes in. What if Dr. Murphy comes by to check on you?"

"He's not my type, but if you're really worried about having an audience, shut the door."

She shook her head. "It doesn't lock."

"No problem." I raised my voice. "Mickey!" He was one of the newer prospects, and he always jumped at the chance to prove himself capable.

Mickey stuck his head in the door. "Everything okay?"

"Sure. Janet and I just need a bit of privacy. You're going to close the door, and I want you to make sure nobody gets in until we open it again. Got it?"

"No one?" He hesitated. "Like not even the doctor guy? Or Ace?"

"Definitely not the doctor guy, but if it's Ace just knock, okay?" I would never ask him to do anything that might endanger his position with the club. Denying the president entrance would definitely fall under that definition. Ace wasn't dumb, though. If he had to knock, he'd have a good idea why. He'd understand.

"Got it." Mickey was smart enough to avoid looking at Janet as he withdrew, shutting the door behind him.

"Now." I kicked the sheet off, wincing when the sudden movement sent a dart of pain lancing through the knife wound. "Let's get down to business."

## Chapter Four

**Janet**

"I don't think so." There was no way I was doing anything that might rip out Thor's stitches or reopen the wound. Thor was not a slow and gentle kind of lover, which was fine with me most of the time. Right now, though, it was a bad idea.

"You want me to chase you around the room? Because I'm in the mood to do just that." He raised one brow.

I believed him. But that didn't change the fact that he had a serious knife wound and any strenuous exercise was out of the question. "No, but how about a compromise?"

He frowned. "Not sure I like the idea of that. It means I don't get what I want, doesn't it?"

I tilted my head, warming up to what I had in mind. "No, you just get it in a different way."

He tilted his head. "How so?"

"Well, it isn't so much the sex that's forbidden, it's all the movement involved that's dangerous for you right now."

He tried to look offended and didn't do a very good job of it. "So, you want to have sex without me moving?"

"Something like that." I started to hum, swaying my hips in time to the sound. Grasping the bottom of my T-shirt, I slowly lifted it up. "I was thinking I could put on a little show for you." I lowered my gaze to his massive hard-on that he was currently stroking. "And you can do that."

"This usually ends up in sex," he pointed out.

"But it doesn't have to."

He didn't look convinced, but his hand slid from

the base to the tip of his cock and back again.

I lifted the shirt a little higher, exposing the lacy confection that barely covered my breasts. Expensive underwear was one of my addictions. If Victoria had a secret, it would be how much money she scammed me out of every month.

Thor's eyes darkened, and his hand moved a little bit faster. The sight of his cock swelling as he ogled my breasts gave me a feeling of power. Thor might be a big bad biker boy, but I wasn't powerless in this affair.

I pulled my shirt off over my head and twirled it a few times before tossing it onto the bed. Still humming one of my favorite tunes, I tossed my hair back and slid a hand up my belly to the clasp at the front of the bra. With the flick of a finger, the lace prison sprang open, releasing my breasts.

"Fuck yeah." Thor growled low in his throat. "Play with your nipples, sweetie. I love it when you play with them."

"Like this?" I'd always been a little self-conscious about my breasts. At least, I had been until I met Thor. I was what people referred to as well-endowed, a polite way of saying my breasts were too big for the rest of me. The other kids had made fun of me all through high school, and I'd done my best to disguise them, never daring to wear tight shirts.

Thor didn't have a problem with their size, though. Far from it.

I cupped the sensitive mounds in my hands, massaging gently before I scored my thumbs across the plump red nipples. They hardened into pebbly peaks, and I kept my gaze locked on Thor. His reaction stoked my own. Heat raced down every nerve ending as I slipped my tongue out to wet my lips.

I'd never done such a blatant striptease, and it hadn't occurred to me that it would have as great an effect on me as it had on the audience. I could feel the dampness gathering at the apex of my thighs. I'd never been able to come without something inside me, either my trusty vibrator or Thor's massive cock.

I threw my head back, watching Thor from under my lashes as I played with my breasts for a few more minutes, running my fingers over the nipples, and massaging the generous mounds.

Hooking my fingers in the waistband of my pants, I slid them down over my hips. They pooled around my ankles, and I kicked them aside as I took a step closer to the bed.

Thor reached out and wrapped the slender elastic band holding the thong in place around his hand. A quick twist, and the lace gave way, leaving my pussy bare to his gaze.

Thor's eyes lit up as he fixated on the bare mound. "Finger fuck yourself."

Even laid up in a hospital bed, with a line of stitches holding his side together, he liked to be in control. I have to admit, it turned me on. I knew he'd never hurt me or ask me to do anything I wasn't okay with.

"Like this?" I lifted one hand to my mouth and sucked my finger in, getting it good and wet. Then I traced a path down my belly to my aching center, leaving a damp trail from my breasts to my pussy. I slipped one finger inside and realized it wasn't enough.

Two fingers.

Better, but still a far cry from how it felt when Thor was inside me. I eyed up that massive hard-on wistfully. Such a waste…

As if he could read my mind, Thor gave his cock a long hard pump.

Maybe this hadn't been such a good idea. It was torturing me as much as him. Possibly more.

Moisture leaked from my pussy as if inviting an invasion.

Thor slid his hand down his cock one more time, and the sight drew me one step closer to the bed.

I couldn't tear my gaze away from his rock-hard cock. Maybe if I did all the moving, it wouldn't be such a bad idea. He needed to rest, and he wouldn't get any sleep with that monstrous thing distracting him.

Amazing how I could justify getting what I wanted.

"Lie back, hands behind your head." I tried to sound bossy, but it came out as a breathy whisper.

Thor complied, his eyes shining in anticipation.

I moved to the side of the bed and clambered on top of him, a knee on each side of his thighs. Leaning forward slightly, I lowered my head and sucked his cock into my mouth.

Thor let out a low growl and placed one hand behind my head, urging me to take him deeper.

I obliged, sucking hard enough to hollow my cheeks. My head bobbed up and down as I worked his cock with my tongue and my lips.

"I want to be inside you when I come." He grunted the words out as he grasped my shoulders.

I lifted my head, frowning. I doubted there was a condom anywhere handy, but I was almost certain neither of us had been with anyone else, and I wasn't anywhere near my fertile period. "Bare?"

He nodded. "Bare. You okay with that?"

*Hell yeah.* Right now, I was okay with anything that meant that delicious cock would be inside me.

"Yeah. But we have to be careful -- stitches. I'll get on top and do all the work."

In reply, he lowered his hands to my hips and helped me straddle his hips so his cock slipped between the soft folds guarding my entrance. He paused, locking his gaze on me. "You sure?"

I loved that he had enough control to asked me for consent while his cock nestled against the damp proof of my willingness. "Positive."

He helped me slide down onto his cock. Slowly. Carefully. Making sure I felt every inch of that massive shaft as it invaded my welcoming body. When he was fully seated inside me, I started to move, riding him like a prized stallion.

My breath came faster and faster. Flashes of white-hot desire blazed through every nerve and pooled low in my belly as it built toward an orgasm. With nothing between us, no condom to dull the sensations, my body raced to the inevitable. I raised my hands, cupping my breasts so as not to give into the temptation to touch him, to caress his massive Viking like chest.

Thor's hands came up, covering mine and holding them in place. He moved his hips in time with each thrust I made. Moments later, my orgasm washed over me like a tsunami on a deserted beach, wiping out everything in its path. I bit back a guttural scream as my inner channel clamped down on his cock and sent Thor into an orgasm of his own.

Having his naked cock inside me was magnitudes better than anything I'd ever felt. I opened my eyes to find him watching me, a satisfied smile playing around his lips.

"You know if you just agreed to be my old lady, we could do this all the time."

"We already do this most of the time," I pointed out.

He shook his head. "Not nearly enough. And half the time you have to go home right after, so we don't get to cuddle."

"Cuddle?" Did the big tough biker just say he wanted more cuddles?

"Yeah, cuddle up and fall asleep in each other's arms. Every night. Grow old together and all that shit."

*Damn, that sounded tempting.*

Just for a second, I let myself dream.

Then, a knock on the door had me scrambling for my clothes.

* * *

**Thor**

Sometimes, Ace's timing sucked. I raised my voice to make sure he heard me through the solid metal of the hospital door. "Give us a minute." No way I wanted anyone else to see Janet naked.

She threw me a panicked look as she shimmied her pants back up over her hips. Fuck, my cock started to harden again, just watching her.

"You okay? I didn't hurt you, did I?" Her brows drew together in a worried frown as her gaze zeroed in on the bulky bandage covering my stitches.

She'd just ridden me like a cowgirl at the barrel races, and she was worried about me? That was adorable. "I'm fine. Didn't even break a sweat. We gotta do that bare thing more often."

She shook her head. "Too risky. The last thing I need right now is a mini-me to worry about."

"If we were exclusive, you could go on the pill."

She paused, a wrinkle marring her brow. "I thought we were exclusive. Are you telling me you're screwing other women?"

She couldn't seriously think that. "Hell no. You're more than enough for me."

She tossed her head back. "Well, I'm not screwing other guys, so I guess we're exclusive."

"Not formally. You need to have my cut on you so everyone knows you're off limits."

She got that funny look on her face again. The one that said there was something she wasn't telling me. "That makes me your old lady. We've talked this over ten ways to Sunday. Not happening."

She was right. We'd talked this in circles that went nowhere, so I dropped the subject for now. She finished getting dressed, running her fingers through her hair in an attempt to straighten it. I liked it all mussed up, but I had a feeling she didn't want to hear that with Ace standing on the other side of the door.

"Do I look okay?"

"Good enough to eat."

She rolled her eyes. "Not what I need to hear right now."

"Okay then. You look like a woman who had been well and truly fucked and enjoyed every minute of it."

She let out an exasperated snort. "That's not what I meant. I don't want all your brothers to know I go for quickies in a hospital bed."

I raised one brow. "They're not dumb. I doubt they think we closed the door so we could discuss grocery shopping lists."

"True." She wrinkled her nose. Adorable. Yup. I was doomed. She needed to have my cut on her. And soon. Before I had to kill some asshole for looking at her sideways.

Another knock sounded on the door, louder this

time. I slanted a look at Janet. "You ready?"

She nodded. "Yeah."

I raised my voice. "Come on in."

The door opened and Ace stood framed in the doorway. He swept a quick look from me to Janet and back again before stepping inside and approaching my bedside. "How you feeling?"

"Like someone shoved a knife in my side, but you should see the other guy."

"Yeah. One ain't talking, but the cops caught up to the other guy. Stupid enough to let the security camera get a full-on face view. Seems he's a regular at the station."

"Rival gang?" We generally didn't have issues with other MCs unless they tried to muscle in on our territory. We weren't one percenters, but we weren't above bending a few rules if it kept our turf safe.

Ace didn't answer immediately, slanting a pointed look at Janet.

She grabbed her purse and slung it over her shoulder. "I should be going."

She knew the rules about club business. We didn't discuss it in front of anyone but patched in members, and occasionally the prospects if they needed to know something. Definitely not the wives or girlfriends. It was as much for their protection as anything. What you didn't know, you couldn't be expected to tell anyone. Like the cops. Or an attorney. Or a judge. Or a member of a fucking rival club stupid enough to touch one of our women.

Ace dipped his head in acknowledgement. "Thanks again for looking out for our boy."

She dropped a quick kiss on my forehead and headed for the door. "No problem. I'm kind of fond of him myself." She pulled the door closed behind her.

I turned my attention back to Ace. "What's the scoop?"

"Not a rival gang. A couple of low-life guns for hire. The one survivor swears he has no idea who hired them, or if you were the intended target or just in the wrong place at the wrong time. The dead guy was the main contact, and he's not talking."

I snorted. "So, what you're saying is that I killed the wrong guy?"

"Kind of looks that way. The survivor swears he wasn't the one who knifed you, so they charged him with aggravated assault and let him out on bail. The only good side is since he fingered his partner as the one with the knife, you're definitely off the hook on any kind of charges. Given his testimony that it wasn't your knife, it's cut and dried self-defense."

My hands went to the bulky bandage on my side. "The gaping hole in my side wasn't enough? So now what?"

Ace shrugged. "As soon as the doctor clears you, we get you back to the clubhouse. Shadow is checking online to see if he can find anything but so far, it's crickets. Unless you can think of a reason why someone would go to that much trouble to off you, we got nothing. It's starting to look like you really were just in the wrong place at the wrong time, but you need to be extra careful until we know that for sure."

I rolled my eyes. "Yeah. I have a feeling Janet's going to make sure of that."

"You two serious or what? You haven't got your cut on her."

I rolled my eyes. "I'm working on it. She's stubborn as shit."

Ace grinned. "Playing hard to get?"

I gave him a sour look. "Yeah. Maybe you could

get Deuce to ask Sophia to have a word with her. You know? Tell her how great it is to be a Riptide old lady?"

"Not a chance." Ace held up both hands. "I'm staying out of your love life, and I'll bet Deuce is too." His face got serious again. "Shadow will keep his eye on the dark web, see if anything about you pops up. Meanwhile, keep your head down and try to think if there is anyone you may have pissed off enough to want to slaughter you. It could have nothing to do with Riptide. Gotta think you weren't an angel before you joined the SEALs program."

He had a point there. I'd been in a few scrapes in my teenage years, but I couldn't come up with anything I might have done to provoke this drastic an attack. Just the usual shit kids do before they realize they're not invincible. A thought occurred to me. "If this was a hit, it had to be someone with serious money. Murder for hire isn't cheap."

"True." Ace narrowed his eyes. "I'll have one of the prospects keep an eye on the guy they cut loose on bail. Whoever hired him might get in touch. They would be pissed if they paid and didn't get results."

I nodded, struggling to look alert. I could feel my strength waning. Probably had something to do with the liquid dripping into my arm from the IV. I needed a nap, but damned if I was going to let that show in front of Ace.

It was as if Ace could read my thoughts, part of what made him a natural leader. "I need to get back to the clubhouse. Beast and Rattler have been scouting real estate and they have some likely properties they want to go over. Market is ripe for investment right now." He reached out to grip my hand. "If you need anything, just holler. Give the prospects something to do besides hold the wall up out there."

I gave his hand a squeeze and let go. "Thanks."

His mouth narrowed into a thin line. "You're family. We find out this was aimed at you, we'll take care of it."

A knock sounded at the door.

"What?" Ace barked out the question.

"The doc is here to check on Thor. Should I let him in?"

Ace slanted a look at me. "Yes. I was just leaving." He lowered his voice. "You can update me when he's done. You have your phone?"

I nodded. "Yeah. Janet brought it in for me."

He studied me for a moment. "She's a keeper, Thor. Nail her down."

"I'm trying."

A ghost of a smile crossed his face. "Good. Talk soon." Spinning on his heels, he brushed past the doctor, who looked pretty spooked. Likely more used to giving out orders than taking them.

The doctor picked up the clipboard from the bottom of my bed, and studied the monitor hooked up to me. "How are we feeling today?"

I snorted. "Don't know about you, but I feel like I got run over by a bus."

"Not surprising. This says you have a knife wound, not to mention assorted bruises and scrapes." He carefully removed the bandage and checked out the stitches, poking gently at the skin around them. "That is one nasty cut. The stitches are starting to heal already, though. No infection, which is good. Knife wounds are notorious for that."

"You're not the same guy that stitched me up, are you?"

He shook his head. "No, that would have been

Dr. Murphy. He's the emergency room doctor, but once you stabilized you got stuck with me. I'm the local on-call guy."

"Fair enough." Not that I really cared, but there had been something about the Murphy guy that sent a bad vibe through me. Probably nothing, but trusting my instincts was what had kept me alive in combat when there wasn't enough time to think things through. I was okay with trading him out. "What's your name?"

"Dr. Samson." He pulled a prescription pad out of his pocket and scribbled something down. "I'm going to give you some antibiotics just in case that knife wasn't as clean as it could be, and a painkiller so you can relax. We're going to keep you here for the night, and unless anything changes you can go home tomorrow. But you need to take it easy for the next couple of weeks until that cut is well on the way to healing. You try anything strenuous, you could pull out the stitches and start it bleeding all over again."

I wasn't about to ask him what he classified as strenuous. If he didn't say no sex, I wouldn't have to lie to Janet when she asked me.

Just as if I'd summoned her, Janet appeared in the doorway. "May I come in?"

Dr. Samson looked up. "Hi, Janet. Sure. You know the patient?"

She locked her gaze on the bandage as he taped it back down. "I'm afraid so. He going to live?"

The doctor chuckled. "I think it's likely so long as he doesn't do anything stupid."

She shook her head. "If he didn't do anything stupid he wouldn't be here, so that's not comforting."

"I'm right here. I can hear every word you say." I pretended to look hurt, tamping down a twinge of jealousy at the sight of Janet joking with another man. "I was being a hero, rescuing a damsel in distress."

"Of course you're a hero." She grinned. "But I kind of like you as a live hero, so you're going to do exactly what Dr. Samson here tells you, okay?"

I sighed theatrically. "Okay, fine."

The doctor ignored the byplay, addressing Janet. "I'm going to have some antibiotics and some more painkiller added to the IV. He'll probably be pretty groggy for the rest of the night. Unless complications set in, I'll sign his discharge papers in the morning and he can go home. He'll need to take it easy for a few weeks and go to his regular doctor to check on it and get the stitches out."

"Sounds good. Thanks."

"No problem. You need anything else, you know where to find me." He turned and left the room.

Janet approached the bed and leaned over to kiss me on the lips. I brought my hand up to cup the back of her head, sliding my tongue along her lips to coax them open. The sound of someone clearing their throat interrupted us.

Janet straightened up and turned. A stern looking woman in scrubs bustled in, pushing a cart in front of her.

"And you are?" I'd never been known for my tact.

"I'm the nurse who's going to spike that drippy thing for you." She raised one brow. "I'd ask if you were okay with that, but I follow the doctor's orders, not the patient's."

Janet reached over and picked up the two vials sitting on the cart, reading the labels. She reached for my hand. "You need these, and you need some rest. I'm on shift shortly, so I need to get ready. I'll check in on you on my break." She dropped a disappointingly chaste kiss on my lips and headed out of the room.

The nurse fussed with the IV for a few minutes, adding the contents of the vials. When she was satisfied with the setup, she packed everything on her cart and glared down at me. "Not sure what's going on between you and that girl, but she's one of the good ones. Be nice to her." With that she swept out of the room.

I stared at the empty doorway. I was getting the feeling everyone thought Janet was too good for me.

Maybe they were right.

## Chapter Five

**Janet**

The move from the hospital to the clubhouse went as well as could be expected. Thor was grumpy and impatient. You would think an ex-SEAL would be good at following orders, but I guess that only applied to orders from people he considered his superiors. Doctors did not fall into that category. Sophia gave me a sympathetic look as I explained to him for the umpteenth time that he could not ride his bike for the next two weeks.

"I wasn't going to race it, just a leisurely ride. I've been cooped up in that fucking hospital. I need to get the stink of disinfectant out of my head."

I glared at him. "You'll survive for a few more days. If you rip those stitches out, you'll be right back there."

Beast grinned from across the room. "Listen to your nursemaid, Thor."

I threw up my hands in exasperation. "I'm not his nursemaid!"

Sophia reached out and tugged my hand. "You need a break from old grumpy there. How about we leave the guys alone while we go get a real cup of coffee. I'm not sure what that stuff in the hospital was, but it wasn't coffee."

"I'm just trying to keep him alive," I grumbled, but I let her lead me out of the room.

The kitchen was empty. It was farmer's market day in town, and Mom liked to go pick up local produce and meat for the clubhouse. Of course, Jake went with her. Those two were practically attached at the hip. If you found one, the other was close by. I had a feeling the Riptide boys were better fed than most bikers.

Sophia crossed to the coffee pot and poured the steaming liquid into two mugs. Carrying them over to the table, she pointed at the seat with her chin. "Sit down and have a coffee. Surviving on the crap they serve at the hospital is likely half your problem."

"The other half is back there trying to convince people he didn't almost die." I dumped some cream and sugar into the mug and stirred it a little harder than necessary.

Sophia narrowed her eyes. "Deuce says Shadow couldn't find anything online to suggest this was a deliberate attack on Thor."

I took a sip of the coffee. She was right. This was heavenly compared to the crap at the emergency ward. Even the coffee in the staff room was barely mediocre. "It sure smacked of an ambush."

"Yes, it did." She pursed her lips. "I'm guessing this must have occurred to you already. Any chance your family found out you were dating a biker and decided to take care of the problem? I know they're fixated on marrying you off to that senator's son."

I shook my head. "I already checked with Montgomery. He said the family had nothing to do with it."

"How about the senator's son? You two have been friends since grade school. Is he upset you're not giving him a chance?"

I sighed. "Can you keep a secret?"

"Of course. What is it?"

I hesitated. If this got out, a lot of people could get hurt, the senator's son being at the top of the list. "Maxwell has a vested interest in me not wanting to marry him. He's in a relationship with his driver, and as long as everyone thinks he's waiting for me to come to my senses and fall in line, he doesn't have to pretend to be interested in another woman."

"Holy shit!" Her jaw practically dropped. "He's gay? You're kidding me, right?"

I shook my head. "I am not. You know how badly his family are going to react when they find out."

"So, the longer you play like it's you resisting, the better it is for him."

I nodded. "And me. If my family changes their mind out about Thor, I'm afraid of what they'll do. They didn't get rich by playing nice."

Sophia let out a deep breath. "You are in one hell of a lousy position. What are you going to do?"

I took a sip of the coffee. "I'm not sure. I'd love to agree to be Thor's old lady, but that would be selfish. It could put him in the crosshairs." I frowned. "Any advice?"

"Not really. Maxwell is going to have to come out at some point, and you can't live your whole life avoiding your family. Maybe they'll see how happy Thor makes you and be okay with it."

I snorted. "And maybe unicorns really roam the earth looking for virgins."

"Does Thor know why you're holding him at arm's length?"

"Not a chance. I just tell him I'm not into commitment, and that I want to keep things the way they are."

"He's only going to buy that for so long. Has he ever asked about your family?"

I shrugged. "Yeah, but I just say we're not close. He gets it. Most of these guys aren't close to their families. It's one of the reasons they're here. This is their family."

Sophia looked unconvinced, but she let the subject drop. "What about your other plans? Are you still thinking of opening a flower shop?"

"Absolutely. It's just taking a little longer than I thought it would. I have some money saved, but commercial rents are high and that's if I can even find a place with the right kind of setup. It needs to have a storefront, decent parking, and a cooler for the flowers. Not exactly the kind of place that comes on the market every day."

"True. You'll probably have to renovate, especially for the cooler. Most retail spots won't have one."

"I know. I have the inheritance my great granny left me, but I'd want a decent lease in place if I'm going to spend that kind of money."

Sophia took another sip of her coffee. "I'll keep my eyes open for you, but real estate isn't really my thing. I can mention it to Deuce. He's got the club looking at real estate investments. I know he was leaning toward apartments or houses they can rent out, but if they come across anything that would work for you, they could let you know. Hopefully the right place will just pop up when you least expect it."

I reached out and covered her hand with mine. "Thanks. I know it will. I just have to be patient and put up with Dr. Murphy a little bit longer."

Sophia cocked her head. "Isn't he the one who stitched up Thor?"

"Yeah. He's a great doctor, one of the top ER surgeons in the state. As a surgeon he's awesome, but as a person he sucks. And he seems to have it in for me." I trailed off as Joker sauntered into the room.

"Someone giving you a hard time?" He reached for a coffee mug and helped himself to the last of the pot.

"Just one of the doctors at work." I stood up and carried my cup to the sink. "Not a big deal."

"As long as it's not one of us. Wouldn't want to upset Thor." He took a gulp of the dark liquid.

"You checked him out yet?"

He shook his head. "Just heading in there. You want to come along, or are you squeamish?"

"I work front desk in a hospital emergency room," I pointed out.

He shrugged. "It's a little different when the blood and guts are spurting out of someone you care about."

He had a point there, but I doubted there would be any spurting going on. "I'll be fine."

"I think Deuce needs me." Sophia stood up and headed to the sink with her empty cup. Sophia had an aversion to seeing anyone in pain, especially if there were wounds involved. Her therapist said it was some form of PTSD and would fade in time. Gunshot wounds definitely bothered her, but I guessed a knife wound wouldn't be much better. I stepped over to give her a big hug. "Talk to you soon."

I turned and followed Joker.

* * *

**Thor**

I watched Janet walk toward me. The sight of her never failed to thrill me. Joker was with her though, which meant my cock wasn't going to get what it wanted. I shifted position to mask the growing bulge at my groin.

Technically, I was on bed rest, but I wasn't about to spend the next week naked and flat on my back. I was propped up in my bed, shirtless, but wearing my jeans. I knew Joker would be up to see me soon, so I'd left my shirt off on purpose. I'd checked the wound myself earlier and while it still looked raw and ugly, it was healing nicely with no sign of infection.

Janet padded over to the bedside and dropped a kiss on my forehead. I snagged her around the waist and pulled her in closer for a decent kiss. Joker was right behind her, but I didn't care. She might not be willing to wear my cut, but she damn sure belonged to me.

The little minx brought her arms up and wrapped them around my neck, deepening the kiss. I'd make sure she paid for that later. She knew I wasn't into exhibitionism, and I wouldn't take it any further with Joker in the room.

Joker cleared his throat loudly. "How about you let me check him out before you start mauling his sorry ass?"

Janet straightened up, and I grinned. "No problem but make it quick. When my woman wants me, I deliver."

Janet snorted, retreating to the far side of the room. "You are so full of yourself."

Joker rolled his eyes, stepping up to carefully remove the bandage. He poked around, watching my reaction. "Looks good. Stitches are clean. I'm going to put a new bandage on it just to be safe. Stops your clothes from rubbing on it, or any dirt getting in. I shouldn't have to say this but be careful. No pressure on the wound, and do not overexert yourself." He looked meaningfully over at Janet. "There's as many stitches inside as there are on the surface, and you do not want to rip any of them out."

"So, no sex?" Janet stuck her tongue out at me.

Joker shrugged. "I'm sure you two can figure

something out. I'm just saying be careful." He turned his attention back to me. "You need to stay off your bike, though, for at least another week."

I frowned. "Why? I can be careful."

"No doubt, but what about all the other idiots on the road? All it's going to take is one asshole to force you to swerve aside to avoid getting creamed, and those stitches will rip right out. You don't even want to think about what it would look like if you laid the bike down."

He had a point, although it didn't make me happy. "Fine. No bike."

Joker carefully rebandaged the wound. "You're free to wander around the clubhouse. In fact, it's good for you to be up on your feet. If you feel woozy or dizzy, have someone come fetch me. I'll update Ace on your condition."

"Thanks, Joker." Janet padded back over to my side while Joker packed up his supplies. "I'll make sure he behaves."

The corner of Joker's mouth lifted in a faint smile. "I'm sure you will." He picked up his bag and headed out the door.

I reached out to grab Janet's hand and draw her to my side. "You heard the man. Sex is back on the table."

Janet giggled, watching for the door to close behind Joker. "I don't think the table is an option, but if you could manage to sit up, I've always wanted to try a naked lap dance."

My cock leapt to full attention. "Woman, you are a fucking genius."

She grinned. "I thought you'd never notice."

I swung my legs over the side of the bed and fumbled with my jeans. Sliding them down over my hips, I kicked them out of the way. "My lap is yours to dance on." I reached over to grab a condom off the side table. Ripping it open, with my teeth, I quickly sheathed myself. After doing her bare in the hospital, I felt a twinge of regret but neither of us were ready for a little biker baby. Hell, she wouldn't even agree to being a couple.

I fisted my hand around my shaft and gave it a slow pull from base to tip.

Janet pulled her top over her head, and her breasts strained against the scrap of lace that confined them. She reached up and undid the front closure, and the bra dropped to the floor, leaving her gorgeous breasts to spring free. The rosy tips hardened into pebbled peaks under my heated gaze, and she cupped them in her hands like a pagan offering, scoring her thumbs across the nipples.

"Fuck, woman, quit teasing or I'm going to come before you ever touch me." I gave my cock another leisurely pull.

She reacted by slipping her tongue out to wet her lips. Letting go of those luscious mounds, she hooked her thumbs in the waistband of her yoga pants and pushed them down to her ankles. Gracefully stepping out of them, she watched me from beneath her lashes for a long moment while I marveled at my good fortune in finding such an amazing woman.

Completely naked now, she stalked over to me and placed her hands on my shoulders. Her gaze dropped to my lap, where my rigid shaft waited eagerly for her attention. A slight smile curved her lips, and she worried her bottom lip with her teeth.

She slung one leg over me, reached down between us and fisted her hand around my cock, aiming it at her moist entrance. I locked my gaze on hers, grasping her hips as she slowly lowered herself into my lap.

*Fuck, that felt good*!

With my cock buried deep inside her, she started to move. She rode me slowly at first, and I gritted my teeth at the exquisite torture. She quickly increased the pace as I thrust my hips upward to meet her movements. Her nostrils flared, her breath came in harsh gasps as we quickly forgot about taking things easy. Her sexy ass ground into my groin with each stroke, and my cock reacted by stiffening even more.

We fit together like we were made for each other. I didn't understand why she refused to become my old lady. It frustrated the hell out of me, but I was damned if I was going to give up on her. She was mine. Period.

She threw her head back as her pussy clenched down hard on my cock and she let out a loud cry as her orgasm overtook her.

I thrust upward one last time, letting out a triumphant growl as I came seconds after her. Her movements slowed, and then stilled and she collapsed against me, careful not to place any pressure on my wounded side.

"Thor…" She breathed my name out so quietly I barely heard her.

"Yeah?"

"Nothing. Just… Don't ever do that to me again."

I frowned in confusion. "Don't fuck you?"

She lifted her head to stare into my eyes. "No, not that. Don't ever almost get killed. I don't think I could handle it."

I cradled the back of her head and placed a gentle kiss on her lips. I cared about her more than life itself, but there were some things I just couldn't promise.

# Chapter Six

## Janet

"Where are we going?"

It had been ten days since the incident, and Thor had behaved admirably. Well, not really, but he'd behaved better than I expected. He grumbled when we took my Jeep instead of his bike to go somewhere, but on the whole he'd been pretty good about it.

"It's a surprise." He grinned at me from the driver's seat. He may have agreed not to ride his bike, but as he'd pointed out more than once, he had not agreed to be ferried around like a disabled armadillo. He refused to let me drive my own vehicle.

I refrained from asking why anyone would drive an armadillo anywhere, disabled or not. Sometimes his logic left me confused. As long as he followed doctor's orders and stayed off his bike, I let the subject drop. For once, I was happy I'd opted to buy a Jeep and not some cutesy car. It was hard to picture Thor happily settling in to drive a Mini Cooper or a VW Bug.

I wrinkled my nose. "Is this a surprise I'm going to like?"

"Sure hope so." His grin widened.

Well, that wasn't encouraging. His idea of a surprise could be anything up to, and including, front seat tickets to a prize fight. Or worse, although I'm not sure what that would be. I let out a sigh and snapped my seatbelt in place. "Is this surprise close to here?"

"Close enough."

That didn't narrow it down. "Does it involve food?"

"Are we playing twenty questions?"

"You don't get to answer a question with a question."

"Is that a rule? Because you know I don't like rules." He sounded much too cheerful.

"Yes, it's a rule, and I don't care if you like it. You have to follow the rules."

He geared down and slid around a corner without coming to a full stop. "I do? Says who?"

"Me. It makes me happy when you follow rules, and you like it so much better when I'm happy."

He straightened out the Jeep and reached over to settle one hand on my thigh. "I can think of lots of ways to keep you happy without following rules."

I giggled despite myself. "You're bad!"

"Me?" His innocent act wasn't very believable.

"Yes, you."

"You like me when I'm bad."

"Only sometimes. Depends on how bad you are."

"In that case it's a good thing we're here."

He pulled into the parking lot of a building with a *For Sale* sign in the front window. A couple of bikes were already parked in front, along with a sporty looking red car.

I frowned. The building looked well maintained, the windows clean, and the parking lot free of the debris that inevitable gathers in abandoned lots. "Why are we here?"

Instead of answering, Thor got out and stalked around to my side of the Jeep. He opened my door with a flourish. I stepped out onto the pavement.

We entered the building through a side door that was conveniently unlocked and walked right into a beautifully open retail area. The front picture windows were currently covered in brown paper, but I could see how the natural daylight would stream in once that was removed. A wide window display area behind them would be perfect to display items to entice customers to come in and browse. I turned and saw a glass fronted display case behind the checkout counter. Good chance it was a cooler, meant to display perishable merchandise.

Speechless, I turned to Thor.

"What do you think?" He looked eager for an answer.

"It's gorgeous, but why are we here?" It would make the perfect flower shop, but this place was for sale, not rent. I definitely could not afford to buy a building.

"You said you wanted to open a flower shop, but you just needed the right place."

"To rent, not to buy. I can't afford this."

"But Riptide can." Ace entered from a hallway behind the counter. "We've been looking for ways to diversify our income. We were looking for residential units, but this works too. It's an estate sale. The owner passed away and it's been vacant for almost a year now. The sellers are motivated. The cost of upkeep is eating away at the value of the asset so they're eager to unload."

"I'm confused." I looked from Ace to Thor. "What does Riptide's investment policy have to do with me?"

Deuce, the club treasurer, appeared behind Ace, along with a guy I didn't recognize. Deuce glanced up, acknowledging me with a jut of his chin before turning to the stranger. I couldn't make out what they were saying, but they looked serious.

"Simple." Ace stepped back, away from the two newcomers. "Sophia mentioned to Deuce that your dream is to open a flower store and get out of the hospital gig. Deuce tells me that interest rates on our passive investments suck. Solution that benefits both of us? Riptide pulls its money out of investments that are paying less than one percent interest and buys this place. We hire you to oversee the renovations it needs to become a viable flower store, which was not its original purpose." He gestured at the cooler behind the counter. "Of course, Riptide will cough up for the renovations. When it's ready to reopen, you can lease it from us at a reasonable rate with a buyout provision at the end of the lease. That gives you time to see if this is really what you want to do with your life. If you decide to bail, we have a viable business to sell, and we make a profit. If you decide to keep going, we negotiate a way for you to buy it from us. Everything will be in writing, nice and legal so we all know where we stand. It's a win-win for both you and the club."

It sounded too good to be true. I turned to Thor. "You arranged this?"

He shrugged. "I was part of it. I know you're not thrilled with that Dr. Murphy guy chewing out your ass all the time, and you did tell me this was your plan. Seemed like a no-brainer when Deuce said we needed to change our investment strategy."

"This doesn't mean I'm going to agree to be your old lady." I blurted it out, maybe because the thought was so tempting.

"I'm not trying to buy you." He looked offended. "If you agree to be my old lady, I want it to be because you can't imagine living the rest of your life without me in it."

I nodded sheepishly. I knew he wasn't that kind of guy. We weren't there yet, though, and maybe we never would be. "What happens if we split up?"

"I said it would all be legal, and that stands," Ace broke into the conversation. "It's not contingent on the state of your relationship with Thor. If that becomes an issue and you don't want to see him, I can order him to steer clear of the store."

"Really?" I raised my brows, looking at Thor. "And you'd do it?"

Thor nodded. "I wouldn't be happy about it, but I'd do it."

My head was spinning. It was one thing to dream, quite another to have an opportunity like this land in your lap.

"You can take some time to think about it. Talk it over with someone." Ace nodded toward the back. "That's the realtor over there talking to Deuce. We're still negotiating terms so we haven't gotten a solid offer in yet. I just wanted to make sure you might be interested before we finalized anything."

"I'm interested. Just a little stunned."

"I get it. You're considering it, though?"

I nodded. "Hell, yeah. I'm just not the jump-in-before-you think kind of person."

Thor slung an arm around my shoulders. "Fuck, I can attest to that."

I poked him with my elbow. "This is different."

Ace grinned. "Totally different. A flower shop is a whole lot less trouble than agreeing to be Thor's old lady."

"Hey! Whose side are you on?" Thor shook his head, addressing Ace.

"There are no sides to that. It's my decision," I pointed out. "I already told you I'm not ready to become your old lady."

The realtor's voice interrupted us as he headed for the door. "I'm out of here for now. I'll get back to you once I've had a chance to talk to the sellers."

Ace waved his hand at the man, then turned

back to me. "It's going to take him a few days to get back to us. We're just clarifying property lines, etc. You think about it, and if you decide you might be interested we can discuss terms and timelines for a lease."

I nodded. "That's fair."

Deuce wandered over, giving me a friendly nod of the head before addressing Thor. "You pitch the idea to her?"

"Yeah. Maybe I should have mentioned it to her before we got here." Thor shrugged. "It was a bit of a surprise."

I rolled my eyes. "That's an understatement. But a nice surprise. It sounds almost too good to be true. I just don't want to make a snap decision. I need to do some calculating and see if I'm ready to dive into being self-employed."

"Fair enough." Deuce tilted his head. "It's a fairly gigantic leap. But you're considering it, right?"

"I'd be an idiot not to." I sighed. "Let me get used to the idea, okay?"

"Okay. If you have any questions, Thor knows where to find me." He glanced over at Ace. "You ready to go?"

Ace gave a nod. He looked at Thor. "You two lock up when you're done."

"No worries. Just going to show her the rest of the place, and the apartment."

The apartment? My brows rose in surprise.

"Let me or Deuce know when you make a decision." Ace grabbed his helmet off the counter and jammed it on his head before following Deuce outside.

I turned to Thor. "Apartment?"

He nodded. "Upstairs is an apartment. Not a huge one, but it would work for us."

"Us?"

"You." He grinned. "But you're going to be so happy, you'll invite me to stay over lots."

I shook my head. "How about you finish showing me the store and then we can go look at my" -- I emphasized the word 'my' -- "possible living space."

"Good idea." He headed toward the hallway Deuce and the realtor had come out of. "There's a walk-in fridge back here, and a workroom for doing all those flowery things."

"You mean arrangements?" Although I had to admit, flowery things sounded so much more fun. I followed him down the narrow hallway that ended in an open room with a stainless-steel working table in the middle. Off to one side was a deep double sink. I could already picture me working in here. It needed more shelving, and some counters on either side of that sink but those were easy fixes. The floor was painted concrete which would be easy to clean, especially since there was a big drain in the middle of it.

"This is the fridge." Thor gestured at a steel door at the far side of the room.

I had a bad feeling about that. It looked like the kind of walk-in cooler you'd find in a restaurant and that's not what you needed for flowers. Unlike cases of drinks, or sandwich meats and cheese, flowers needed a very gentle air flow to keep them as fresh as possible. The glass display cooler out front was ideal but not big enough. I'd need a second one to have enough room for stock. Bigger would be better, but unless I was doing a wedding or another type of event it would do. I'd probably be able to order larger amounts close to the date of a big event. I made a mental note to check the cost of coolers, and to see if there were any places where I could pick up a used one.

Thor broke into my train of thought. "You look worried."

I shook my head. "Not worried. Just thinking." I opened the cooler door and confirmed my suspicions. This wouldn't do for flowers at all. I explained the problem to Thor.

"A flower cooler would be part of the renovations." He put his hands on his hips. "Not much room in here for that though. Could you have it out front?"

"Out front would work better, actually. People could see what we had in stock that way. Often people can picture what they want, but they don't know the flower's name."

He nodded. "Yeah. Makes sense. We would have to update the wiring if you're putting a second cooler out front. Deuce mentioned having an electrician and a plumber in to check things out before we put in an offer. We could have them add hookups for a display cooler as part of their estimates."

* * *

**Thor**

I felt a surge of satisfaction. She'd take the shop.

I could tell by the adorable wrinkle in her brow that she was already cataloguing what she needed to do to get the place in shape. Adding a cooler wouldn't be a big deal. The place needed a good scrubbing down, and maybe a coat of paint. Nothing major.

As if she could read my mind, Janet commented, "It would be brighter in here if we painted the walls a lighter color. Maybe an off-white or a really pale yellow? I could get Sophia to come look at it. She has a knack for that kind of thing."

"Do you want that walk-in cooler in the workroom taken out to give you more room?"

She shook her head. "No, it could be useful for other supplies I need to keep cold, like fruits and things. It just won't work for flowers. And this room is plenty big enough to work in."

She pulled out her phone and started to dictate notes into it. I trailed behind her as we toured the entire ground floor. She investigated every nook and cranny, speaking into the phone as she went.

She was already hooked, and we hadn't even gone upstairs yet. Once she saw the living space, she wouldn't be able to say no. She paced into the retail space and chattered away, pivoting in a circle as she talked.

When she finally fell silent, I took her by the hand. "Want to see the living quarters?"

She glanced around. "Yes please. I don't see a stairwell."

"The suite is separate from the shop, so the stairs are outside. We could add an entrance from here if you want one, but it would take up room. Just let the guys know when they are renovating." I led her out the side door and around the back. Ace had left a set of keys with me, and I unlocked the door. The stairs were in good shape and led to a landing outside the apartment. I unlocked the door and pushed it open, stepping aside to let Janet enter.

Her swift intake of breath sent a curl of satisfaction sliding through me. She loved it. How could she not? The open living area had been painted in muted tones of pale pink, fading into a creamy white in the kitchen. The floors were oak hardwood polished to a high shine in a soft hue that matched the kitchen cupboards. A built-in shelf unit covered one wall in the living area, with a gas fireplace set in the middle.

The kitchen had granite counters on three sides, and shiny stainless-steel appliances. A shiny chrome faucet with a pull-down sprayer graced the double sink. Having a window over the sink that looked onto the parking lot would be helpful for watching customers.

"It's way nicer than my current apartment!" She turned to me, her eyes taking on a worried slant. "How am I going to be able to afford this? The apartment alone is worth a fortune."

"You haven't seen the whole place yet. There's still the bedroom and a bathroom."

"With a tub?" Her constant complaint about her current place was the lack of a tub in the bathroom. It had a shower, but she wanted to be able to soak in a tub.

"Yes. There's a tub." I smiled indulgently. "A deep one."

She squealed and raced over to the hallway. It wasn't much, just a few feet long but it had two doorways. One opened into the bedroom, which was pretty standard -- a ten by twelve-foot square room with a window and a closet. Mirrored sliding doors on the closet made the room appear bigger than it was.

The bathroom, which was right next to the bedroom, clinched the deal.

"A clawfoot tub! I love it!" Janet clapped her hands in delight. I swear she hadn't been this excited when she'd been touring the flower shop. "And a separate shower stall!" She ran her hands over the tiled wall. "Look! It has one of those rainforest showerheads. And it's so big! We could both fit in it."

A picture of the two of us sharing the shower

filled my mind, her generous breasts gleaming wet and droplets dripping from her puckered nipples.

My jeans were suddenly uncomfortably tight. Yup, the shower thing was definitely top of my to-do list.

She turned to face me, her expression suddenly sober. "Do you think I can really afford to do this?"

I shrugged. "It's a risk, sure. But life is a risk, so we just gotta do the best we can. You want a flower shop, you make it happen."

Her eyes sparkled, and the corner of her mouth quirked up in a ghost of a smile. "You know, sometimes you sound so wise it's hard to believe you're a biker."

"Bikers are fucking brilliant!" I paused. "At least, when we're not busy getting knifed in an alley."

She laughed then, a light tinkling sound that I loved to hear.

"And you could get a roommate." I waggled my brows suggestively.

She snorted. "Yeah. I could look into that. I think one of the medics at the hospital is looking for a place."

"Like fuck you'll take some asshole of a medic as a roommate!" I grabbed her around the waist, ignoring the twinge as my stitches pulled tight. "The only guy you'll be giving a key to is me."

"Jealous much?" She grinned as I pulled her in tight against me. "And Timmy is a nice guy, not an asshole."

"Well, he can be a nice guy somewhere else."

"So, if I need a roommate, you'd be willing to cough up some cash?" She leaned back in my arms, batting her eyelashes.

Me paying for things had been a bit of an issue between us from the word go. I had money. More than

I needed. I saw no reason why I shouldn't spend it on her. Janet, on the other hand, seemed to see it as some kind of trap. Like I expected some fucking return on my investment. I knew I was old-fashioned, but in my world, if you took a woman out on a date, you picked up the tab. To hell with this whole going Dutch thing. I wasn't Dutch, and I wasn't a pussy-assed, new age wimp. "You know it, babe. Just say the word."

She wrinkled her nose. "I think we're getting ahead of ourselves. I'd love to live here, and the flower shop would be a dream come true, but we're not at the live-together stage yet."

I shrugged. "So, you say. You want the shop, it's yours. The rest is just details."

She shook her head. "It can't be that easy. There's leases and legal things, and the club hasn't even bought it yet. They can't give me something they don't own."

"Technicalities." I lowered my head to devour her lips. I'd never get tired of kissing this woman. She tasted like sunshine and goodness and second chances.

She parted her lips, and I deepened the kiss, sliding my hands up her back. Oh yeah, this was going to be our first love nest and now was as good a time as any to baptize it.

* * *

"Looks like the attack on you was a one-off."

The attack had been almost two weeks ago, and Ace sat behind his desk, his fingers steepled on the polished oak in front of him. Shadow sprawled in a chair off to the left and Rattler was perched on a chair to my right. As president of Riptide, Ace had called me in to talk about the attack and let me in on what they'd managed to find on the perpetrators so far. Shadow and Rattler had been tasked with digging up whatever they could on the assholes and liaising with the cops assigned to the case. At least I'd been cleared of a murder charge.

I frowned. "One-off? Felt like an ambush to me, and those are usually targeted."

"Either you were just in the wrong place at the wrong time, or the perps mistook you for someone else." Rattler shrugged. "The second guy swears he wasn't in contact with the people who ordered the hit. He was just brought in as muscle. Given his previous encounters with them, the cops think he's telling the truth. He's not the brightest bulb in the lamp. The girl was smart enough not to let her face get caught by the camera so they haven't made any advances in finding her. It was definitely a setup, but it looks like you might have taken the bait before the intended target."

Lucky me. "I don't suppose you know who the intended target was?"

Shadow spoke up. "That's the strange part. Can't find any chatter on the web, dark or otherwise, about a botched hit or a dead assassin. Whoever is involved is either not in the dark web world or has enough money and sense to make things go away."

That was not comforting. Enough money and sense meant mafia or cartel. I didn't think I was important enough for either though, so maybe I was overthinking this.

"Really, the only thing we care about is that the intended target likely wasn't you." Ace shifted position, leaning forward. "That place was crowded. There's no way to tell who was there that night and supposed to notice and follow the perps outside. And honestly, we don't care. No point in poking our nose into something that doesn't affect us. We're just concerned with your safety."

"So, I should just forget about it?" Sounded like a plan to me, except for the nasty scar. That damn thing was ugly as sin.

"Always good to be cautious, but I don't think you have much to worry about." Shadow pursed his lips. "It's been a while now and nothing else has happened. If this were mafia or cartel out to kill you, they'd have taken another shot at it by now."

Rattler nodded. "True. If this was a targeted hit, the guy left alive would have made a second attempt right way, most likely at the hospital."

"You had two of the prospects guarding my room," I pointed out. "Even the nurses had a hard time getting into my room to change bandages."

"True, but when you got out, a drive-by shooting could have been arranged. They would know you were Riptide and could have staked out the club compound with a sniper or waited for you to leave and followed you to finish you off. Lots of options for a second chance at you."

I looked from Rattler to Shadow. "Wow. Way to make a guy feel fucking safe."

Rattler shrugged. "Just saying, if I fucked up a hit I'd be right on it. I wouldn't give the target time to heal up and come back at me."

He had a point there. I looked at Ace. "So, I'm in the clear, everything goes back to normal?"

He shook his head. "Not yet. You might not be a target, but I want Joker to okay you as one hundred percent fit before we put you back on the duty roster."

I suppose I should have been unhappy about that, but it meant I could spend time with Janet getting the shop up and running. Deuce had finalized the purchase offer on the building, and the seller was eager for a quick closing. Barring any last-minute surprises, she could move into the apartment at the end of the next week and start working on renovations to the retail space. She'd given her two weeks' notice at the hospital and would be finished up there soon. That would give her time to pack. The rent on her current apartment didn't run out until the end of the month, so she could take her time moving things over to the new space.

She hadn't actually agreed to me moving in with her, but I could work on that. Besides the obvious financial benefits, I could provide security, muscle to move heavy things, and stress relief.

That last one was my ace in the hole.

## Chapter Seven

**Janet**

You know that thing where if something feels too good to be true, it probably is? That's how I felt about Riptide practically bending over backward to get me set up in my dream career. Everything on my wish list had suddenly fallen into my lap. Yeah, it definitely felt too good to be true.

Jason Witherspoon was a good lawyer and I'd known him since I was a child, but he was also a family friend. Knowing how close he was to my parents, I'd debated the wisdom of calling him, but I really need to have someone I trusted go over the legal stuff that Riptide's lawyer had prepared. I'd called his office after hours, knowing his receptionist would be gone but he'd still be there. Guys like Jason didn't work the nine to five.

He answered the phone with his usual charm, his voice gruff. "This better not be a scam call or I'm going to sue your ass."

"Well, hi to you too, Jason. We haven't talked in ages, but you're as charming as ever."

"Janet?"

"Yup, It's me."

"How the heck are you? Your parents said you had a big blowout and ghosted them."

"Depends on how you look at it," I answered wryly. "They said if I didn't agree to marry Maxwell, I was out of the family. I'm definitely not marrying Maxwell, so it seemed best to move on."

"I'm sure they didn't mean that literally. Your parents just want the best for you. Maxwell's family has money and connections. You'd never have to worry about anything again."

I doubted that, but I let it pass. "I have a legal question for you, but first I need to know if what we discuss is going to get back to my mom and dad."

"Absolutely not." He sounded all professional now. "Client-lawyer privilege is sacred. You can tell me anything up to and including who you murdered, and I will not tell a soul."

"Well, it's not quite that serious." I took a deep breath. "It's a business deal I'm looking at, and I need someone I can trust to look over the contracts and make sure there's nothing in there that can trip me up."

"What kind of business deal?"

"A lease with an option to buy on a building. I plan to open a flower store and the place is perfect. With a few changes, it will work just fine. It just needs a bit of sprucing up to get it ready to open. The owners will pay for the improvements that I want."

"Sounds ideal. Are you working with a realtor on this?"

I shook my head and then realized he couldn't see me. "No. The guy I'm seeing belongs to a group that is looking to invest in real estate." I explained the situation to him, trying to make it sound more formal than it was.

"It sounds like a great opportunity for you. Right place at the right time and all that." He paused, and I held my breath, waiting for the "but." It didn't come. "Can you bring me a copy of the contract before you sign it? I can give it a look over and make sure it's as good as it sounds."

"Absolutely!" I felt a weight lift off my shoulders. I would trust Thor and Riptide with my life, but it made sense to get an outside opinion before jumping into such a big commitment. "I'll let you know when I have it."

"Great. I'll let my receptionist know to squeeze you in, and I'll make sure you don't accidentally run into any family while you're here. And, Janet?"

"Yes?"

"Consider giving your parents a call. They miss you."

"I'll think about it. But I'm not marrying someone just to please them."

He chuckled. "If you did, I'd have to feel sorry for the guy. Talk to you soon."

I ended the call and turned to see Thor toweling his hair dry, a second towel wrapped low around his hips. He'd slept over last night. We'd ordered pizza, and he'd picked up a case of beer. The plan was to figure out what I wanted to take to the new apartment, and what I needed to get rid of. There was a woman's shelter a couple of blocks from the hospital, and they were always looking for donations for the women who needed to start a new life from scratch. Whatever I didn't need they'd be happy to come and pick up.

We'd spent hours making lists, packing, and sorting. I couldn't believe how much stuff I'd accumulated in the few years I'd been living here. After we called it for the day, we ended up sitting on the sofa, eating pizza, drinking beer, and watching stand-up comedy on YouTube. We fell asleep wrapped around each other and stumbled to the bedroom in the middle of the night when I woke up with a cramp in my leg from the awkward position.

I stifled a giggle when I realized how domesticated that was. I kept saying I didn't want to be Thor's old lady, but we sure fit the picture of an old married couple.

I sobered up when I caught sight of the angry

looking scar where the stitches had been just days ago. It reminded me that his life wasn't exactly safe.

"It will fade. Give it time."

It always amazed me that he could tell what I was thinking. "I know, but it kind of jumps out at me."

"You mean it makes me look rakish, like you can't wait to jump my bones?"

"You are so full of it. No, more like you're hurt, and I want to kiss it all better."

He grinned. "We could start there, but I've got a meeting to get to at the clubhouse and Ace can be a real fucking prick if guys are late."

I could see that. They might not be in the SEALs anymore, but Ace ran Riptide with a military type of discipline. Mention of the club reminded me of the conversation I'd just had with Jason. "Can I ask you something?"

"Sure." He lowered the towel and shook his head to straighten his hair out. "What is it?"

"Are you okay with me getting my own lawyer to look over the contract for the building?"

"I'd expect you to." He stalked over to me, slinging an arm around my waist. "This is a business deal, and Daryl will insist on it just to keep things on the up and up. I want you to be absolutely sure about this deal before you sign anything."

I felt a surge of relief. If I were honest with myself, I would be crushed if this fell through now but there was a tiny voice in the back of my mind telling me that my family could still come between Thor and me, and I didn't want my dream shop to be the leverage they used. "Thank you. Once I have the contract, I'll call and set up an appointment with a lawyer."

Thor nodded. "Anything else bothering you?"

I shook my head. "Nope, not a thing." I crossed my fingers behind my back. I still had to call Maxwell, the guy my parents wanted me to marry, and make sure we were both on the same page, but I wasn't sure I wanted to involve Thor in that. I hadn't explained my family situation to him yet, which was one of the big reasons I couldn't commit. I had a feeling he'd just barge into my family's mansion and tell my parents to go to hell.

Only not that nicely.

He tossed the towels into the hamper just inside the bathroom door and sauntered toward me, buck naked. Not a great move if he wanted to get out of here any time soon. I admired the way his muscles glided beneath his skin as he walked. The man made my pussy cream just looking at him.

He caged me between his outstretched arms and lowered his head to sear a kiss across my lips. I wound my arms around his neck and kissed him right back.

"Got to get to the club." He murmured the words against my lips.

"I'll miss you." The admission slipped out before I had time to think.

Thor slid one hand down to fondle my ass through the thin material of the T-shirt I'd pressed into service as a nightie. "I'll be back tonight. Ace would have warned me if we were going to be out of town. Okay if I come by?"

"You think you need to ask?"

He gave a faint shrug of his shoulder. "Maybe. Not like you're my old lady or something."

I ignored the dig. "It's okay. If it's going to be late you might want to let me know in case I fall asleep."

"You could give me a key, so I could come in

without waking you up."

I had a feeling he could get in without the help of a key, but it was nice of him to ask. It showed respect. "Good idea." I slid out from his embrace and crossed to the kitchen. The spare keys were in one of those magnet things stuck to the top of the fridge. They were secure and there was usually enough crap up there to keep them out of sight.

Standing on my tiptoes, I reached up and snagged them. Pivoting, I tossed them to Thor. "Catch."

He plucked them out of mid-air. "Thanks. I'll try not to be too late."

"If you are, try to be quiet." I tipped my chin back and gave him a haughty look. "I need my beauty sleep."

"Babe." He grabbed me for another steamy kiss. His eyes twinkled as he lifted his head and swept me with a heated gaze. "If you get any more beautiful, I'm going to have to keep you hidden away so you don't break any more hearts."

"More?"

"Yeah. It's too late for me."

I laughed, rolling my eyes. Palms on his chest, I pushed him away from me. "Go. I need to get dressed and get down to the store. The electrician is coming in today to get things ready for the new cooler, and the sign guy needs to take some measurements."

He headed back to the bedroom. "Not so fast. I need to get dressed."

I wanted to say no he didn't, but then neither of us would get any work done today.

* * *

**Thor**

I shrugged into my cut and grabbed my helmet off the table by the door. Turning to give Janet one last kiss, I headed out to my bike. I'd be happy when she moved to the new place. The rent on her current apartment might be good, and it was close to the hospital where she'd worked up until now, but the neighborhood was a fucking nightmare. Drug deals went down right out in the open, and the cops avoided the area if they could.

I wasn't worried about me, or about leaving my bike in the parking lot. Only a lunatic with a death wish would bother to tangle with a biker when there was so much easier game in sight. Janet often worked late shifts though, and I worried about some druggie looking for an easy score.

Once she was settled into her new digs, I planned to take her out to the shooting range at the club and teach her how to use a gun. All the old ladies knew the basics and could defend themselves if they had to. Hell, Beast's twin daughters were probably better marksmen than half the guys out hunting in the fall. I'd feel better knowing Janet could protect herself when I wasn't around.

I slung a leg over my bike and settled into the seat. My ride of choice was a Harley Softail Fat Boy I'd found in a scrapyard and restored as a teenager. I was an orphan. No known relatives, but my adoptive dad had been a weekend biker, and he taught me everything he knew about restoring the bike to its original glory. Heavier than the Softail deluxe, the Fat Boy gave a smooth ride and handled well at high speeds. Mine was the 1992 model, a couple of years after they first came out. I'd tinkered with it over the years until it was fucking perfect.

The engine purred to life, and I glanced up at

Janet's window one last time before kicking the machine into gear.

* * *

When Ace said he needed to talk to me, I'd assumed he meant just the two of us, but when I entered the office, Rattler, Beast, and Shadow were all there. I pivoted slowly to look at each of my brothers. I had a bad feeling about this. "This is starting to look like an ambush."

"Not exactly. Have a seat." Ace gestured at the one empty chair in the room.

"What's up?" I took the seat, perching on the edge.

"Shadow?" Ace looked over at our IT wizard, and I could see the tension in every line of his body.

*What the hell*?

Shadow cleared his throat, nervously. "I was cruising the web, looking for anything that might show you were in danger. I found a mention of Janet on one of those high society pages."

"*My* Janet?" He had to be kidding. I loved the woman to death, but she was as down to earth as they came.

He met my gaze straight on. "Yeah. Your Janet. Dug a little deeper. What do you know about her family?"

"Not much, but I have a feeling you're about to enlighten me." I narrowed my eyes. "Just so you understand, be real careful here. I love that woman. Nothing you think you know is going to change how I feel about her."

The tension in the room ramped up.

Rattler spoke up. "Easy there. Hear him out."

"Janet told you she'd bailed on her parents, right?" Shadow played with the tablet in his hands.

"Yeah." I nodded.

"Did she tell you why?"

"Not really. Happens all the time. Look at us in this room."

Ace broke in impatiently. "Just tell him what you found."

"Janet comes from money. Big money. Old money. And as I'm sure you know, old money doesn't always come from clean sources. The family owns a pharmaceutical firm in South America, and there are rumors that people who oppose them have disappeared over the years."

"And this concerns me why? We're not naive here. We've done our fair share of making people who deserve to die disappear."

"You could be in the way of one of their bigger plans." He paused.

"You trying to fucking tell me Janet is out to get me? She spent all this time with me just so she could set me up?" I stood. "She's the one who rushed me to the hospital. That's just insane."

"Sit down." Ace used his Prez voice, the one that said you needed to listen to him. *Now.*

I sat, but barely. This was my family, but if it came down to a choice between Janet and Riptide, I'd choose Janet.

People don't just leave an MC. Once you put on the cut, you were in for life. The only way it came off your back was if you weren't breathing. I knew that. But I loved Janet, and I was damned if I'd let them blame her for what her family was like.

Beast spoke up for the first time since I'd entered the room. "It's not Janet we're worried about. It's the family. Her parents want her to marry some senator's son for his connections. She's refusing, but according to our intel, the arrangement is still up in the air. The guy hasn't been seen in public with anyone else since this was announced, making it look like he's onboard with it."

"She walked out, ghosted them, and they still think they can make her go through with this?" I frowned.

Beast cracked his knuckles, a sure sign he wanted to do something physical to release the tension he felt. "These are not nice people. They might figure you're the only thing between them and what they want. They dress good and smile at the right time, but they'd gut their best friend like a fish if it suited them."

"Of course they'd have an alibi. These kinds of people pay others to do their dirty work for them." Rattler shook his head. "And you're in the way of them marrying Janet off to a family they want to have connections with."

"So that's why she won't agree to be my old lady." I turned to Shadow. "Is there anything indicating they were behind the attack on me?"

He shook his head. "No. Doesn't mean it wasn't them, but so far, we're still going on the assumption you were in the wrong place at the wrong time. We just thought you should know what you're up against."

"Yeah, just wanted you to be aware." Ace stood up, pacing the space behind his desk. "Sophia and Janet are tight. I had Deuce ask Sophia if she knew about this or if Janet had told you and she told me it was none of my business. It was between you and Janet." He stood still and pinned me with his gaze. "If you plan on having a future with that woman, you need to sort this out. Make sure you don't have a target on your back."

"I appreciate that." I wasn't sure how I was going to bring this up without telling Janet the club had been spying on her. I was damn sure that wouldn't be okay with her. "Anything else?"

"Yeah." Ace looked at Shadow and Beast. "You guys can go, and send Deuce in." He looked at me. "The whole club isn't in on Janet's family ties. I thought it best if we kept it on a need-to-know basis for now. When you finish with Deuce, we have a run to make today. They asked for escorts, at least six of us. You up for that?"

That's why Ace was the Prez. He kept his cool and thought things through. Me? I tended to jump first and look later.

Beast placed a hand on my shoulder as he headed for the exit. "We've got your back. And hers too, if she needs it."

I nodded. Yeah. I might not have any blood ties to family, but sometimes a found family was better than one you were born into.

Beast and Shadow left, and a few minutes later Deuce came in with one of those file folder things. People tended to underestimate him when they found out he was an accountant, but I had a feeling he saw a lot more than he let on. When his old lady had been in trouble, I had no doubt he would have killed anyone who hurt her.

"This is the leasehold agreement for the flower shop." He handed the folder to me. "Janet needs to get her own lawyer to look it over and explain it all to her before she signs. Daryl was very clear on that."

"What's in it?" I had a vested interest in making sure she got a good deal.

A half-smile tugged at the corner of his mouth. "Normally I'd say that's privileged information but it's between Riptide and Janet, and you're part of Riptide so I guess it's okay."

He gave me the Cliff Notes version of what it entailed, making sure to emphasize the part where nothing in the deal hinged on my relationship with her.

I nodded. "She mentioned she's got a lawyer she trusts, so we should be able to move ahead once he looks this over. I'll send her a text and let her know I'm bringing it over." I pulled my phone out of my pocket and fired off a quick text to Janet. I'd have to figure out how to open the subject of her family to her later. Right now, it wasn't my top priority.

Her answer came back almost immediately. She was at the shop with the electrician. She'd contact her lawyer and see when he could fit her in. I let her know I'd pop over to her place once we finished escort duty. Hopefully it wouldn't be too late, and she'd be up and ready for me.

# Chapter Eight

**Janet**

I called Jason and set up an appointment for the next day. His receptionist sounded almost too cheerful as she told me she could manage to squeeze me in just before lunchtime. Things were moving fast.

When Thor brought it to me, I'd sat down and read the whole contract over, and I couldn't see any issues with it. It was written in plain language, without a lot of legal jargon, and spelled out everything I'd already agreed to. It even had a paragraph dealing with what would happen if Thor and I split up.

Butterflies were having a party in my belly. It felt like I was about to take a huge leap into the unknown, but another opportunity like this wouldn't likely ever come my way. I just needed to have faith in myself and my abilities.

I tucked the paperwork into my backpack so I'd have it handy the next day. I'd been using the backpack to carry things when Thor used his bike to chauffeur me to places. It worked better than trying to sling a purse over my shoulder. Of course, there were always the saddlebags, but I preferred to keep my wallet and whatnot on me.

I loved riding behind my big Viking, with my arms circled low around his waist. I could slide my hands up under his shirt and feel his warmth. The thrum of the engine and the vibration of the machine beneath my butt were something I'd never expected to enjoy as much as I did. It had its drawbacks though, the main one being the ability to carry things. Grocery shopping required the Jeep.

* * *

The next morning came fast, and not surprisingly

Thor had slept over the previous night. One thing I'd learned in the past few weeks was that Thor was one of those people who could roll out of bed cheerfully at first light. I wasn't quite as jolly until I'd had at least one coffee.

"You ready to go?" Thor had made a habit of coming into the store with me in the mornings to help me to get the place in shape for the opening. Riptide had him on what they called light duty. As near as I could tell, that meant unless it was just riding around on his bike, he wasn't doing it until Joker okayed it. His knife wound had healed well, although the scar still looked raw. Joker said it would take at least six months for it to start to fade, and more likely a year or two to be completely faded. By then I'd probably be used to it.

I grabbed the backpack and made sure the paperwork for the lease was in it. Thor promised to drop me off at the lawyer's for my appointment later in the morning. Satisfied I had everything I needed, I slipped it on. My boots were by the door, a cute pair of biker boots I'd picked up last week when Sophia and I had gone shopping. The twins had gushed over them so much we'd promised to take them with us the next time we went shoe shopping.

I straightened up. "All ready!"

We walked down the stairs hand in hand, nodding to one of the neighbors heading in the other direction. We really were starting to act like a couple.

The bike ride was quick. Not many people on the road at this hour of the morning. Thor parked at the side door, and I unlocked it and went in. We'd already cleaned the retail space and painted the walls. I needed to set up the displays shelves and make a list of supplies I needed to order.

I was hoping to do a soft opening at the end of the month to work out the inevitable kinks. I'd already set up the sales system using an online program that tracked inventory. Shadow had helped with that and made sure there were backups in place in case something went wrong. Actually, he said for when something *did* go wrong.

The delivery van with the new flower display cooler showed up at ten a.m., right on schedule. I let Thor supervise the unloading and placement of it. It was nice having him around to help. We worked well as a team, each of us doing what we did best and allowing the other to work without interference. It was getting harder and harder not to give in to the desire to make our relationship official.

The delivery guys left, and I reached for the glass cleaner to remove all the labels and fingerprints from the glass. Things were coming together nicely. I glanced at the clock, a large antique piece with whimsical flowers marking each hour. The hands were shaped like stalks with leaves at the tips to point to the time. I'd found it at a garage sale a few years back and hung it on the wall of the living room in my apartment. Every time I looked at it, I swore I'd have my own florist shop someday to hang it in. Now it was here. And the decorative hands showed eleven fifteen. Time to go see the lawyer and make this official.

Thor sauntered over, dusting his hands off on his jeans. "Time to head out?" He already knew where the lawyer's office was and promised to wait outside for me. He said it was important that I have no pressure from him or anyone else in Riptide while I discussed the contract with the lawyer of my choice. I thought he was being a touch paranoid, but if it made him feel better, I was fine with it.

I nodded and grabbed the backpack. Thor double checked the lock on the front door and followed me out the side one. "So how long have you known this lawyer?"

Something in his tone made me do a double take. "You're not jealous, are you?"

"That's not an answer."

I tried to stifle my laughter. The big bad biker was jealous of a happily married man old enough to be my father. "He used to bounce me on his knee when I was a toddler, so I'd have to say a long time. A couple of decades or so."

"Good to know." He mounted the bike and motioned me behind him. "You sure he's not going to go running to your parents with anything you tell him?"

"Positive. I already confirmed that with him, but why would you ask?"

"No reason. Just asking." He started the bike, and I wrapped my arms around his waist as he kicked it into gear.

The ride to the law office was short. I have to admit I felt a little trickle of disappointment deep down in my belly. I would have been happy to sit with my legs spread and my head resting against Thor's broad back for another hour, minimum. Definitely too short. I let out a sigh as he pulled into the parking lot and killed the engine.

Reluctantly, I sat up straight and slid off the seat. Thor leaned over and wrapped an arm around me, drawing me in close for a searing hot kiss.

"Is that in case he saw us pull in?" I teased.

A mischievous smile curved my biker's lips. "Maybe."

I laughed. "Then I won't tell you he has the

corner office on the far side of the building."

He dipped his head. "I appreciate that. It's important to humor me." He reached down to swat me on the ass. "Now go discuss the contract so we can get back to the flower shop and see if the workbench in the back is the right height."

I tilted my head. "Right height for what?"

He just grinned. "Go. Your lawyer friend is waiting."

I stuck my tongue out like the mature woman I was and turned to walk over to the front door. As I pulled it open, Thor let out a low wolf-whistle from his seat on the bike.

I pretended I didn't hear it.

The law offices were on the second floor, and despite what I'd just told Thor, I had no idea which one belonged to Jason. I approached the reception desk manned by a blonde dressed in an impeccable three-piece suit. She gave me a professional smile. "Can I help you?"

"I'm here to see Jason Witherspoon. I have an appointment."

The woman pulled up something on her computer, and her smile became more genuine when she looked back at me. "You must be Janet. Mr. Witherspoon said to send you right in."

"Thank you." I looked around at the array of tightly closed doors. "Which office would be his?"

"I'm sorry. He said you were an old family friend, so I assumed you'd been here before." She nodded her head at the second door on the right. "I just started a month ago so I'm not up to speed on everything yet."

"No problem." I stepped toward the door she had indicated and grasped the door handle. Taking a deep breath, I opened it and stepped inside.

Jason stood as I walked in, stepping around the desk to take me in his arms and give me a big hug. "You're not a little girl anymore."

"No, I'm not. But you still look the same." I wrinkled my nose. "Maybe one or two extra gray hairs, but they just make you look more distinguished."

A wry grin crossed his lips as he let me go and went back to his chair. "More than a few, I'm afraid, but thanks."

I looked around. I'd never been to his office before. Legal things were always handled by my father. Everything in the room was carefully chosen to create an impression of power and wealth. From the high-end leather seats to the signed artwork on the walls and the gleaming hardwood flooring, the subtle message clear: this was the office a man to be reckoning with. I was glad he was on my side.

"So, tell me what's going on." He leaned back in his chair.

I slid my backpack off and unzipped it. Pulling out the folder Thor had given me, I laid it on the desk. "As I mentioned on the phone, I'm going to open a flower shop, and I've been offered a lease for the premises with a buyout option at the end." I went on to explain the deal, making sure to stress the fact that my relationship with Thor wasn't a factor.

Jason narrowed his eyes, flipping through the papers in the folder. He looked up for a minute. "Can I have my assistant get you something while I take a look at these? Coffee? Water?"

I shook my head. "No, thanks, I'm good." I was much too nervous, afraid he'd find something in the paperwork that would torpedo the deal.

He went back to reading, and I sat back in my

chair, willing my body to relax. It seemed like hours as he carefully read all three pages of the contract and studied the pictures of the property. He finally raised his head. "That is the least complicated document I've seen in decades."

I frowned. "Is that a bad thing?"

"Far from it. There's no clauses or fine print to trip you up. The building is freehold. The lessor has already made sure they have clean title to it. There's a set payment schedule with a very reasonable buyout clause at the end. And you have the option, without penalty, of not buying it out if circumstances change. It's most likely the best deal you'll ever see."

I let out a sigh of relief. "So, I can go ahead with it?"

He nodded. "Definitely. Now tell me about this new beau of yours."

I hesitated. How to describe Thor? "He's an ex-SEAL. He's part of the group that is offering me this deal, but he's a really good guy. He makes me feel special."

"Riptide is a motorcycle club, correct?"

I nodded. "But they're not one-percenters. They don't sell drugs or run prostitutes or anything like that. They mostly do security work. They're kind of like a little family all of their own. Most of them aren't close to their real families. Thor is actually an orphan who was adopted out as a baby so he had a family, but no blood relatives that he knows of."

The lawyer raised one brow. "Thor?"

"My boyfriend." It felt silly calling him that. "His teammates nicknamed him that back in the SEALs because he looks like one of the old Norse gods."

"Sounds fascinating. Do I get to meet this Viking god of yours some day?"

I nodded. "Once I get things settled, we can arrange to have lunch or something. I'd say I'd invite you over for dinner, but my cooking leaves a lot to be desired."

He laughed. "If you're going to stay away from the family and settle down with a biker you might want to take some cooking lessons. I'm guessing there isn't going to be kitchen staff in the new life you're building for yourself."

"Nope, no staff at all. I've gotten fairly good at simple fare like grilled cheese or meatloaf. And I'm a pro at ordering pizza!"

"I'll take your word for that." He glanced down at his watch. "I don't want to rush you, but I've got another client coming in a few minutes. It's been really great to see you."

Standing, I gathered up the papers and zipped them back in my backpack. "No problem. I appreciate you squeezing me in. Should I leave an address with the receptionist so you can bill me?"

He shook his head. "Not necessary. I'll put this down as an initial visit which makes it no charge. I do expect you to keep me in the loop though and let me know if you need a prenup."

I tilted my head, confused. "A prenup? We haven't even considered marriage." I wasn't going to try to explain the concept of an old lady to him.

"You're still the only child of a very wealthy family, even if you're not talking to them right now. If you and this Thor person get serious, you're going to want to arrange a prenup to protect your assets. I know it can be a touchy subject, but if he refuses to sign, that raises all kinds of red flags."

"He has no idea I have any assets so he's not with me for the money. I've never given him details about my family."

"Then he shouldn't have an issue signing a prenup. It could be to his benefit as well, if he has joint assets with this Riptide company. They could insist, depending on the legal structure."

I smiled and slung the backpack over my shoulder. "That's a future problem, but I will be sure to let you know if things get to that point."

He came round the desk and gave me another hug. "I'm proud of you for sticking up for yourself. I can't picture you being happy with the senator's son. Call me any time you need me."

* * *

**Thor**

I relaxed when Janet came out of the lawyer's building. She looked confident and happy, which meant the meeting went well and the flower shop was going to be a go. I'd worried that the lawyer would talk her out of it, being an old friend of her parents and all. Yeah, I knew that would be unethical on his part, but I didn't have a lot of faith in the legal shit.

"He said it was the most straightforward contract he's seen in decades." She beamed at me as I crossed the lot to meet her.

"That's a good thing, right?"

She laughed. "That is exactly what I asked him. And he said yes, I'd never get a better offer. He asked about you too."

"Did you tell him I was the best thing that ever happened to you?"

She shifted the backpack to a more comfortable position. "I told him you made me feel special, and you look like a Norse god."

I grinned. "That's me. A Norse god with the

ability to keep a florist happy."

She rolled her eyes. "If you come back to the shop and help me get that new cooler ready for opening day, I'll be happy."

"Your wish is my command, fair lady." I mounted the bike with a flourish and patted the back seat. "Your chariot awaits."

I couldn't see behind me, but I was willing to bet that she rolled her eyes again as she slid into place and cuddled up against me.

I started the bike and kicked it down into first. We didn't have anywhere we had to be at a certain time, so I circled around the downtown core, taking the long way around town to the shop. It gave me a few more minutes to enjoy the feel of Janet plastered against me. The woman was addictive. I couldn't get enough of her.

We eventually arrived at the flower shop, and I parked my bike in the shade around the front of the store. I lowered the kickstand, and Janet slid off and pulled off her helmet. I took mine off as well, handing it to her.

"Can you take mine in too?"

Janet cocked her head, as I was still sitting on the bike. "Why? Aren't you coming inside?"

"In a couple of minutes. I just want to check the bike out. Something feels a bit off."

Her gaze swept the machine, and she shrugged, that happy smile she'd had at the lawyer's office still on her face. "Okay. I'll leave the side door unlocked for you."

We'd been locking the side door while we worked in the store, just to make sure no one thought we were open and wandered in. She'd given me a spare key, but I'd left it sitting back in my room at the club a few days ago and I hadn't been back there since to retrieve it. I spent most nights in Janet's bed. She wasn't quite ready to admit it yet, but we were a couple in all but name. Once I moved in here with her, I'd double down on that.

She disappeared around the corner, and I pulled the emergency tool kit out of the saddlebags. It was a bare bones kit, but that was all I needed for now. I pulled the bike up onto the center stand and crouched down to check it out. I used a clean rag to wipe all the road grime off the outside and kept an eye out for anything that would indicate a fluid leak.

It all looked good. I set the rag down on the ground beside me and reached for the wrench. My hands came up empty and I turned my head to look at the spot I'd left it. Damn thing had slid several feet away. In the back of my mind, I could hear my adoptive dad telling me to always set the tools on something to stop them from moving. As usual, he'd been right.

I stretched my arm out and grabbed it. I spent the next half hour checking the spark plugs, the oil level, and a few other common issues. If it turned out to be the timing, I'd take it back to the club and fix it in the garage. That would take more tools than I had with me, and a dedicated workspace.

Satisfied I'd done all I could do for now, I wiped my hands off and stowed the tools back in the saddlebag. Pulling the bike down off the center stand, I started it up and listened. It sounded better so it had probably just been a minor issue.

I dropped it into first gear to move it around to the side door.

I heard the crack of a rifle shot and something whizzed past my head, right in the space I'd occupied seconds ago.

*Fuck*!

Someone was shooting at me.

Automatic reflexes kicked in and I jerked the bike to the left as another shot sounded. I geared up, moving around the corner and out of range as quickly as possible. I saw a movement across the road on the roof of an apartment building.

*Sniper.*

I pulled my gun out of the shoulder holster, but the distance was too far. The shooter was already breaking his rifle down and heading for the access door. I jammed my gun back in the holster and revved up the motor.

Out of the corner of my eye, I saw Janet coming out, and I waved her back inside where it was safe. When she ducked back into the door, I turned my attention back to the rooftop.

I saw the shooter exit the apartment by way of the side door and jump into a little green convertible. Looked like a Miata. He took off with a screech of rubber, heading down the cross street.

*Fuck*!

I slammed my open palms down on the handlebars in frustration. By the time I managed to make my way through the traffic in front of the store and hit the crossroad, the shooter would be long gone.

## Chapter Nine

**Janet**

Amazing how quickly I could lose things. I'd had the glass cleaner before I left to see the lawyer. The glass cleaner and a whopping big roll of paper towels, all set to clean that new display cooler. Could find them now that I needed them? Not at all.

I grumbled to myself as I wandered around the store, looking on, under, and behind everything I could think of. Just when I was sure some magical creature had spirited them away on me, I stepped into the little cubicle of a bathroom just off the workroom, and there they were, sitting innocently on the sink.

Good thing Thor was still outside tinkering with his bike, or he'd be laughing. Absentmindedly misplacing things was one of my bad habits, and for some reason he found it hilarious. I carried them back out front and set to work cleaning the case.

I knew Thor was out front, but I couldn't see him or his bike. I hadn't taken the brown paper off the windows yet. I wanted to have the inside looking pretty and full of flowers before I did that.

I hummed as I worked. Life was good, and I was happy. It had been a little dicey when I first walked out on the family, but things were falling into place now. I had an awesome place to live, a guy who really cared about me and came with his own version of a family, and soon I'd have the floral shop I'd always dreamed of.

My phone chirped and I pulled it out of my pocket. The twins sent me a picture of Willow, Sophia's dog, dressed in biker style complete with goggles. The furry little mutt was adorable, and she had the patience of a saint. Another picture came in and I scrolled to see it.

A thunderous crack broke my happy bubble.

*Can't be a gunshot. Not in the middle of town. Must be a car backfiring.*

A second crack followed on the heels of the first.

*Shit. That* is *gunfire.*

*Thor*!

The front door was locked, and I didn't have the code memorized yet. I raced to the side door and opened it cautiously, peeking outside. I could see Thor -- he must have moved to the side of the building when the shooting started. I couldn't see any blood on him, and other than being super angry he looked okay. I followed his line of sight and saw the shooter on the roof of the apartments across the street.

Thor glanced over and motioned me to get back inside. My phone was still in my hand, so I lifted it and snapped off a few pictures before the shooter disappeared through the access door.

I retreated inside. This was not a wrong place, wrong time attack. It was too deliberate, and the gunman must have been up there for some time, just waiting for a clear shot.

I tried to wrap my head around that.

Someone wanted Thor dead. My Thor.

I looked at the pictures on my phone. They were blurry, and at that distance I couldn't make out any details but maybe someone with better tech skills could blow it up enough to recognize the shooter.

Thor lowered the kickstand with a little more force than necessary before sliding off the bike and stalking to the door. I backed up to let him in, and then threw my arms around him, burying my face in his shoulder so he wouldn't see how close I was to freaking out. His arms came round me and his head rested on top of mine, enclosing me in his solid presence.

Yeah. I loved him. I could admit it to myself, but I wasn't ready to say the words out loud. Not until I was sure I wasn't the reason he was in danger.

Other than being really angry, he appeared to be safe. He held me tight for a few minutes. "I'm fine, just fucking pissed. I could see the fucker plain as day. Had him in my sights. If I'd had my damn rifle I could have ended this right here."

"They'd just send someone else."

"I know." He snorted. "Assholes. Whoever is after me is too damn cowardly to show their face. Hiring someone else to do their dirty work."

I remembered my phone and lifted my head to look up at him. "I have pictures. Not good ones but maybe someone can make something out of them. Maybe trace the sniper back to whoever hired him."

"Pictures?"

"Yeah. On my phone. Of the guy with the gun." I pulled my phone out and turned it on, pulling up the photo app and scrolling to the last few images. "See?"

Thor took the phone from me and squinted at the screen thoughtfully. "Shadow might be able to do something with that. He's a fucking magician with this kind of shit. Okay if I send them to him?"

I nodded, and he keyed in Shadow's info and hit SEND before handing it back to me. "I need to let Ace know about this." He pulled out his own phone, and it lit up with an incoming call before he had a chance to do anything. A wry smile curved the corners of his mouth. He hit accept and held the phone up to his ear. "Yeah, Ace?"

I attempted to slip out of his grasp so he could talk to his Prez privately, but he tightened his arm around me. The conversation was short. Ace had been with Shadow when the pictures came through. Thor explained what had gone down. I could hear Ace, plain as day as he barked out the order for Thor to get our asses back to the compound ASAP. The call disconnected, and Thor pocketed his phone.

He let out a deep breath. "You heard?"

"Yeah."

"You okay with it? Prez will likely want both of us to stay at the clubhouse until this is over."

I nodded. "Whatever it takes. I want this over too. I don't have to be out of my other place till the end of the month, and it's probably not a good idea to open the store until this is over." The last few glorious nights flashed through my mind. "And I've already brought over enough clothes and things here for a few days. I can pack them up to go."

"Thank you," he said softly. "I know you're still on the fence about the whole old lady thing, so this means a lot to me."

I didn't have an answer for that, so I kept quiet. Now was not the time to bring up my family connections. Soon, though.

I went to pull away so I could go pack, but he grabbed my hand and drew me back into the circle of his arms. Sliding his fingers through my hair, he tugged my head back and seared a sizzling kiss across my lips.

When he lifted his head, he looked calmer. "Let me check outside first and make sure the coast is clear. Just grab what you need. I can send a prospect back to get anything you miss. I'll lock up down here."

I took a deep breath and nodded.

Thor pulled out his gun and checked to make sure it was loaded. I'd never seen him do that before.

He'd always made a point of shielding me from the rougher parts of his life. Motioning me to stay back, he sidled up to the door and slid outside in one fluid move.

Suddenly, he wasn't the comforting, loveable guy I knew. He looked tough. Dangerous. Every bit an ex-SEAL turned bad-assed biker. I suppose it should have scared me, but it just made me realize anyone who thought he was an easy target was in for a surprise.

I just hoped they weren't related to me.

* * *

**Thor**

This shit had to stop. There was no longer any doubt. I was the target. Not like it was the first time, but now I had Janet to worry about, and I'd be damned if I'd let her end up as collateral damage.

I prowled the perimeter of the building and parking area. I couldn't see any visible threats, so I waved Janet out, sweeping the rooftops around us with my gaze as she made the run from the side door and up to the apartment. I backed into the stairwell and kept watch, gun at the ready.

I knew from countless operations in hostile territory that the danger was likely over for now. The enemy would want surprise to be on their side when they launched the next attack, but it never paid to lower your guard. Janet came back out in less than five minutes, a bulging backpack slung over her shoulders.

"Ready?"

She nodded and followed me to the bike. We strapped on helmets in record time, and I fired up the engine.

"Hold on tight," I hollered over my shoulder. On

the off chance that some fucking asshole was watching us, I had no intention of being predictable. Yanking the handlebars around in a tight circle, I headed straight for the vacant lot behind the shop.

Janet's arms tightened around my waist as the bike jumped the curb and bounced over the rough ground. The lot extended past the main road, and we exited onto one of the older side roads. I zigzagged my way through town and headed out to the club's compound.

As we approached the club, I could see four prospects guarding the gate, twice the usual number. I took that as a sign that Ace expected trouble. The prospects recognized me and opened the gate wide enough for me to blast through without slowing down.

The long line of bikes in the parking area showed most of the guys were here already. I pulled up at the top end of the row and killed the engine. Janet slid off the bike and pulled off her helmet. Shaking out her hair, she gave me a wan smile and placed her helmet on the back seat. "That was… intense."

"But fun, right?" I hung my helmet on the handlebar.

She wrinkled her nose, a doubtful look on her face. "Sure. Might have been, if I hadn't worried about someone taking potshots at us."

I slung an arm over her shoulder, and we headed up to the clubhouse. As we climbed the stairs, Deuce appeared in the doorway. "Prez called church in ten minutes." He nodded at Janet. "Nice to see you. I think Sophia's out back at the shooting range with the twins."

"Thanks." Janet shifted her gaze to me. "I'll go catch up with Sophia while you're in church. I haven't talked to her much since this all started."

She didn't quite meet my gaze, and I put a finger under her chin to lift it. "Cheer up. I'm not that easy to kill, and we're safe here."

She gulped and nodded her head shakily. I wished there was something, anything, I could say to ease her mind. Sometimes shit got real, and as much as I wanted to sugarcoat it for her, this was the life.

We entered the clubhouse, and a wall of noise hit us. I wasn't kidding about most of the guys being there and they weren't a quiet bunch. We made it through to the kitchen without stopping, and I nodded at Mom who was busy making piles of snacks. She loved cooking for large groups, the more the merrier.

Willow, Piper's little terrier was guarding the floor, making sure no crumb that fell from above accidentally landed on it. She glanced over and wagged her tail when she heard us but didn't make a move to come over and greet us. She had her priorities.

Mom stopped filling little pastry tarts with some kind of meat mixture. "Glad to see you two in one piece."

I grinned and snagged a cookie from a heaping plate. "Pushing up daisies isn't in my five-year plan."

She shook her head. "Plans change. Make sure yours don't. You've got an old lady to worry about now. Time to settle down and take things a little more seriously."

"I'm not his old lady." Janet's voice lacked conviction.

Mom tilted her head. "You might not be wearing his cut yet, but it sure looks like you two are joined at the hip. I'm betting if you go sit on anyone else's lap out there in the common room, we'd have a fight going in no time."

This wasn't the time to get into the old lady

argument again, although I appreciated Mom coming down on my side. I could hear the noise in the other room quieting down as my brothers started heading to the cabin out back where church was held.

I always thought church was a good name for it, although it didn't fall that way with some people. None of that holier-than-you crap. For bikers, church was a place where we met and talked about shit that was important to us. We listened to each other and made decisions based on who was in favor. Everyone got a vote. That's how decisions were made, and we all stood by those decisions, even if we didn't agree with them. Majority ruled. A brother didn't do anything that could affect the rest of us without taking it to church. If a brother wanted to make someone his old lady, he'd go to church and make sure it was okay with everyone. I'd already let them know I planned to make Janet my old lady, so to them it was a done deal even if she hadn't agreed yet. Most of my brothers thought it was fucking hilarious that she wasn't on board.

"Almost time for church. Let's go find Sophia and the twins." I urged Janet toward the back door.

"You should get the twins to give you shooting lessons." Mom opened the oven and stuck a tray of those tiny meat pie things in. "They're better shots than a lot of the guys."

A bit of an exaggeration. The twins were good, but as ex-SEALs the Riptide brothers were all crack shots. I'd be happy if she got the twins to teach her though. "They taught Emma, and it saved her life."

"Yeah, she told me. She thinks I should learn. Sophia does too."

We headed out the back door. I could see Sophia and the twins over at the shooting range. I glanced down at my watch. Two minutes until church. Ace wasn't okay with a guy being late. "You okay if I leave you and head over to church?"

"Yeah, I'll be fine." She turned toward me and brushed her lips over mine. "Go do what you gotta do."

* * *

I made it to church just as Ace motioned to Rattler to close the doors. The noise quieted down and everyone's attention focused on the Prez.

He didn't beat around the bush. "Someone's targeting Thor. We don't know who, and we don't know why, but we're going to find out. You all know about the ambush behind the bar where he got knifed. Well, today a sniper took a couple of shots at him. They set up on a roof overlooking the flower shop his old lady is leasing from us and waited. That's not random. We need to get the assholes behind this before they try again. Any ideas?"

It was a tough one. Hard to make a plan when you didn't know who you were targeting or why. Ideas were thrown out, considered, and then discarded. Beast, always a fan of immediate action, wanted to put up a reward on the dark web for info. Shadow pointed out that would just bring out every crackpot looking to make a buck and cloud the issue.

We debated ideas for almost an hour without any results when the door burst open and Sophia stumbled in.

Her eyes wild, she screamed at the top of her voice. "She's gone! They have her. They took Janet!"

## Chapter Ten

**Janet**

When Thor headed over to church, I figured this was my chance to call Maxwell, the senator's son that my parents wanted to marry me off to. For my own peace of mind, I needed to hear from him directly that he wasn't behind these attacks in some twisted way. I knew he was gay and had been in a committed, although secret, relationship with his driver for the past few years. Surely he didn't want to marry me. The fact that I was the one refusing the match was convenient from his point of view, and even explained his lack of interest in dating. Having me dating someone else would only reinforce his position as the patient suitor waiting for me to come to my senses.

I sauntered up to the gun range as if I planned to stay there, keeping tabs on Thor out of the corner of my eye. I had no doubt that if he saw me veer off, he'd be right there to see why. I reached Sophia just as Thor disappeared inside the little cabin they used for church, and the doors closed. Two of the prospects were standing outside guarding the doors.

The twins were busy taking shots at a target attached to a stack of hay bales. Jasmine turned to wave at me before turning back to take another shot at the outline of a man holding a chicken by its neck. I'd have to ask her what the heck that was supposed to mean after I dealt with Maxwell.

"What's going on?" Sophia stepped up to greet me with a quick hug. "Deuce just said things with Thor were getting serious and Ace called church."

I nodded. "There was a sniper set up on a roof overlooking the flower shop. He took a few shots at Thor, but he missed." I glanced over at the twins to make sure they were out of hearing range. Both of them had on those big headsets to muffle the noise of the guns. "I need to call Maxwell to make sure he isn't behind this. Can you cover for me for a few minutes?"

She frowned. "I thought you said Maxwell was gay."

"He is. But maybe he thinks me hanging with Thor will make people think he should move on. It's better for him if it looks like there's a chance I'll change my mind and agree to marry him."

She just looked confused, and I sighed. "I just want to make sure this whole mess isn't because of me. Montgomery said it wasn't my parents, so that leaves Maxwell."

Sophia pursed her lips. "I can just stand here while you call him, if that's okay. From a distance it's going to look like we're catching up. Unless you don't want me to hear what you say?"

"Good idea, and it's not private so you're fine." I pulled out my phone and dialed up Maxwell's number. He answered on the second ring, and I motioned Sophia to be quiet. I might be okay with her hearing the conversation, but Maxwell would freak out at the idea of anyone else finding out he wasn't straight.

It didn't take long for Maxwell to confirm he had nothing to do with the attacks on Thor. He seemed genuinely happy to hear I'd found someone and confided that he was almost ready to come out and consequences be damned. He and his partner were tired of pretending they didn't care about each other. I congratulated him and wished him well before I disconnected the call. That lifted a weight off my shoulders, although I still needed to talk to Thor about my family.

Given the current crisis though, it seemed like a good idea to wait until things calmed down.

"You want to watch the twins?" Sophia pivoted and headed toward the twins.

"Sure." I didn't have anything better to do while Thor was at church. "Just give me a minute to go use the washroom."

"You want me to come with you?" Sophia looked back at me over her shoulder.

I shook my head. "No, it's not like I'm leaving the compound. I'll be right back." I headed back toward the clubhouse.

I was partway there when I saw a flash of brown off to my right. I stopped and stared at the spot where it had been and heard a muffled whine from the bushes. Had Willow gotten herself tangled up in something? She had a habit of chasing rabbits and rodents. It wouldn't surprise me if the silly thing had gotten herself stuck in a thicket. I glanced back at Sophia, but she was already back at the range, talking to the twins.

"What have you got yourself into, you furry little menace?" I stepped toward the bushes, looking for the little mutt.

A man jumped from behind a tree and grabbed me around the waist. I opened my mouth to scream, and he slapped a moist cloth over it.

I started to struggle as the world faded to black.

* * *

My mouth felt like it was full of cotton as I slowly became aware of my surroundings. I was lying on the floor in a small room. I could hear the muffled sound of conversation from beyond the door in front of me but couldn't make out what was being said.

Realization hit me. I'd been kidnapped. Again.

Unlike the first time, I didn't panic. The brothers at Riptide had made a point of teaching the old ladies and any other female interested in learning what to do if they found themselves in a situation like this. Beast had been particularly diligent in making sure we understood our options. He had two daughters, and he wanted to make sure they were able to defend themselves.

Besides the usual self-defense moves, in which he stressed that playing fair was not a consideration, he went over escape protocols. The first was to see if you still had your phone and activate the find-me function. I pushed myself upright, shaking my head to clear the last wisps of whatever they'd used to knock me out before I reached in my pocket for my phone. Damn. It wasn't there. Either I'd dropped it at some point, or the kidnappers had taken it and trashed it. Either way, I couldn't call for help or activate the find-me function.

I wasn't sure how much time I had before the thugs who'd grabbed me would come to see if I was conscious. The fact that they'd left me untied seemed to indicate they didn't expect me to regain consciousness for quite some time. Or else they thought I was dumb enough to just lay here and wait for whatever they planned to do to me.

Not a hope in hell of that happening.

I looked around the room they'd left me in. There was a door on one side, and I could hear my captors beyond it, and one window on the wall opposite the door. It looked big enough for me to squeeze out of. I stood and walked over to it, being careful to keep quiet. The latch gave way easily enough, but when I tried to open it, it wouldn't budge. It looked like someone had painted the damn thing shut. It was glass though, and glass could break.

I stepped over to the corner by the door where a bunch of cleaning supplies were piled. Despite the condition of the room, it looked like whoever owned this place was big on cleaning supplies. There were five different mops, each with a sturdy handle. I picked one with a thick wooden shaft and hefted it in my hand.

A wave of dizziness swept over me, and I reached out to steady myself against the wall. Whatever they'd used to knock me out wasn't completely out of my system.

I could hear the conversation in the other room clearer from this position. It sounded like there were two men, and they were gloating over how easy it had been to get to me. One of the prospects had been bribed to look the other way while they snuck into the compound.

*Sketch.*

I needed to remember that name. When Thor came to get me, and I was positive he would, he needed to know who'd betrayed the club.

The dizzy spell passed, and I twisted the mop head off, leaving me with a nice solid stick. I was no longer weaponless. I could hear Beast's voice in my head, explaining all the ways to take down someone bigger than you if you were lucky enough to have a long stick or branch.

There were at least two men in the other room, possibly more. I had to assume they weren't above hurting a woman and were likely armed with more than a stick. I didn't like those odds.

I grabbed some rags, trying not to wonder what they'd been used for. They definitely weren't clean. I wasn't going to be the helpless victim waiting to be rescued. Not this time.

I crossed to the window and tried to open it again. Nope. Not happening. I examined it closer. It was single paned, and probably older than my grandfather.

*Did glass get brittle with age?*

*Did it make a lot of noise when it broke?*

I was about to find out, but first I needed to know what was outside the window. No point in breaking it only to find a couple of vicious dogs waiting to have me for lunch. I used one of the rags to wipe the grime off the window. The only thing visible was trees. Lots of trees, with ribbons of moss trailing off them. It wouldn't take long to sprint across the open ground and gain the cover of the woods.

I took another look around the room on the insane hope there was something else I could use to free myself, like maybe a loaded gun someone forgot to take with them.

A rickety old chair in the far corner of the room caught my eye and I remembered Beast talking about not only defending yourself and escaping but slowing down pursuit any way possible. It took a bit of fumbling to wedge the chair under the doorknob but hopefully it would be enough to slow the kidnappers down if they tried to enter. It might just give me enough time to get out of the area.

*Time to escape.*

I took a deep breath and glanced upward, praying to a deity I wasn't sure I believed in that I could get out of here and find a hiding spot before the kidnappers realized I'd escaped.

I wrapped one of the rags around the end of the wooden pole and swung it at the window.

The glass exploded outward, and I was sure the sound was loud enough to be heard for miles. I threw a fearful glance back at the door before using a handful of rags to knock the rest of the glass out.

*Slicing an artery while trying to escape defeats the purpose.*

I could hear Beast's grumpy voice in my head, telling us to make sure to pad the edges of the hole if we were trying to climb out of a broken window.

I quickly lined the edges of the window with the remaining rags and hoisted myself through the gap. I landed awkwardly on the glass-covered grass on the other side, gaining a few nasty scratches on my bare arms. Thankfully, I was wearing long pants, socks, and shoes or it could have been much worse.

Throwing a panicked glance behind me, I stumbled to my feet and headed into the woods.

* * *

**Thor**

*They took Janet.* Those words sent a dagger right through my heart.

Janet was in danger. Because of me.

This was the second time she'd been kidnapped for the sake of someone else. The first time, she'd been used as bait when the real target was her BFF, Sophia. This time I had no doubt it was because of me.

I surged to my feet and made a rush toward the door, but Rattler caught me by the arm. "Slow down, bro. Think. You have no idea where she is, or even if it's really about you. Could be her family. Remember what Shadow found?"

"I don't a flying fuck who took her or why. I'm going to get her back."

"You can't get her back until we figure out where she is." Ace sounded way too fucking calm for my liking.

"She have her phone on her?" Shadow flipped open the laptop he'd brought with him.

I shrugged. "Maybe. Unless they took it."

His fingers flew across the keyboard. He paused, staring at the screen. "Got it."

"You know where she is?" Rattler relaxed his grip.

"I know where her phone is, and given the location if it's not on her, then it's close. There's a chunk of property northeast of here with not much on it except some abandoned sharecropper's cabins. The signal's coming from one of those."

I made a move toward the door, and once again Rattler stopped me. "We need a plan. You rush in there, you're just giving them what they want and there's no guarantee they'll let Janet go once they have you."

"Fuck, fuck, fuck!" He was right and I knew it. Didn't make me happy. "So what's your plan?"

Ace looked around. "Anyone?"

Beast stood up. "They know he's a biker. I say half a dozen of us go in the front way, loud pipes, not attempting to hide who we are or that we're coming. The rest sneak in the back, get Janet out, and once she's free we kill the assholes. Of course, we interrogate them first to make sure we get the whole crew. We can always hunt down any loose ends and take care of them later."

Sounded like a good plan to me. "I want to be the one to take the fuckers out. Once I have Janet safe."

Ace looked around the room. "We vote on it. Who's for Beast's plan?"

The vote was unanimous.

"Who's for letting Thor take care of loose ends, with whatever help he needs?"

Again, all hands went up. We worked on democratic principles, but there were no such thing as secret ballots. Votes were by show of hands. If you voted on something you needed to be willing to stand behind your decision. The Prez might run the club, but major decisions were decided by a majority vote.

"Who's in the rescue group?" Deuce ground out the question. "She's my old lady's BFF. If I ever want to get laid again, I need to make sure she gets back here safely."

Ace nodded. "Fair enough. That makes you and Thor. Who else?"

"I want to be in the frontal assault." The smile on Beast's face was terrifying. "I want to scare the shit out of those assholes before we send them to hell."

"I'll go with Thor, and Shadow should come as well. He can sneak in and out better than any of us," Ghost spoke up. He'd just transferred in from our sister club up in Tennessee and usually didn't say much at church. I didn't know his whole story, just that he'd been in jail for a few years and when he came out, he wanted a fresh start in a new place. The Prez of the Tennessee club assured us what went down wasn't his fault.

Ace nodded. "Done. Thor, Deuce, Ghost, and Shadow go in quietly. When they let us know they're in position, the rest of us blaze in the front making as much noise as possible. Should draw the assholes attention long enough for them to get Janet out."

Prez closed the meeting, and I headed back to the clubhouse to get my gear. I donned my bulletproof vest under my cut. If I had been wearing it that night in the alley, I wouldn't have been wounded. I checked the load in my pistol before sliding it into the shoulder holster and tucked my favorite knife into my boot. I slung a couple spare clips in my ammo pouch, tossed it over my shoulder, and headed out.

We were ready in minutes. The cabin Shadow had tagged was a bare twenty minutes from the compound. The main assault party waited far enough away that the sound of their bikes wouldn't tip the thugs off. The four of us in the rescue group parked a mile out and hiked in through the woods. We were almost in sight of the cabin when we heard a rustling sound in the bushes up ahead. Probably a wild animal of some sort, but I wasn't taking any chances with Janet's life at stake. I held up my hand to signal the team to halt and crept forward. As I got closer, the noise stopped.

*Had the assholes actually been smart enough to set a perimeter guard?*

If they had, I prayed the guy hadn't caught wind of us and sent a warning back to the cabin.

I crawled forward on my belly, making as little sound as possible. As I got closer, I caught a glimpse of a person.

I blinked.

*No!*

*Janet!*

She was crouched down in the middle of a clump of weeds and would have been almost invisible if I'd been standing up. She wasn't moving, and her attention focused forward, away from me. In her right hand, she clutched a wooden stick about four feet long. It looked like the handle of a broom.

I took a deep breath to calm myself. I wanted to jump for joy and grab her and never let her go. Unfortunately, that wasn't an option in the current circumstances. I needed to get her attention without scaring her. I thought for a moment and then started to hum her favorite song.

I had no fucking musical ability at all. I was always off-key. It was a long-running joke between us.

I saw her head come up and slowly pivot until she was looking right at me. Her whole face lit up, but I held a finger to my lips to make sure she knew she had to keep quiet. I had no idea how the hell she'd escaped, but we weren't out of danger yet.

I took out my phone and fired off a text to Ace to let him know Janet was safe and they were good to go. Putting the phone away, I motioned Janet to move back to me.

She crawled back and collapsed against me. I wrapped her in my arms and held her tight. I could have lost her. Shit. Those assholes could have tortured her, raped her, done any fucking thing their depraved minds could come up with. And all because I'd failed to keep her safe.

"I knew you'd come for me." She whispered the words against my throat.

"Damn right I came for you." I frowned. "You should have been safe in the compound."

The sound of approaching motorcycles drowned out her reply. Ace and the Riptide crowd were moving in. Between the bikes and the sound of gunfire it was impossible to talk. I motioned my team to move out. We'd accomplished our objective, albeit faster and easier than we'd expected. Janet was safe.

We made it back to the rendezvous point at double time, safely out of gunfire range. Shadow, Deuce, and Ghost stayed right with us, making sure there weren't any nasty surprises coming our way. Our bikes were right where we'd left them with Tiny guarding them.

"Any problems?" I asked.

Tiny shook his head. "Haven't seen a soul since you left."

"Good."

The gunfire in the distance died off and my phone pinged, signaling an incoming text from Rattler.

*Threat neutralized. All clear. Meet and debrief at the compound.*

I looked at Shadow, Deuce, and Ghost. "We're headed back to the compound."

"Wait!" Janet grabbed my arm. "You need to know you have a traitor back at your clubhouse."

Everyone turned to look at her. I frowned. "A traitor?"

She nodded. "Yes. I heard the kidnappers talking. Someone named Sketch or Skeetch, maybe. It was a little hard to hear through the door, but they said he let them into the compound so they could grab me. They were laughing, saying you guys thought you were so close and yet one of you was willing to sell you out."

I exchanged a look with Deuce, Ghost, and Shadow. That explained a lot. No one should have been able to breach our perimeter. I had no idea why a prospect would have done that, but it would be his last mistake. I fired off a quick text to Beast. By the time we got back, Sketch wouldn't be a problem.

"Thanks, we'll take care of it. He won't be doing anything like that again." I handed Janet her helmet. "I don't suppose they mentioned what their issue with me was?"

She shook her head before slipping the helmet on. Flipping the face shield up. "Sounded like someone hired them, but I didn't hear a name."

"That's okay. We'll figure it out." I put my own helmet on and threw a leg over the bike. Janet climbed on behind me and we headed back to the compound, riding formation between Ghost, Deuce, and Shadow.

Two of the prospects were at the gate, and they opened them up so we could ride through. Sketch wasn't one of them. I tried to remember why we called him Sketch, but I drew a complete blank. It didn't matter. He'd betrayed the club, his brothers. There was no going back from that.

The other team had made it back before us. I could see Ace's bike sitting alongside Rattler's as well as the rest of the brothers who'd gone with them. I pulled my bike up alongside them and glanced up as Jake came out onto the porch. He nodded his head ever so slightly in the direction of the interrogation shed.

That meant the team had brought back at least one person to question. Good. Because I wanted answers and I wasn't overly squeamish about how I got them. When whoever the fuck was behind this escalated to include a woman, they gave up any chance of Riptide showing mercy. There was an unwritten rule in the MC world that excluded old ladies and all the other females from attack.

"You should go let Ace know you're back. Janet, you okay?" Jake leaned against the porch railing.

"I'm fine, thanks. Just a little shaken up." Janet lifted her helmet off and grinned at the old man. "I escaped all by myself this time. Beast will be proud of me."

We held hands as we climbed the stairs.

"I'm sure he will." Jake reached into his pocket and pulled out a phone. "This is for you. It's got Thor's number in it already, along with a few others, just to get you started."

Janet looked from the phone to Jake. "You got me a new phone?"

He shrugged. "You need to be able to call if you need help. Shadow said your old one was toast. The kidnappers smashed it, but they didn't do a good enough job. The tracker was still active. That's how they found you so fast."

I wrapped an arm around her shoulder and pulled her in close. "She was waiting for us in the woods. Didn't even have to go near the place. To hell with Beast, *I'm* proud of her." I dropped a kiss on the top of her head.

Mom was waiting in the kitchen. When we entered, she threw her arms around Janet and hugged her tight. "I was so worried! You have got to stop getting yourself kidnapped!"

Janet hugged her right back. "I intend to. Any idea how I go about that, because I thought I was doing everything right and they still got me."

Mom's face turned grim as she narrowed her eyes, pinning me with her gaze over Janet's shoulder. "Well, that's been taken care of. You won't be seeing Sketch around here anymore." She sighed. "I could understand if they had something over him, like threatening his family or something, but he did it for money." She shook her head. "Like money is worth more than what Riptide can offer."

Jake wandered in and snatched a warm cookie from the counter. "Amen to that. But she's home and she's safe so let's just be thankful."

I agreed with Jake. I couldn't even begin to imagine how I'd deal with it if something had happened to her. I cleared my throat to get her attention. Both Janet and Mom turned to look at me.

"I hate to do this when we just got here, but I need to go check in with Ace. You okay with Mom and Jake?"

Janet nodded. "What I really want is a shower. I'll just head up to your room and wait for you there, okay?"

I immediately pictured her naked with water streaming down over her breasts. "Yeah. I'll be as fast as I can."

"You do that." She grinned and blew me a kiss.

## Chapter Eleven

**Janet**

Something about standing under a hot shower helped me to relax. I stood with my face tilted up and my eyes closed for a long time, letting the water stream over me. So much had happened in the past few weeks. Thor was in danger. That much was very clear. Riptide might have found me and brought back one of the kidnappers to question but I had no doubt they were just hired guns, doing the dirty work for someone who wanted Thor dead. There was a good chance they didn't even know who had hired them.

That was the part I had trouble understanding. Thor. *My* Thor. The Thor who played with Willow and teased the twins like they were his little sisters. He was the kindest, most gentle man I'd ever met. How could anyone possibly want him dead?

I knew he'd been in the SEALs and he'd probably done his share of things he'd rather not talk about. I was equally sure he had never deliberately harmed anyone unless under direct orders. Ever.

I gave my head a mental shake. All this thinking was giving me a headache and not doing anyone a lick of good. Ace and Beast and the rest of them would figure it out and make sure he was safe. I had to believe that.

What I needed to do was decide how to bring up the subject of my family. Somehow, I couldn't picture myself telling Thor I came from a super-rich family that had made their money by exploiting orphans and poor children in their factories. Admittedly, it had been generations ago, but far from being ashamed of the fact, or trying to do good to make up for it, they'd used that money to finance other ventures, some almost as bad. They attended church on Sundays, and had other people do their dirty work.

Now they wanted more. They wanted to enter the political arena, so they'd arranged to marry me off to a senator's son. My mother, all excited at the prospect, had pointed out that if I produced a son, we'd have a shot at putting him in the White House. What a coup that would be! She truly did not understand why I wasn't thrilled with the idea of being treated like breeding stock.

As if thinking of them summoned their attention, my new phone rang. I glanced down and saw my mother's name on call display. I hesitated. How had she gotten my new number? We hadn't talked since I'd walked out, and I wasn't sure I was up to sparring with her now. The phone kept ringing, and I realized I hadn't set up messaging on it yet, and I had no idea how long it would ring before it stopped. Sitting on the edge of the bed, I took a deep breath and picked up the phone. I hit *ACCEPT*.

"Janet?" My mother sounded hesitant. Almost scared. Not at all like the self-confident mother I knew.

"Yes, it's me."

"We want you to come home." She said it so fast I almost didn't understand what she was saying, like she had to get it out before I hung up or interrupted her.

I felt calm, almost sad. Too much water under the bridge. It was much too late. "Why? Why now? It's been years since I left. I'm not going to marry the person you want me to, and I'm not going to be part of the family business. You know that. Nothing has changed. I've moved on." I hesitated to tell her I'd met someone and put him in the crosshairs. That was assuming Montgomery had been right, and this hadn't been my family's doing all along.

My mother sighed. "We know."

Of course they knew. They'd probably had me followed since the day I left. "Well then you know I'm happy. I've found someone that cares about me, and we're going to move in together."

"Thor. The biker. Yes, we know. And he sounds like an impressive young man." She paused and her voice trembled just a bit. "We would like to meet him."

"Why?" Not that I was paranoid or anything, but Thor wasn't part of their world, and neither was I. Not anymore. I liked the life I'd built for myself. I didn't want them to interfere.

"We know that he makes you happy. Your dad and I miss you and want you back in our lives. On your terms. However you're willing to do that. And we understand that means this Thor gentleman will be part of it."

"Mom, we haven't talked in years. What's changed?"

"Just things. You're my daughter."

"I was your daughter before today. It didn't matter then."

She let out a dramatic sigh. "Okay, here it is. I watched the news last night. About those kids that were murdered in the school shooting? They interviewed one girl's mother. She talked about all the things she'd never get to do with her daughter, and I realized unless I made the first move, I'd never get to do those things with you either. I know we've never been close, but I want to change that. Listening to her, I realized how much I've been missing. How much *we've* been missing."

She'd always been dramatic, and I wasn't sure what to make of this sudden about face. "What have we been missing? Because I'm happy now, and I'm not about to go back to being manipulated by you and Dad."

She hesitated. "That's not going to happen. Are you married to the gentleman?"

So they didn't know everything. Interesting. And rather amusing that she referred to him as a gentleman. Maybe their influence didn't extend to this area of society. "Not yet, but it's likely in the near future." Of course, he'd have to ask me first.

"I'm sure your father would like to walk you down the aisle when the day comes. And I could help plan a beautiful wedding."

My head throbbed. On top of the day I'd had, this about-face on their part was just too much to comprehend. "Mom, I've had a tough day, and I'm really tired. This call is completely out of the blue. How about you give me a few days, and I'll call you back? Maybe meet for coffee or something." Despite everything that had happened, she was my mother and a part of me missed her, missed the relationship we could have had. Should have had.

"You promise you'll call?"

"I promise." I hesitated. "I miss you too." I almost whispered the last bit as I disconnected the call.

"Who was that?" Thor strode into the room and sat beside me.

"My mother." I guess now was the time to have that talk. "It's been years since we last talked."

He pulled me over to sit on his lap. "You don't have to tell me anything if you don't want to."

"But I do." I tried to sort the words out in my head. "When you were knifed, my first thought was to wonder if they had anything to do with it." I explained my family as best I could, and the hardest part was admitting I still loved them and wished we could have some kind of relationship.

Thor held me close. "Of course you do. They're your family, and that's important. Trust me. I don't have a family, and I envy everyone who does. If they're holding out an olive branch, take it. Maybe they've had a change of heart."

I turned to face him. "You are the wisest man on the face of the earth. I love you. You know that, right?"

He grinned. "Does that mean I can finally put my cut on you?"

I lowered my head to capture his lips in a passionate kiss. When we finally came up for air, I traced a finger across his rugged jawline. "Yeah. I guess it does."

He looked shocked. "Are you sure?"

"Yes, I'm sure."

He reached past me to slide open a drawer on the bedside table. Reaching inside, he pulled out a leather vest and held it up for me to read the back. On the rocker panels surrounding the Riptide logo, it said *Property of Thor*. I stood up and let him put it on me.

"How long have you had that hiding in there?" I straightened the vest.

"Too long. You are one hard-to-pin-down woman."

I grinned, turning so I could admire my reflection in the mirror on the back of the door. "I'm going to have to wear this when we go meet my parents."

Thor raised a brow. "We're going to meet your parents?"

"Eventually." I wrinkled my nose. "I'm going to make them work for it, though."

Thor pulled me back into his arms. "That's my

girl -- play hard to get." He lifted my hair and nibbled at my neck. "I want to fuck you in nothing but your cut. And maybe those boots. They're sexy as sin."

I laughed. "You are bad!"

"Bad to the bone!" He grinned. "Wanna see my boner?"

"Damn right."

I completely forgot to ask him if they'd figured out who wanted him dead and why.

* * *

**Thor**

I leaned down to brush a stray lock of hair off Janet's face. She'd fallen asleep snuggled up against me after we made love. We'd had a fucking hell of a time lately and exhaustion had finally caught up with her. I liked to think it was because she felt safe surrounded by the Riptide family. She looked adorable, curled up against me with her new cut still on. I'd pulled off her boots while we were making love. They were sexy as hell to look at but kind of tough on my hide.

My phone chirped, and I glanced over at the screen. *Shadow.*

The kidnapper we'd brought back for questioning hadn't known much. Basically a gun for hire, he'd followed orders and had no idea who was paying him. He didn't care as long as he got paid.

Too bad for him, that wasn't going to happen. Beast made sure he'd never hurt anyone again. No one fucks with our women and walks away.

His phone had proven a whole lot more helpful. It unlocked with facial recognition and luckily Beast hadn't worked his face over so bad that the phone didn't recognize him. Shadow found a whole string of text messages between the asshole and the guy who'd hired him. Went by the name of "Joe Smith" according to his text handle. It might as well have screamed *alias*.

Asshole was supposed to send "Joe Smith" a picture to prove I was dead and then he'd be paid by cash drop in a storage locker on the far side of town.

Shadow worked his magic and traced the fucking idiot back to his home base. Joe Smith my ass. Turns out the guy was a financial manager who had a lot of very rich clients. None of that made sense of him wanting me dead, but Rattler and Ghost were on their way up to Atlanta to invite him down for a visit. He could explain the connection when he got here -- the easy way or the hard way.

I was hoping he chose the hard way. He'd fucked with my woman, and that was a killing offense.

I texted Shadow to let me know when our guest arrived. In the meantime, I'd catch a few z's with my woman. Setting the phone back down on the bedside table, I wrapped myself around Janet and closed my eyes.

* * *

We had one peaceful day before Rattler and Ghost returned. Randolph Amundsen -- alias Joe Smith -- hadn't come willingly. I left Janet with the rest of the old ladies having a gab fest and admiring her new cut while I headed down to the interrogation shack.

Ace opened the door to let me in. "Glad you could tear yourself away from your old lady."

Beast snorted from across the room where he was busy arranging assorted supplies on a table in front of the captive. "Took him long enough to win her over."

"Fuck off," I said calmly. "Some things are worth waiting for."

"That she is." Beast nodded.

I grinned. "I meant me."

I stalked into the center of the room and raked my gaze over the man who'd ordered my death. Not much to look at. Probably mid-fifties, with a pudgy face and the start of a beer belly. The torn and dirt-streaked suit he had on must have cost him more than most people made in a month.

"What the hell?" I turned to Ace. "I've never seen this asshole before in my life. Why is he trying to kill me?"

"That's what we're about to find out." Beast picked up one of the knives on the table. The look on his face was enough to scare a serial killer.

"How's he supposed to answer questions if he's gagged?"

Beast shrugged. "Not my problem."

Ace walked over and yanked the cloth out of the man's mouth.

The asshole struggled against his bonds, not managing to do much more than rub his wrists raw. "Who are you people? I want a lawyer!"

Ace raised a brow. "Does this look like a police station? That's not how this works. You see, you tried to kill one of us, and we don't take kindly to that. We already took care of your little team of assassins who, by the way, upped the game by threatening one of our women. Not cool."

I could see the moment the fucker realized how much shit he was in. "That's not my fault. I never told them to take the woman. They did that on their own."

"But you ordered them to kill my brother Thor, here."

"Thor?" He looked confused. "Who is Thor?"

I spoke up. "I am. And it makes me angry when people try to carve me up in an alley or take potshots at me from rooftops. Makes me fucking furious when they threaten my woman."

Comprehension lit his face. "You're John Stennson?"

I narrowed my eyes. "How do you know my legal name?"

He gulped and shook his head. "No. Not going there."

Ace slapped a hand on my shoulder. "You might have to answer questions on this if the police stumble across the corpse. Let Beast and me find out what the hell is going on, and we'll fill you in later."

Beast picked up a leather strap and ran the knife over it a few times, stopping to test the sharpness of the blade with his thumb. He glanced over at me. "Go. Your woman is waiting for you."

I turned and strode toward the door.

"What the hell does he mean, corpse?" Behind me, I could hear Randolph Amundsen struggle against the ropes that held him to the chair. "Hey! You can't just leave me here with these psychos."

This was a game we'd played out more than once. Good biker, bad biker? Cute that he picked me as the good guy, after paying to have me killed. I turned back toward our captive. "Tell me why, and maybe I'll see what I can do."

"Why?" He looked confused.

"Why you want me dead. Better make it good."

The man looked from Ace to Beast with a terrified expression. "It wasn't personal. Honestly. "He gulped, his eyes fixated on the knife shining in Beast's hands. "I have a client, an old lady. Mary Lansky. She didn't have any kids, never got married, and she was going to leave her fortune to my charitable foundation. I already had plans for that money. Then she did one of those stupid DNA things that tracks down relatives you never knew you had. It turned up you, and she hired a private investigator to track the connection. Luckily, I managed to have him report to me. She trusted me, you see. I've been handling her affairs for decades now. Turns out your father was some kind of distant cousin she'd never met. So she asked me to try and find you. Stupid bitch wanted to meet you, get to know you, all that shit. The cunt planned to rewrite her fucking will in your favor."

"Watch your language." Ace's tone was mild, but that just made it more terrifying.

Randolph whimpered, and a wet stain spread across the front of his pants. Damn wussy pissed himself.

I felt like someone had hit me with a two by four. "I have a blood relative?" I'd grown up knowing I was an orphan, and I'd accepted that a long time ago, but I'd always longed for a family. That was the reason Riptide meant so much to me. They became the family I desperately wanted to belong to.

"We'll need information on this lady." Ace pinned the asshole with his gaze. "Where to find her and that sort of thing. In case Thor here decides to look her up."

The captive nodded eagerly. "I can give that to you. It's all in my cell phone." He made to get it and then realized he couldn't move his hands. "It's in my pocket."

Beast reached over and plucked the phone out of the coward's pocket, holding it up to his face to unlock it. He thumbed through it for a few minutes, before looking over at Ace. "He's telling the truth. I can see her name, address, all kinds of shit about her. Looks like she's worth a lot."

"A fortune. You can see why I did what I did. Think of all the good my foundation could do with that kind of cash." The pleading note in Randolph's voice turned my stomach.

"So you think it's okay to murder someone so that you can use their inheritance to do good? Explain how that works, because it sure sounds like bullshit to me." Ace shook his head. "What happens to this foundation of yours if you die?"

He blinked. "If I die? I guess my wife and son would take it over, or hire someone to run it."

Ace turned to me. "We'll take it from here." He handed me the phone. "Give that to Shadow. He can get the information about your relative and you can decide if you want to make contact or not."

I nodded and took the phone from him. What he said earlier still applied. I needed to be elsewhere when this fucking waste of a life breathed his last. "Thanks, man."

I turned on my heel and walked away, closing the door on the panicked screams of the man who'd ordered my death when he realized it wasn't me who was going to die today.

## Chapter Twelve

**Janet**

I'd tried to pretend I wasn't worried, but as I chatted with Sophia and the rest of the old ladies, I kept one eye on the door. When Thor walked in, I jumped to my feet and ran to him. "It's over?"

He wrapped an arm around my waist and lowered his head to sear a kiss across my lips. "It's over."

It felt like a great weight had been lifted off my shoulders. "Thank goodness. Let's celebrate!"

"My thought exactly." He scooped me up in his arms and headed out of the room to the sounds of whistles and laughter from the rest of the old ladies.

He entered his room and tossed me on the bed. Our room. I was wearing his cut, which meant more than any state issued piece of paper, although I still wanted the legal wedding thing. Especially now that I had a reason for it. I placed my hand on my belly, and for a brief moment, I wondered how he'd react. We'd never seriously discussed children. We'd never gotten past the part where I kept telling him I didn't want to commit. I'd only done the tests yesterday when I realized I was late, so I hadn't had time to get used to the idea myself. I hoped whatever the kidnappers had used to knock me out hadn't harmed the baby. I'd have to make sure to mention it when I saw the baby doctor. I'd have to find one first, though. I doubted a bunch of ex-SEALs had one of those on speed dial.

So many changes in such a short space of time.

"What happened? Is it really over? Did you find out who was trying to kill you?"

Thor shrugged out of his cut and laid it on top of the dresser. "Yes, it's over and turns out it was all about money."

"You don't have any money." Or at least none I was aware of.

"No, but apparently I have a distant aunt or fourth cousin or something and they do." He pulled his shirt off over his head and tossed it aside. "I haven't quite wrapped my head around it yet. Some old lady up in Atlanta did one of those DNA things to find her relatives, and it came up with me."

"Wow." I knew how much he'd always wanted a family. "Are you going to get in touch with her?"

"Probably. I'll have Shadow see what he can come up with on her." He slid his pants down over his hips and kicked them over to the corner of the room.

Suddenly I had no interest in his new relative. His shaft was rock hard and just begging to be sucked. He took a step toward the bed, and I rolled over and took his cock in my mouth.

Thor groaned and fisted his hands in my hair while I sucked and licked, running my tongue down the sides of his gorgeous shaft. Damn, the man was hung! I tilted my head back to take him all the way in. The head of his cock hit the back of my throat, and I gagged a little but kept sucking. Every time he let out a little groan, it sent a thrill right down to my toes.

"Honey, stop." He tugged on my hair. "I want to be inside you when I come."

I thought about it for a minute, and he gave another tug on my hair, harder this time. "Janet, please."

I lifted my head, letting his cock slide out and he flipped me over on my back. "You have way too many clothes on," he said before proceeding to undress me.

I lay on the bed and let him pull my shirt off, and then my leggings. He flicked the front closure of my bra, and it fell away leaving me completely exposed except for a tiny scrap of lace over my mound. Then he ripped that off as well.

Reaching across me, he snagged a condom from the bedside table. Tearing the packet open with his teeth, he quickly sheathed himself before propping himself up over me on his arms. "Beautiful."

I could see the heat in his eyes as he looked down at me. Heat and desire. The tip of his massive cock teased its way through the soft folds guarding my pussy, and I spread my legs to welcome him in.

"I want to take it slow, really celebrate, but you're so fucking tight I don't think I can last that long." He drew back for a minute, and I let out a low whimper.

"I love you, Janet. You know I do." He surged forward, filling me so full I gasped.

Winding my arms around his neck, I pulled him down. "I love you too, you stupid Viking. I always have. I just didn't want to involve you in my family drama."

He pulled out almost all the way, and then slammed back in. "I can handle your family. What I can't handle is the thought of ever losing you." He started to move inside me, sliding in and out in a steady rhythm. I arched upward, meeting him thrust for thrust.

"Same here. Losing you would destroy me. The thought that someone wanted you dead was giving me nightmares." I gasped as he circled his hips.

"I told you I'm not that fucking easy to kill." He pinned me with his gaze as he reached between us and ran his thumb across my clit.

My orgasm exploded across every nerve in my body, and my pussy clamped down hard on Thor's cock. He let out a roar as his own orgasm engulfed him. Lowering his head, he took my lips in a savage kiss, staking his claim on me as his seed pumped from his cock.

I lay locked in his arms as the aftershocks of my orgasm slowly faded. It felt good. Thor. Me. And baby would make three. A family of our own.

Opening my eyes, I found Thor staring down at me with a bemused expression on his face. "What?"

"You're finally wearing my cut. I was starting to think that would never happen." He dropped a tender kiss on my forehead.

"You know I always wanted to." I reached up to trace a tattoo of an eagle on his chest. Someday I'd get around to asking him what it meant. "I was just scared my family would mess things up."

"I can handle your family. I bet you I'll have them eating out of my hand by next summer."

I peeked up at him from beneath my lashes. "Won't take that much work on your part."

He tilted his head, looking slightly confused. "Because I'm so charming they won't be able to resist me?"

I shook my head, placing my hand over my belly. "Because they'll have something else to focus on by then."

"Huh?"

I took a deep breath and blurted it out, watching his face for his reaction. "I'm pregnant. We're having a baby."

His expression went from confusion to shock to absolute joy within minutes. "You're pregnant?"

I nodded.

"You're sure?"

"Yes, I'm sure. I did half a dozen of those pee

stick tests. All positive."

He placed a hand on my still flat stomach with a look of absolute awe. "A week ago I was an orphan. Today I have a partner, an aunt, and soon, a son or daughter."

I placed my hand over his. "A family. We're a family."

"One more thing we need to do then." He reached back into the drawer he'd pulled the cut from and pulled out a blue velvet box. Sliding out of my arms, he knelt beside the bed and flipped the lid of the box open to reveal a diamond ring. "Janet, will you marry me?"

Stunned, I stared from the ring to Thor's face and back to the ring again. For a split second I was too shocked to reply.

Thor looked nervous. "Janet?"

"Of course I'll marry you!" I threw my arms around his neck, hugging him so tight it was a wonder he could still breathe.

He gently pulled my arms away and took the ring out of the box to place it on my finger. "You had me scared there for a second."

I held out my hand to admire the ring. Three round-cut diamonds were mounted on a white gold band. Simple but elegant. I knew they were supposed to represent past, present, and future but to me they represented family. Thor. Me. And the child we'd created. "I didn't expect this. It took a moment for it to sink in. When did you buy a ring?"

He grinned. "A long time ago, when I realized how very much I loved you. I knew you weren't ready yet, but every time I saw that box in the drawer, it made me feel good. I knew some day you'd agree to be mine."

I threw myself into his arms. "This is the day. I love you from the bottom of my heart."

* * *

**Thor**

I'd arranged the BBQ for Riptide tonight with a couple of special events to announce. Everyone, including the Prez, thought it was just to celebrate Janet finally agreeing to wear my cut and be my old lady.

They were in for a surprise.

Mom and Jake were helping me with the actual work. I'm useless in a kitchen. I could probably burn steak on the BBQ if I had to, but that's about it. I wanted people to be able to eat, so I enlisted some help. Mom had made salads and baked a ton of stuff. She was good at that kind of thing. Jake had agreed to man the BBQ and make sure everyone got fed. I'd ordered a fucking ton of beer and some wine and hard liquor. I had it cooling in tubs of ice out back by the BBQ pit.

I'd ordered some special, alcohol-free stuff for Janet because the baby doctor said no alcohol until after the baby was born. Even then, if she was breastfeeding, alcohol was going to be a no-no. The baby doctor also did an ultrasound and said the baby looked fine, so whatever those assholes had used to knock Janet out hadn't hurt the baby. Damn lucky or I would have brought them back just so I could kill them again.

Yeah. I know that's not possible, but I'd give it a fucking try.

"Did you manage to connect with your aunt, or cousin, or whoever that was searching for relatives?" Janet was in the ensuite, getting ready for the event.

"Not yet. I entered my contact info in the database, but I'll leave it up to her to connect if she wants to. Otherwise, it's like I'm after her money. I don't need that, and I don't need to find a family either. I have one right here."

"Fair enough. I'm okay with whatever you want."

"What about your family? It sounds like they want you back in the fold."

"I'm not sure. I don't want our child treated with anything but love and acceptance. I'm not saying no, but I think we should take it slowly. I haven't told them I'm pregnant yet." Janet came out and twirled around so I could get a good look at her outfit. "Do I look okay?"

"You look amazing. I love seeing my cut on you." I stood and offered her my arm. "You ready to go face the pack?"

She grinned. "No problem. I plan to blame you for everything."

"How so?"

"Well, I didn't get pregnant all by myself. Even a bunch of bikers can figure that one out."

I laughed. "Yeah. They can. I'm sure they'll congratulate me on a job well done."

She shook her head. "Don't let it go to your head. I'll be expecting you to do your share of midnight feedings and diaper changes when the time comes."

I dropped my gaze to her generous cleavage. "I can change diapers, darling, but I'm not equipped for feeding."

She grinned. "Don't kid yourself. I'll pump milk for you to use. The baby can learn to take a bottle." She looped her arm through mine. "Lead the way, oh husband-to-be."

We headed to the back door and were greeted by whistles and clapping as we approached the BBQ area. Most of the guys were sitting around on the logs that served as seating. They'd already started in on the beer and liquor.

Ace stood and motioned for quiet. The noise died down, and he turned and held out his arm to motion us forward. "I'd like you all to help me welcome Thor's old lady into the Riptide family. Janet, we wish you and Thor the very best that life has to offer."

I let Janet precede me into the circle of bikers and their old ladies. She held out her arms and executed a perfect pirouette, turning slowly so that everyone could admire her cut. I was so fucking proud of her. She managed to look like a princess accepting the homage of her court.

Sophia jumped up from beside Deuce and ran to hug her. "Welcome to the family! We're practically sisters now!"

Emma followed, then Jasmine and Jewel. Pretty soon all the women were standing with Janet in the middle of a circle of bikers, hugging and laughing and talking excitedly. I stood back and let Janet have her moment in the limelight.

Every time a Riptide brother managed to find his old lady, the circle got bigger and louder and more joyful. We weren't kids anymore and we were getting to the settle-down stage of life. It felt fucking good. It probably wouldn't be long before more of the old ladies were in a family way.

I cleared my throat, and the women ignored me. Ace slapped me on the back good-naturedly. "Better get used to it. You're not in charge anymore."

At the sound of Ace's voice, Janet looked over at me. I raised my brows, and a slow smile curved her lips. She whispered something to the women surrounding her, and they scattered back to their seats. She held out her hand to me and I crossed to her side.

Clasping her hand tightly, I cleared my throat again. This time a hush fell over the brothers, and they looked at us expectantly. I turned and grabbed Janet's other hand so that we stood facing each other. "We have something else to announce."

"Actually, two things," Janet said.

"Two things, then." I gazed into her eyes. "The first is that Janet and I are getting married on December 21st, the winter solstice."

Janet gave my hand a squeeze. "And the second is that I'm going to have a baby."

I'm sure the resulting noise could be heard for miles. Hoots and whistles, clapping and cheering. Everyone came up to slap me on the back or place a reverent hand on Janet's still flat belly.

A new generation was beginning, and this child would know love from its very first breath.

## Author's Note

If you enjoyed this book, I would really appreciate you leaving a review on whatever platforms you participate in such as Goodreads, Barnes and Noble, Amazon etc. Reviews help readers find my stories.

And, if you're not already subscribed to my newsletter, follow the link on my website and you can get Cyclone and Rylie's story free, just for signing up!

## Anne Kane

Anne Kane lives in the beautiful Okanagan Valley with a bouncy little rescue dog whose breed defies description and an Aussie Shepherd who's too smart for her own good. Anne likes to write spicy stories with sassy heroines and protective, sexy male heroes who love those women. Her stories all have one thing in common: a happily ever after ending.

Her hobbies, when she's not playing with the characters in her head, include kayaking, hiking, swimming, playing guitar and spoiling the grandkids.

Anne at Changeling: changelingpress.com/anne-kane-a-116

## Changeling Press LLC

Contemporary Action Adventure, Sci-Fi, Steampunk, Dark Fantasy, Urban Fantasy, Paranormal, and BDSM Romance available in e-book, audio, and print format at ChangelingPress.com - MC Romance, Werewolves, Vampires, Dragons, Shapeshifters and Horror -- Tales from the edge of your imagination.

## Where can I get Changeling Press Books?

Changeling Press e-books are available at ChangelingPress.com, Amazon, Apple Books, Barnes & Noble, Kobo, Smashwords, and other online retailers, including Everand Subscription and Kobo Subscription Services. Print books are available at Amazon, Barnes and Noble, and by ISBN special order through your local bookstores.

ChangelingPress.com

www.ingramcontent.com/pod-product-compliance
Lightning Source LLC
LaVergne TN
LVHW020539100826
845148LV00010B/1535